Select

BOOK ONE

Select

BOOK ONE

MARIT WEISENBERG

Charlesbridge
TEEN

For Jeff—M. W.

Published by Charlesbridge
85 Main Street
Watertown, MA 02472
(617) 926-0329
www.charlesbridgeteen.com

Library of Congress Cataloging-in-Publication Data
Names: Weisenberg, Marit, author.
Title: Select / by Marit Weisenberg.
Description: Watertown, MA : Charlesbridge, [2017] | Summary: Julia Jaynes of Austin,
Texas, is one of the select, a secret group of humans with abilities bordering on the
supernatural, but, unlike her younger sister, she has never been entirely
comfortable as part of the "perfect" family—and when she falls for a normal human guy
and draws attention to her more-than-normal family she finds herself banished to that
most ordinary of institutions: public high school.
Identifiers: LCCN 2016043041 (print) | LCCN 2016051812 (ebook) |
ISBN 9781580898065 (reinforced for library use) | ISBN 9781632896421 (ebook)
Subjects: LCSH: Secrecy—Juvenile fiction. | Identity (Psychology)—Juvenile fiction. |
Dating (Social customs)—Juvenile fiction. | Sisters—Juvenile fiction. |
Families—Texas—Austin—Juvenile fiction. | High schools—Juvenile fiction. |
Austin (Tex.)—Juvenile fiction. | CYAC: Secrets—Fiction. | Identity—Fiction. |
Dating (Social customs)—Fiction. | Sisters—Fiction. | Family life—Texas—
Fiction. | High schools—Fiction. | Schools—Fiction. | Austin (Tex.)—Fiction. |
LCGFT: Romance fiction.
Classification: LCC PZ7.1.W4347 Se 2017 (print) | LCC PZ7.1.W4347 (ebook) |
DDC 813.6 [Fic] —dc23
LC record available at https://lccn.loc.gov/2016043041

Printed in the United States of America
(hc) 10 9 8 7 6 5 4 3 2 1

Display type set in Freeland by Trial by Cupcakes
Text type set in Adobe Garamond Pro
Printed by Berryville Graphics in Berryville, Virginia, USA
Production supervision by Brian G. Walker
Text designed by Susan Mallory Sherman

In all things of nature there is
something of the marvelous.

—Aristotle

Select

Chapter One

"Julia!"

That startled me. I turned my head, tucking my hair behind my ear so I could see Angus come to stand beside me.

"Hey." He stopped and focused on the wall-length curved panel. The light of the TV sliced into the dimly lit room, rudely cutting through the Zen-like atmosphere. I thought my family would just flash across the screen, but the camera held on them.

"Novak Jaynes and his wife, Dr. Victoria Jaynes, major donors to the new University of Texas Medical School, are here with their daughter." You could tell the commentator was unsure of what he was allowed to say, and that he wished the camera would move on. Due to a well-publicized Securities and Exchange Commission investigation, this year there would be no hailing "the Oracle of Austin"—my dad, the investor with preternatural abilities.

Angus was temporarily still while he watched Novak,

Victoria, and my sister in their suite at the football stadium. I was impressed with Liv. I knew the toll this must be taking on her, trying to keep the public from penetrating the imaginary wall of glass Novak had taught us all to erect. No one in my family looked overwhelmed by the sensory overload of the football game or by the fact that people—now a cameraman—were studying them. It was impossible not to stare. Even for me. They were a perfectly matched, elegant family, with their sun-streaked brown hair and beautiful, fine features, although now my sister was taking it to a different level. It was like they'd externalized being members of the One Percent.

Angus paused to look again—at my almost-grown-up sister, I knew—a second longer than I would have liked before getting back to business.

"Come on. They're waiting for us," he said.

To my surprise Angus ran his hand down my tattooed arm before catching my wrist, then my hand, and pulling me out of the room. We interlaced fingers. He didn't ask why I wasn't at the game. He knew. Everyone knew I wasn't invited. But Angus was maybe the only person who actually seemed more interested in me than in them.

A voice in my head whispered that maybe he only wanted me for what he thought I could teach him.

"You suddenly interested in UT football?" Angus joked lightly.

I laughed and said, "Very interested in football."

But I was embarrassed I'd been caught watching.

We walked hand in hand through Paul's parents' many living rooms. Through the windows we could see some of our group wrestling on the grass in the side yard. When we stepped outside, Angus immediately dropped my hand.

I didn't understand why it hadn't happened between us yet. Every night this summer I thought he would make the first move. Maybe he was waiting for me to take the first step, but I wanted it to come from him. He got everything he wanted, and I didn't want to fall in his lap too.

The moment I stepped outdoors, I felt as if I were enveloped in a swamp. Not everything could be controlled, I guess. But the landscape was lush. Only money could tame a garden like this into submission in the August heat of Texas. The harshness of the black gravel contrasted with the softness of the flowers, the symmetry of the stone pathways, and the soothing paleness of the white-brick monolith behind me.

The boys were unusually sweaty. T-shirts clung to shoulder blades, and I could see beads of perspiration on those necks not covered with light-brown hair. They looked uniform with their honey coloring. I was always aware of how I stood out.

Angus and I came to stand near the boys, waiting patiently for them to finish playing. Next to me, Angus removed his hand from the back of his neck, revealing one tattoo. His arms were covered with ink as well—designs of black bands around them, as if he were in mourning. I wasn't sure if it was in honor of our ancestors or if it was a statement about his current situation. I could tell he felt me appraising him, and I quickly looked away.

We watched the dog pile. The boys looked like they were going to kill each other tonight. Their cuts and bruises would be unusually bad, but at least they would disappear quickly.

I noticed Paul standing off the path and directly on top of some landscaping, size-thirteen boots crushing flowering ground cover—a minor fuck-you to his parents. He lit a cigarette and, through that first cloud of smoke, squinted up at us as we joined the all-male group. Instantly Paul's body language changed, now less the punk and ready to defer to Angus. And when they realized Angus was there, none of the boys resisted the instinct to turn their bodies to face him, in an act of deference and respect—the same as we all did when my father was in the room. I wasn't sure if Angus was aware of it, but when it was just the two of us he in turn angled his body toward me.

Sebastian had been blocking my view of Ellis, and when he shifted I saw what was going on. A knife was plunged into Ellis's right hand—a steak knife with a curved silver blade protruding from his golden flesh. There wasn't the least sign of blood. The boys stopped wrestling all at once and gathered around, watching and taunting, voices too loud for the serene setting on the water. Driving it deeper, Ellis maintained his impassive face, and the group, fiercely competitive with one another, attempted to look unimpressed. Ellis was getting good.

All at once he crashed, turning white as the blood drained from his face. Angus broke through the group, grasped the handle, and in a smooth, confident maneuver removed the knife. I saw the deep wound between the knuckles begin to seep just a bare amount of dark-red, almost-black, blood. *Well done,* I thought. Ellis had almost controlled his response to the pain. Now he seemed to be recovering. He hid his compromised hand behind his back, wanting to protect it from the critical eye of the group.

"I should go," I said, always aware I was the only girl.

"She didn't like the trick," Cyrus said, laughing.

Despite that I'd grown up with these seven boys and that no one in this group would ever think of doing anything to hurt me, I felt vaguely uneasy when I looked around. Over the past year they had transformed their appearance like I had. They were deeply attractive, but they appeared hardened now with their abundance of tattoos and scars. And they were in fact hardened after a year of living with their wings clipped.

I reminded myself it didn't matter that I was the only female. It had just been me for the past year. I couldn't help thinking that if any other girls had been included in our particular group, things wouldn't be as out of control. There was too much testosterone. Every night the boys wanted to play in secret, practicing skills we didn't understand and weren't supposed to explore—thanks to me and my moment of weakness telling Angus what had happened last spring.

I had explicitly disobeyed Novak when I shared my secret, wanting to impress Angus. Novak had warned me not to say anything after I'd gathered my courage and told him about the odd experience I'd had on a ski trip to Park City, Utah.

It had started with a stupid mistake. I'd locked myself out on my bedroom balcony when I went to smoke a cigarette in the middle of the night. For hours I'd been trapped in the well-below-freezing temperature in shorts and a T-shirt, kicking myself because the cigarette wasn't even worth it—it had no short-term or long-term effects on us. It was just something to do. I told my father how, instinctively, I had closed my eyes and focused inward, visualizing the color blue turning to warm red, and I must have raised my core temperature because I didn't feel cold while I was stranded out there. Then I showed Novak how, if I concentrated my energies on an object, I could move it or even break it—like a door lock, which is how I got back into the ski house after I eventually grew bored waiting for someone to come rescue me.

I was surprised how fast he shut me down. "Those are only tricks. We're capable, but we don't practice them because they aren't worth the exposure. Don't tell anyone what happened, and don't do it again. Understood?"

Immediately I felt like an idiot because I actually thought I'd done something extraordinary. Apparently it was nothing. I had irrationally hoped it would be enough to get me moved to the other set of teenagers in our group. In keeping with tradition, those sixteen- and seventeen-year-olds were finally getting answers about themselves and all the inexplicable things we could do. Those of us who remained, myself and the other teenagers in my group, were the first of our kind ever to be kept in the dark. I thought of us as the Lost Kids.

Paul suddenly began to back away from the group, walking toward the driveway. We understood. We could all sense there were suddenly more of us in the vicinity. His parents were almost home. Moments later we could hear their car driving toward us, just a few blocks away now.

"Come on." Angus breezed past his friends, walking toward his brand-new and badly dented black BMW without giving them a glance. He knew they would follow.

"Where to?" Rob unfolded his long body from a steel bench and stretched, showing off defined abs.

"Julia!" Angus pulled my attention away from Rob. I could

tell Angus noticed I was noticing, and he didn't like it. I smiled to myself, feeling more optimistic about tonight. I walked down the path to join him and arched an eyebrow. Whatever trepidation I was feeling inside, I had almost complete confidence I was masking it. Even if I was the bastard child and a Lost Kid, I was Julia Jaynes, Novak's daughter. And I owned it. Because if I didn't, I'd have no place in the world.

"Where do you want to go tonight?" Angus looked in my eyes and, briefly, we shared a moment. I knew he was wondering if I would play along tonight and that he was willing to try to charm me into it. I didn't totally trust Angus, not after he broke his promise to me at the beginning of summer and showed these boys what I'd taught him how to do. They had taken the idea that they could assert their minds over their bodies and quickly gone to extremes. I understood: it felt good. It was a way to channel that pent-up feeling that physically hurt. But I couldn't show them anything else or Novak would kill me and he might punish the boys.

The ultimate threat of being left behind was almost enough to dissuade us from breaking the rules. Almost. More often the residual anger at being demoted and segregated from our other friends just empowered us to rebel.

Still, for tonight I could go along for the ride and enjoy as Angus continued to try to make it up to me for telling my secret.

"The train tracks," I said. I tossed my hair and stood at my full five feet four inches. It was an announcement, not a question. I saw surprise and respect on Angus's face.

"You going to jump trains with us tonight, Julia?" he asked flirtatiously. We all started pairing off and climbing into the collection of luxury sports cars in the circular drive of Paul's parents' contemporary monstrosity. We weren't that far from my house.

"We'll see," I flirted back. I wished I could stop the blush that warmed my face when Angus opened the passenger door for me. I hated it. No one else in the group did that. Everybody seemed to have near-perfect command over their emotions and only showed what they wanted others to read.

Car doors slammed behind me in perfect unison. Angus and I would lead them where I wanted to go. It was a powerful feeling. Train jumping should distract them. It was challenging enough. They might not ask for more.

Chapter Two

~~❧~~

"Julia. Wake up."

I was in such a deep sleep—finally—it took me a moment to surface and realize my sister was standing over me. Her hand was on my shoulder, gently shaking me awake. My eyes snapped into focus, and I quickly sat up.

I was so glad to see her, but then I was scared. "What's wrong? What's going on?" She never came into my room anymore. I knew it was because she was uncomfortable. In keeping with Liv's new status, her mother had had us switch bedrooms this summer—my old bedroom had been the bigger one with the better view. Now it was Liv's. I didn't blame her, though. It hadn't been her decision. She could have it. We wouldn't be here too much longer anyway. I smiled indulgently, having missed spending time with my little sister. It was only a bedroom, I told myself.

"No. Nothing, nothing. It's okay. I didn't mean to scare you. I just came to say hi." Liv perched on the side of my bed, blocking the clock, dragging a finger along the white blanket. The blackout shades were drawn, but she was fully dressed, giving me the feeling I'd slept in and it was afternoon.

"What time is it?" I sounded like a frog, so I cleared my throat. My mouth felt like an ashtray. Liv remained where she was. It felt like we hadn't been this physically close in months. Reluctantly, it seemed, she stood up and walked over to the shades. Disappointed, I realized this interaction would still have the tinge of awkwardness.

"It's ten. Do you mind?"

"Go ahead."

She stood up and slapped at the panel on the side of the wall. The shades retracted and an expansive view of Lake Austin appeared, but I had seen it a million times. I took in my sister instead.

Liv could have been from my dreams. She was so beautiful. Like me, Liv had my dad's blue eyes, but that was the extent of any similarity between us. She had high cheekbones that set off the small, perfect features of her heart-shaped face. Her thick, long hair almost matched her skin tone. Tall and willowy at five ten, she somehow also had curves. I wasn't used to it yet. She had been a late bloomer, and it had happened so fast over the course of this summer, just as she turned sixteen. It felt strange to live with someone your whole life, and then suddenly need to adjust to their physical appearance every time you saw them.

"So, what's up?" I felt self-conscious in my tank top, and smelling like cigarettes. And I was sure my hair was a mess. I didn't like being surprised.

"What'd you guys do last night?" Liv asked, then wandered over to where my guitar sat in a corner and picked it up. *Help yourself,* I thought, mildly annoyed. Liv tuned the already perfectly tuned guitar while pretending she wasn't listening intently for my answer.

"Nothing. The usual," I said.

"What's the usual?" she asked.

"Just hanging around. I don't know. Why?" There was an edge in my voice. Had she heard something? Why was she suddenly so fascinated by what the Lost Kids and I were doing?

"No, I just—you guys make it seem like you're always off having so much fun."

She had to be kidding. She made it sound like we'd turned a negative into a positive. That we weren't dying for the training they were getting, that we weren't just looking for things to do, biding our time.

"Trust me, we aren't." Liv glanced up at my sharp reminder.

"You all seem close, like a secret club."

Maybe the Lost Kids and I tried to pretend we were the cool ones, but Liv couldn't seriously envy a group of rejects forced into humiliatingly typical teenage rebellion.

I tried changing the subject. "Hey, how was your first soccer practice yesterday?"

"Fine," Liv said shortly, clearly not wanting to talk about it. I could tell she was frustrated. Liv was good at soccer, but she wasn't nearly as good as I'd been. I knew that must kill my stepmother. I wondered if being compared with me ever bothered Liv.

Liv wouldn't look at me, I realized. I heard her heart rate accelerate, which was highly unusual for any of us. So now we were getting to the real reason she was here.

"What are you doing today?"

"I'm not sure. Why? What are you doing? Is Dad home?" I suddenly sat up straighter.

"No, I don't know," Liv said quickly. "I was wondering. . . . You're probably going with that group to swim at Barton Springs?"

"What?" I felt like I wasn't getting what she was saying.

"Angus. You know?" That instantly got my attention. I nodded warily. "He texted me about it," she said.

Many things were strange and wrong about this—mostly, why in the world would Angus be texting my little sister? I didn't like that at all. Also, our two groups didn't mix, and we definitely didn't go out in groups to public places. All those outsiders. All that noise. And most of all, the exposure. What was Angus up to? The risk-taking was escalating. A nod was all I could manage. "Can you hold on for a second?" The lift of her eyebrows indicated, *Of course.*

Attempting to look nonchalant, I let the sheet fall away and swung my legs over the side of my king-size bed, grabbed my phone, and bolted to the bathroom and dressing area. Closing the door behind me, I tried to calm my nerves in the soothing darkness, focusing on the cool marble beneath my feet. A rash was spreading up the insides of my arms. With the back of my hand, I turned on the lights, bringing the bathroom to life.

I had to have some kind of release. With a cracking sound, the hairbrush on the counter split down the middle. Right away I felt calmer. I looked down and saw the rash receding in answer.

I glanced up at the mirror. My heavy mascara was smeared,

and my bottle-black hair was a rat's nest. I looked the opposite of my sister—night to her day. But I enjoyed how tough I looked. It hid how not-tough I was inside. I took a few more breaths.

I checked my phone. Sure enough—and thank God—there was a text from Angus about Barton Springs. I felt better. But how had he gotten my sister's number? And why would he use it?

That Liv and I had been separated into different groups made things tricky. It had been a shock when my dad announced his plan to split up the kids, and even more of one when my name was randomly selected for the group that needed to "lie low" and underachieve for the sake of appearances. It was one thing to have to fake it at school—to not be so smart, so good at sports, so quick at absolutely everything. It was another when Novak told us my group would not be receiving any kind of instruction for now and any natural skills we had would have to lie dormant.

This was why the boys had begun to live for what I'd shown Angus how to do. We were all in the same boat: going crazy having to suppress our instincts. Not to mention that we had to deal with the migraines, the fitful, sweaty sleep, the waking up to find the contents of our bedrooms broken around us. It all felt wrong. We had been assured that our dormancy was just a temporary precaution during our remaining two years before we disappeared from Austin due to the recent scrutiny. So far we'd made it through one year and two months, but it had changed us.

I opened the bathroom door and reluctantly walked back to the bedroom, trying to decide what I wanted to do. Liv looked nervous to be in my room, nervous awaiting my answer. At least one thing hadn't changed: I was still her older sister and, like old times, her ticket to where she wanted to go.

I sat back down on the bed, watching her as she attempted to look uninterested, twisting her brown and gold hair into a messy ponytail. It was a new and scary feeling to be jealous of her. She had always been the baby in my eyes, so sweet, and the bright spot in my life in this house. I had been proud of her when she replaced me as captain of the soccer team and I'd had to watch from the sidelines, the team moving in unison like a flock of birds. Watching them never grew old. It was like they had eyes in the back of their heads, they were so in tune with each other's movements and unspoken signals. I missed it so much, it almost killed me—that beautiful feeling of connection and flow. It had been exchanged for the constant, maddening feeling that something essential was missing.

I was ready to have every privilege restored to us in our next place, to not have to hold back in any way, to stop feeling the emptiness. I never blamed Liv. She had felt guilty, but she'd had to listen to her mother. I saved my resentment for Victoria, though I tried, with every ounce of my being, to hide it.

Liv was waiting. She knew I couldn't say no to her. I didn't think I ever had. But my biggest reason for agreeing to go on this ill-conceived excursion was my absolute confidence that Liv would be scared off when she saw Angus, Lord of the Lost Kids, in his element.

"What time do you want to leave?"

Happy now that she was getting what she wanted, Liv let out a breath and smiled.

"Soon, maybe. It's getting hot." That was the understatement of the year. "Is that a new tattoo?" Liv moved closer to me and pointed to the vine lacing itself across my upper chest.

"Yes, sort of new."

She nodded. "It's beautiful."

"Thank you. I'll have to get rid of it soon enough, I guess. Ten more months." I could tell she noted my sudden coldness. I didn't like that she was idly picking up things on my desk.

Liv consulted the rose-gold Rolex Daytona on her tan wrist. "Meet you in what? Fifteen minutes downstairs?"

I nodded.

"Hey," she said over her shoulder as she left my room. "I'm excited to hang out. We never see each other anymore."

I smiled halfheartedly. As soon as she was gone, I walked over to what she had been fiddling with, hoping it wasn't anything I hadn't wanted her to see.

It was a loose photo of Angus. I was frightened by the sharpness of my anger. Liv clearly knew that Angus and I were close, and she was pursuing her little crush anyway. But then, why wouldn't she? Regardless of her reluctance, what was mine always became hers. It was all she knew. But now she seemed to expect it.

A few months ago I would have thought Liv's fascination with Angus was cute—one more thing that showed she looked up to me, much to my stepmother's anxiety. Now, considering this womanly and newly empowered Liv, it wasn't funny anymore. The question was, what was Angus thinking about her? Even if he didn't see her as a little girl anymore, surely he wouldn't dare go near her, out of fear of Novak? There was no way forward. Even for Angus.

It was the first time Liv had ever disappointed me. I felt the loss of the little girl who wouldn't be coming back.

❧❧❧

I closed my bedroom door softly behind me, leather tote slung over one shoulder. I hesitated, wondering if I should go back and change.

Even though I was inside the house, I wore my large black sunglasses so Liv wouldn't see my eyes. Already I knew putting on the black string bikini was the wrong move. It had somehow ended up in my drawer, and I'd never before had the guts to wear something so tiny. What had felt like an I-don't-care moment a minute ago now felt somehow desperate.

I passed the gallery of photos on the wall of the hallway that spanned the entire length of the upstairs. So many of them were of Victoria and my father that it felt forced, as if Victoria wanted to prove Novak was in love with her, that they were as connected as all the other couples in our group. In some of the photos, they were so young. My father had been with someone else before Victoria, as evidenced by my existence, but in our culture that was atypical. We paired off early—in our late teens or very early twenties—and stayed together for life. I was at that age now. Almost all of us kids were. Which made this Angus and Liv thing even more irritating.

The same photo always caught my attention, as if it wanted to remind me on a daily basis of the reality of my situation. It was one of the few of Victoria, my sister, and me. My sister sat to the side, one of her chubby four-year-old hands at ease on Victoria's knee. I was almost six in the picture and I seemed to be sitting in Victoria's lap. My face was blank. A young Victoria was looking down, her eyelashes demurely on her cheeks, a curtain of long hair casting a shadow on her face.

The picture was hung because it looked like we were a happy family, outside on the lawn, Liv and I with musical instruments in our little hands. What I actually remembered was the staging of the photo and Victoria's hands under my armpits, aggressively trying to reposition me on the other side of her. For me there was never any touching her, let alone sitting in her lap. At some point I realized why my presence was hard for her. She had been left to raise Novak's daughter by a rival, I presumed. But I must have been confused at that age, not understanding why she treated me differently from Liv. As much as I'd tried to be an easy guest in her home, Victoria never softened. At the time the photo was taken, we had been in Austin for five years. All of Liv's life and all but the beginning of mine.

I headed down the floating staircase, the living room below looking sparse and grand at the same time—glass, cool stone, beautiful furniture of various luxurious textures. The living room had a retractable glass wall that opened onto a terrace, the first of three tiered levels of garden leading down to the lake. The basement housed the underground garage and basketball court. At the western part of the property, near the guesthouse, was a more contemporary-style glass-and-steel gym. Most spectacular was how the house itself had a wing that reached almost to the water and connected to a boat garage, making the boats as accessible as the cars.

I wound my way through the other spacious, hushed rooms painted in natural shades and decorated with orchids. I paused midstep when I registered his presence a few seconds before I saw him. When I entered the kitchen, there stood the king.

Once I made the joke that seeing my father was like spotting an elusive elk. It was rare and exciting and you never knew when it was going to happen. Liv didn't get it, or at least she didn't think it was funny.

Since we ran cooler as a whole, I knew the show of affection and exuberance now taking place was for the housekeeper's benefit—a simulation of an everyday family's interactions. Still, I wished I could take a picture. My youthful, handsome dad, in running clothes, bent down to greet Liv with a hug, their golden-brown heads resting together as he gave her a squeeze. He'd just come in from a run, and they were laughing about him getting her sweaty, their identical blue eyes showing genuine fondness for each other. Both of us were daddy's girls.

I didn't realize I'd stopped in my tracks to look at them until I felt someone else in the room watching me watch them. I caught Victoria's eye. I dropped my gaze.

"Hey, doll!" Novak came over to me and wrapped his arms around me too, instantly making every worry disappear. I lived for the infrequent moments when he acted not just like a leader but like a dad.

Even though Novak had a slight build, he was wiry and strong. I didn't even care that he was sweaty from his run. And of course he wouldn't really think we'd mind. He was too used to being adored by all of us. He was the sun. For a second I lost myself in this uncommon hug. He pulled away first and began to loudly chug a green energy drink, the only thing he ever consumed. He raked a hand through his hair. The curls were cut short but still there. It was hard to believe he was my father when he looked like he was twenty-five.

I felt an imperceptible exchange between Victoria and Novak. Lydia, the latest in the line of short-term housekeepers, had left the kitchen, and you could feel a bit of the act fall away. I knew the calm that replaced it would look eerie to outsiders.

"Where've you been, Dad?" Liv asked. As a precaution, Liv continued to speak in a measured tone of voice instead of taking the easier route—speaking quickly and just above a whisper.

"Just working my ass off."

I knew we were alone, but it was so unusual, I felt like looking behind me for the people who almost always surrounded Novak. There were always members from our group around him, even at home. And when he wasn't home, they were here too. We were all related to one another and we instinctively preferred to be together, weaving in and out of each other's homes as if living in mansions separated from one another was an unnatural lifestyle.

I glanced up at Victoria, who was hovering. There was the Victoria, Dad, and Liv family unit, and then there was the Dad, Liv, and me unit. The second was never given a chance to breathe. Victoria was annoyed I'd interrupted her time to enjoy her family. I knew it was my place to stay away at moments like these, and I would have if I had been paying attention.

"I've got to go, gals." Novak lowered his face to Liv's for a quick kiss and then walked over to me. Same thing.

"Do you need me today?" Victoria asked. I wondered if he realized he hadn't kissed her as well.

"No." Novak was already busy checking his phone.

"My dad wants a meeting," she said. Novak had been voted in as leader—already a legend for being the youngest we'd ever had—replacing Victoria's father soon after we'd arrived in Austin.

Novak didn't look up. "It's not a democracy," he joked. It was in fact a democracy. Or it used to be, with everyone's needs equally considered. But if Victor had been a traditional leader, Novak was more like a shaman. He had a small inner circle, but these days it was clearly just Novak calling the shots.

Novak's leadership had been divisive. On the one hand, by making us rich, he'd bought us a kind of security we'd never had before. On the other, we found ourselves living further than ever from how we used to live. According to stories, we had once been a communal culture of what's mine is yours, with no emphasis placed on acquiring personal possessions.

"He—"

"I can't stop everything to have fifty council sessions a month like he had." Novak looked up at Victoria when he said this, and she stared back for a millisecond before breaking eye contact first.

"Do you really have to leave? You just got here!" A whine crept into Liv's voice.

"I'll see you tonight," he said.

We knew it was unlikely.

Liv nodded. For some reason I felt sad, and a flash of the

old protectiveness for Liv. It was never enough. His presence and the energy he exuded made you want more. Always more.

It was what got him in trouble with the people he interfaced with at work. Among us kids there was speculation that maybe Novak had the power to affect people's emotional states and that's why we felt almost high in his presence. The outsiders who weren't too shy to interact with him could too easily become infatuated with him, his intense focus making them feel like the center of the world. Novak came across as deferential and unwaveringly polite to anyone he had dealings with, which was a heady combination in someone so powerful and attractive.

Novak was our liaison to the outside world, but he was maybe too good at it, because now the business world and admirers in general followed his every move. The SEC had been plaguing him now for the past several months.

With Novak gone we were left alone in the kitchen with Victoria, a different energy completely. "Where are you going?" she asked. *Dammit.*

Dressed in an expensive tunic she wore as a dress, Liv was all legs. She opened the glass door of the refrigerator and grabbed a few bottles of water. Except for the fruit, breakfast sat untouched on the table. Presumably Victoria had explained our plant-based diet to the housekeeper, but it had probably seemed so unsustainable, it went ignored. I wondered if anyone else was always hungry like me.

Victoria walked over to Liv and touched her sleeve almost like she was holding on. Victoria was trained as a doctor, but she had never practiced. Instead she waited around, bored, like everyone else in the group, until Novak called on her for her area of expertise to consult on his grand plan. Our goal was to relocate somewhere that would be environmentally more protected and less directly impacted by the climate change that was worsening every year. Not to mention the other man-made messes that were inarguably coming home to roost. Novak knew future wars would be fought over water, just like wars were fought over oil now. None of us felt bad about Novak's plan to pump water for our sole use, not when outsiders had first disturbed our way of life, not when they had almost exterminated us.

The teens in our group never stopped hearing how our generation was lazy in comparison with previous ones, that we lacked any sense of urgency about contributing to the group's well-being. Maybe it was because we had a sense of futility about the future. We were the last generation. Not one child had been born to the group in sixteen years. None of the couples in their twenties and thirties had children. Liv had been the last, and it was a never-ending source of grief.

The childless couples and even the adults my parents' age had done everything they could and had kept trying in spite of Novak's vision, which had predicted it would be futile. From a pure biological standpoint, the group, now numbering fewer than sixty, had stayed too insular. The idea of diluting our DNA wasn't an option anyone ever discussed. It seemed we would rather die out. Otherwise, what would all this have been for—the decades of running, the hiding in plain sight? Everything had been in the name of staying together in spite of the odds.

My eyes flew to Victoria when she loudly placed a water

glass on the countertop. Victoria was tall—in heels, taller than my dad—her hair a darker shade of brown than Liv's. She always kept her lips bare, even though the rest of her face was made up. It suited her to appear always a little edgy and not just a little severe. Today she was dressed in a tight black dress worth thousands.

Victoria and I were both experts at wiping our faces of emotion when we entered each other's company. So proud of her daughter, she melted every time she laid eyes on the younger, almost-identical version of herself. Since I looked nothing like my dad or Liv except for the color of my eyes, I knew I must take after my mother. Whoever she was.

I assumed my birth mother had not been allowed to relocate with the rest of the group when we moved to Austin, that maybe there was truth to the rumor that not everyone had made the cut. I wondered if Victoria had something to do with it. That was the best explanation I could come up with. To keep our identities as protected as possible, everyone was prohibited from talking about the past, even among ourselves.

Years ago, I realized I would never learn who my mother was or why the older members of the group seemed to avoid meeting my eyes. My whole life I had always exceeded expectations, even for our people, but I'd never been praised for it. I'd had to come to terms with never having answers. It was either that or go crazy.

When I'd hugged my dad, I'd left my sunglasses on the counter next to where Victoria now stood. I debated leaving them, but the sun would hurt my eyes and I'd lose that layer of protection that would hide my expression. I left my position behind Liv and casually grabbed my sunglasses from the marble surface where Victoria was leaning. She straightened at my proximity and must have seen down my black tank top.

"Why are you wearing my bathing suit?" she asked acidly.

"It was in my drawer. I thought it was Liv's." Wrong thing to say, I realized too late. She'd think I was saying she was too old to wear it. "I can change."

"No," she said flatly. The resentment aimed at me was subtle, but I was sensitive enough to pick it up. It vanished as quickly as it flared. "Keep it."

Shaken, I walked back to my sister. In spite of our distance this summer, Liv was still my safety in this house.

"Where are you going?" Victoria asked again, as if the thought of Liv and me going somewhere together was completly unacceptable.

"I'm dropping Julia off at Ellis's, and I'm going to Emma's. To swim," Liv lied.

She had actually lied. The old Liv wouldn't have bought into that. I felt like someone had just kicked me in the chest. Even worse, Victoria knew Liv was lying. The trickle-down of that would only land on me.

"Bye, Mom." Liv quickly kissed her cheek. Victoria looked back at Liv, clearly not satisfied. "Come back by three. Remember, I'm taking you to Grandma's tonight." I wasn't included in that plan.

There was a moment of silence, and then Liv and I made our way to the elevator. When the doors opened into the garage, Liv automatically walked over to the black Range Rover without asking me first. She wanted to drive her new car. It was a change for me to ride in the passenger's seat.

For a second it seemed as though Liv was going to say something. I stared straight ahead. Liv apparently decided against it.

When she started the car, the music came on loud, jolting us both, but she didn't bother to turn it down. It made for good filler.

We wound out of our neighborhood, which was lush with greenery and hanging vines, then down the curves with water views and large homes hidden behind tall trees and massive gates. At the base of Scenic Drive, the car was spit out onto flat, hot pavement.

Chapter Three

The first time I saw him, he had on a battered baseball hat and Ray-Bans. I noticed him getting out of an old white Ford Explorer close to where we'd parked, in the dusty lot at Barton Springs. I didn't know why I was immediately drawn to him. I was always vaguely and automatically scanning my surroundings—especially in public, where there was excessive interest in us.

He saw us almost instantly, turning his head, along with the other people in the parking lot who were now staring. As soon as Liv exited the car, everyone tried to place her, wondering if she was some kind of celebrity hiding behind her sunglasses. Teenagers typically didn't look like her or pull up in a car like that.

I felt his eyes on me, but, unlike everyone else, his gaze didn't switch back to Liv. As we walked to the entrance, I was aware of how I looked beside her. Short and thin next to her tall curvaceousness, I was all hard exterior with my tattoos, my chin-length black bob, my skin pale against my black clothing. In contrast Liv was a natural beauty, dressed in all white, her hair cascading down her back. Self-consciously I tucked a strand of hair behind my ear, then kicked myself for allowing an outsider to make me feel self-conscious.

It wasn't just him, I told myself. I wasn't used to all this public gawking. It would be better when summer ended and we went back to school on Monday. It would keep Angus from wanting to push the envelope.

Involuntarily, I turned my head to look at the boy again as he trailed us to the admissions booth. He was over six feet tall and had dark-brown, almost-black hair. There was something in how he carried himself—a type of confidence that made him immediately eye-catching. Confidence meets I-don't-give-a-shit meets calm. Standing right behind me in the long line waiting to pay, he was acutely aware of us. I could feel it. I wondered if I was making it up, but I thought his attention was wholly directed toward me.

So softly that it was impossible for anyone else to hear, Liv said, "He smells good," referring to our usual revulsion at the scent of outsiders. I knew who she was talking about. I'd noticed it too.

"It's probably his sunscreen," I said.

I glanced over my shoulder and saw him deftly juggle his things from one arm to the other in order to take his phone from his pocket. The glass face of the phone had a long crack in it, and a picture of Johnny Cash on the lock screen. He checked it quickly before putting the phone back in his pocket, vaguely annoyed. He wasn't just looking at the time. I could tell he was waiting for a call or text that hadn't come. I felt him bring his focus back to me. I didn't know why he made me feel so self-aware when usually I was a master at blocking people out. At least watching him was distracting me from the nearby crowd.

Once Liv and I paid at the booth and walked through the entrance, it was like stepping into a different world smack in the middle of the city. Shaded by pecan trees and dotted with towels and chairs, the lawn sloped steeply down to the sunlit water. The din of the shouting swimmers and intermittent spring of the diving board carried up the hill. The bathhouse was on the opposite side of the water, that lawn already filling with a different kind of group—mostly people with kids.

It was around noon and not crazy-crowded yet. It was ridiculously hot already. As Liv and I stood at the top of the grassy hill, deciding where to sit, I realized everyone in the vicinity was looking in the same direction.

The Lost Kids were here. It was like a haze of gold surrounded them—partially because of their coloring, but also because they were half in the sunlight and half in the dappled shade beneath the trees. It was jarring to see them together in public like this. With their almost identically colored hair that nearly matched their skin tone, the seven boys looked like an otherworldly grouping of models posed as gorgeous young skate rats. They were all very tall and skinny, reminding me of the ectomorph cross-country runners I'd see running in packs, except that my friends' chests and backs were covered in tattoos. The boys acted like they were in their own private world, but it was far too obvious who they were.

Usually we were so careful to go out alone or in small groups so the public would see just one or two people with tan skin and perfect features. I could feel everyone around us begin to realize who the girl next to me was. And now they were looking at me too, wondering how I could be with her when I didn't match.

People were using their phones to take pictures and to text, presumably about the sighting. Angus and the boys stood on the slope, shoving one another, blatantly oblivious to the stares and the space they were taking up.

Liv, thankfully, didn't walk over to the Lost Kids. She was too wary. Then I saw Liv's friends on a different section of the lawn—another group of seven teens, looking like royals trying to relax at a public pool. They waved her over, but Liv breezed down to the central part of the wet, green hill, putting us squarely between the A-group and the Lost Kids. No way would I have come if I'd known there would be this many of us in public. This wasn't allowed.

"Did you invite George?" I asked.

"No. I told Emma I was coming. I can't believe they're here."

"He's trying to protect you. I heard you're dating him."

Liv laughed a *whatever* laugh.

"This is making me nervous," I stated flatly. "All of us shouldn't be here."

I shook out the turquoise hand-woven cotton blanket that had no business being on the ground and Liv sat down, lounging back on her elbows. I sank down next to her, wanting to get out of the crowd's line of vision.

Angus was watching us. I could sense his smirk from fifty feet away. Shirtless, with shorts falling low on his hips, he had no body fat, just a lot of lean, defined muscle. He turned and I saw the telltale wing tattoo that spanned his entire back. I forgot what meaning it had at the time—freedom, I guess—

but it reminded me of a fallen angel. And he definitely looked like an angel gone bad, with his curls and that fierce gaze in his icy blue eyes. Actually, he looked a lot like my dad.

"You can go sit with them if you want," I said to Liv, gesturing with my chin to her friends. The schism between the two groups of kids—the haves and the have-nots—was stark. Novak's decision to form two groups had been disastrous for our friendships. It was too painful for us Lost Kids to be around the others, knowing they had to keep secrets from us. And they were scared off by our derision, which was mostly fueled by our jealousy.

But Liv was looking at Angus as she said, "No, they can come to us." I couldn't believe she actually thought I was telling her to go to my friends. She's young, I kept reminding myself, making excuses for her self-centeredness.

Sweat trickled down my back. I had a metallic feeling in the back of my throat—I was beginning to recognize this as one of the signs that the rash was coming on. I needed to leave. I didn't want to be the one blamed for bringing my sister here. There was bad energy in the air. The boys continued to draw attention to themselves, doing neat backflips they shouldn't all have been able to manage.

If I had been smart, I would have stood up right then and driven home. Unfortunately a much bigger part of me wanted to stay, in order to stand in the way of whatever might have been happening between Liv and Angus.

Angus lit a cigarette, and I immediately looked over at the nearest lifeguard. I saw the lifeguard quickly look away, pretending not to see the infraction. He didn't want to approach. It felt like everyone in the park was holding their breath—

partially out of wonder and partially from tension. I knew that in their minds it wasn't clear what our group might do next.

Liv angled her body to look behind us. Craning her neck, she stared at something. "What?" I asked, and turned around.

I had been so busy freaking out at the heat and the noise and the spectacle that I hadn't noticed where the boy from the parking lot had landed. He'd spread out his beach towel just behind us, but he was ignoring us completely. The only personal items around him were a bottle of smartwater, a phone, and a paperback book. He had the aura of someone who wanted to be alone. I was wondering if he was about my age—seventeen or eighteen—when he obliged me by removing his hat and sunglasses, and I could see my guess had to be close. Then, almost violently, he whipped his shirt off over his head. Balling it up, he stuck it behind him where he could use it as a pillow, grabbed his hat and sunglasses, putting them back on before he lay down on his towel, and reached for his book. Not even a glance our way, though I'm sure he could tell we were both openly staring. Now that he had his shirt off, I looked a second longer than I should have.

I was embarrassed and wanted to cover. I didn't think I'd ever wanted to really look at an outsider before. At least in that way.

Liv seemed fascinated also. "What do you think his story is?" she asked, finally facing forward.

"I don't know—some guy here feeling sorry for himself. He's wondering why his girlfriend hasn't called." I was just trying to sound dismissive, but as soon as it came out I knew with certainty it was true. I knew his girlfriend was cheating on him at this very moment. And that he was far too good for her.

Liv laughed at that.

"Since when do you care about outsiders?" I asked her, wanting to blow it off.

She shrugged. "Since never." But she turned back around again and stared. Suddenly she looked like she was actually about to call out to him.

"Liv!" I said quickly.

"What?" she asked, annoyed, as if I'd just interrupted something.

"Emma's trying to get your attention." We could feel Emma and the other swan-like girls staring Liv down from across the substantial distance.

Liv looked over in her best friend's direction but made no move to get up. Luckily I'd managed to distract her, and she was facing the water again. Her persistent interest in the person behind us was peculiar.

We both trained our eyes back on the boys.

I saw Ellis take a pull from a flask, in full view of the roving lifeguard now swiftly walking toward them. My eye caught the flash of silver traveling from one point in the circle of boys to another, but by the time the lifeguard approached, there was no sign anyone had been drinking anything. The lifeguard looked baffled, probably wondering if he was crazy and had never seen a flask to begin with. The boys blatantly laughed in his face, and the lifeguard instinctively backed away.

"Hey, man." It was the boy behind us talking on his phone, his voice low and gravelly. I realized with a shock that if we could hear him, he could hear us. Liv and I had automatically switched to the way we spoke to one another in public, like we were supposed to. He'd most likely heard everything we had said, about a girlfriend, about "outsiders." We were in a pocket where sound carried perfectly. It sounded like he was speaking directly to us.

Liv and I both listened. It was impossible not to. He spoke quietly, probably assuming—correctly—that we were eavesdropping.

"What's up?" Pause. "I forgot. Sorry. I can be there in thirty minutes." I surreptitiously looked behind me and saw him, phone in hand, head bent and looking at the ground, trying to be as private as possible. Then, reluctantly, he said, "Barton Springs. No, by myself." It was like he was shy about revealing his location and that he'd come alone. "I don't know. I haven't been here since I came back. . . . I'll tell you next time. I gotta go—my phone's about to die. I have one of your rackets in the car. Okay. Later."

He checked his phone again before tossing it aside. He picked up his book, *All the King's Men*, and acted like he wanted to shut out everything around him for just a few more minutes. After a second he gave up and closed it. I found myself wondering where he'd just come back from. I knew that had been his brother on the phone.

I knew *information* about this person. That had never happened before. My first instinct was to blow it off as a fluke. I mostly felt weak that some regular person had broken through the barrier I was so good at maintaining between outsiders and myself. Why him?

All of us had better senses than outsiders. Just like we were faster, stronger, and smarter than regular people. We were also healthier and lived longer. It had always been a fact of life that we were biologically different—better—and that this had to be kept secret.

We were also more perceptive. English felt like a secondary mode of communication. We were more like other animals—constantly reading body language for unspoken signals and information. Outsiders had no idea what they were always unconsciously conveying. In turn we maintained such a state of calm that it made it almost impossible for us to read one another.

Our contact with outsiders was typically brief and minimal—with teachers, housekeepers, restaurant servers—but if we wanted to we could tell you things about them that were lost on most people. We knew when a stranger hadn't slept or was distracted, angry, in love. The rhythm of their heartbeat and their scent also gave details about them away. Mostly we'd been taught to block those signals out. Novak said outsiders were a bad influence—caught in their never-ending cycles of fear and desire.

But this was different for me. I was positive that what I knew about this person was correct. *Jesus.* I didn't know if Novak could read anyone's mind, if the other adults could. . . . It felt hard to believe it was commonplace.

For the next several minutes, I tried to refocus on what was happening around me—on pretty, upstanding George staring at Liv like he owned her, on Angus, on needing to get Liv out of here.

"Let's just relax. We're making people nervous." The exact moment I said it to Liv, it was like the boy behind me held up a hand and asked for it all to stop. All of the tension I felt, he was feeling too.

I instinctively sat up and turned to him. I knew I was looking at him like I was asking him a question. He didn't respond like I was crazy. He took off his sunglasses as if his instinct was to let me see him. Just the two of us existed at that moment. I had never felt anything like it—as if he were looking into me and I suddenly wanted him to.

He knew who we were. He'd heard about us before. He'd picked up on my calling him an outsider. He also thought we were elitists, and he was offended that I thought he was a loser waiting for his girlfriend to call. He'd only wanted to get away from his life for a few hours, and he disliked the keyed-up atmosphere we brought with us.

And he thought I was so incredibly beautiful.

I could only describe it as recognition. I knew him even though I didn't know who he was. And he felt it too. It was the oddest, most right moment of my life.

Liv broke the moment. "Here comes Angus." And then the feeling was gone. I turned my back on whatever was happening, hoping my expression conveyed that he was no longer worth my time. I wanted no part of it. It was the last thing I needed right now.

After I turned around I waited for the flash of excitement I felt whenever I saw Angus. That ridiculous longing and unrequited crush was something I could grab on to.

Angus strutted up to us, all cocky half grin and knowing blue eyes. A sheen of sweat was on his hairless, tan chest, tattoos covering almost every available inch. I tried to see him through Liv's eyes and couldn't tell if she would be repulsed, or attracted the way I was. But when I saw them look at each other, they suddenly made perfect sense to me. I knew they would end up together. I felt a beat behind, like I'd shown up too late to the party to put a stop to what was happening in front of my face.

"Livvy Jaynes, you slummin' today?"

"Apparently." A huge smile played on Liv's face. God, she could light up.

"What took you so long?"

"I wasn't sure I could make it."

I rolled my eyes at that one.

They eyed each other intently for a moment. I was surprised to know Angus was slightly nervous, which was not something I'd ever seen.

"I'm sitting down. Sorry, assholes." Angus pointed his chin in the direction of George and friends, who were staring down hard at Liv from their position.

Angus sprawled next to me on the blanket, putting me between them. Then he proceeded to plaster himself against my side as he leaned across me to talk to Liv. I inched away and wondered if he cared. Angus was always overfamiliar—touching me all summer by leaning against me, holding my hand. I had thought it was because he liked me. Now I felt sadness, disgust, and an *Of course* feeling all wrapped together. I felt another surge of unrecognizable and totally unacceptable anger. She could have everything. I'd given her everything. Why this . . . ?

What a total d-bag.

I looked up to see who had called Angus a douchebag and was about to get the shit kicked out of them. It hadn't been said in a joking way by one of the Lost Kids. It had been said in the most derogatory tone you could imagine. But there wasn't anyone near us, except for the person behind us. Then I realized Liv and Angus had had no visible reaction. Liv sifted her hand back and forth through the grass while Angus tried to make her laugh. They hadn't heard.

I whipped around.

It had been *his* voice. But he was looking off into the distance, pretending to study the people swimming down below. It sounded like he had said it to himself, in his head. I stumbled on that thought for a moment before deciding he must have murmured it and I was the only one listening. It actually kind of cracked me up that he had such disdain for Angus, who was starring in the worst love triangle anyone had ever seen. A one-sided love triangle, I guess. And then I felt uncomfortable that this stranger was seeing this.

"I had your sister out late last night," Angus was saying to Liv.

"I know. What were you doing?"

Angus looked off into the distance at his friends, who were not-so-discreetly watching him in amazement. He was talking to Liv. It was a big deal. He was going to catch a lot of shit from them.

Angus turned back from the Lost Kids and looked at Liv, deliberately not answering her question. I wanted to say, *Angus and I were out and he begged me to teach him more of the tricks I know. In fact, he had a knife through his hand at one point in the night, and then he hung himself from a tree, to see how long he could last, until I threatened to leave.*

I tried to tell myself that if I hadn't shown Angus my "tricks," these guys would be deep into mind-numbing drugs. That's where they'd been heading before this near-death crap. I completely understood they needed a release of some sort.

These small tricks kept me sane so I could quash my instincts for the rest of the day. But if our families found out . . . I absentmindedly watched the sparkling water below. Of all the eyes on us, I was most conscious of the gaze coming from directly behind me. I tried again to block him out.

"I'm going for a swim." Liv stood up suddenly and with two hands grasped the bottom of her short white dress and whipped it over her head. It was like all of Barton Springs turned to her in unison.

Liv clearly expected Angus to join her. But to my surprise and Liv's, he didn't move an inch.

"Enjoy." He gave her a Cheshire grin. Liv pretended she didn't care that he wasn't following her like a puppy, and she walked lightly down the hill, resplendent in a white bikini setting off the glow of her tan skin.

Angus openly watched. I couldn't believe it didn't make Liv want to bolt, but she carried herself like she was impervious to scrutiny. I had to resist the urge to look over my shoulder to see if *he* was looking at her too.

Now that there was room on the blanket, I shifted so I could see Angus. He was looking at the water, momentarily lost in thought. I concentrated hard on maintaining a neutral expression so he wouldn't have the satisfaction of knowing I was hurt.

From the intensity I'd felt in the air between them, it struck me that maybe Angus had spent the whole summer getting even closer to me in order to gain access to Liv.

That sudden realization made my stomach hurt. As if on cue, the sun broke through the trees and blazed onto my side and legs. Suddenly I wasn't able to keep the noise from the water, the groups of people all around me, and the intensity of the stares at bay. I needed to process what had happened seconds before Angus sat down. I felt the tingle on my arms. The rash was about to appear. I didn't know where I planned to go, but I made a move to stand up.

"Hey! Hey." Angus's voice suddenly gentled, and he grasped my wrist to pull me back down next to him. "Julia, it's going to be okay. Shhhhh. Breathe." He knew. He was the only person who understood what I was feeling and that I needed a release. As much as I hated myself for it, I let myself be soothed by him because it would work. When I let Angus hold me, I had the distinct sense the person behind me was reacting to the sight of Angus touching me. He didn't like it.

As angry as he could make me, I had never been able to distance myself from Angus for long. He changed when he was around me. With his friends, he was the alpha dog whose moods were unpredictable. When he wasn't playing mind games, he was outright taunting them into the next dare. But with me, when he wasn't teasing and flirting, he was kind. I have to admit I loved it because I thought maybe he understood how hard my situation was in my family. He knew why I'd showed him the tricks. It was just one way to secretly be special in a family that said you couldn't be. He'd wanted what I had so badly. I'd had no idea he'd be smart enough and talented enough to take it to a new level, using his own body for practice.

Angus examined me to see if I had pulled it together, and then his attention moved on again. He looked back at the water, searching for Liv. Without glancing at me he said, "Are you okay?"

"Why did you want to come *here* today, of all places?" I asked, my whisper so soft, I knew only Angus could hear. Too many confusing things were happening. It was rare for me to feel so out of control. I realized Angus must feel it too, but it was feeding him, giving him some kind of thrill.

Angus spoke softly, taking my cue. "What? You don't like big groups of people?"

"No. Why would I?"

Angus shrugged. "I like watching them. You should too. There are well over seven billion of them, and they're the ones in charge."

"I think you like the chaos," I said.

"I don't know. They're pretty predictable in their stupidity." Angus suddenly changed the subject. "I heard your dad is back in the country. Do you know where he was?"

I shook my head. The whole point of Relocation was no one knowing where we were going. It minimized the risk and enabled us to start fresh someplace where no outsiders knew who we were, where it would hopefully take another twenty years before there was too much suspicion of our abilities, like there was now in Austin.

"I hear it's going to be different this time."

"What do you mean?" I asked, squinting at him.

"Like, not just changing identities and location. Not just removing this shit." Angus held up an arm, referring to his tattoos.

"But how else would we do it?"

"I don't know." Angus sounded pissed. "Maybe Novak tells *them*." He looked over at Liv's group of friends and gave them a dead-eyed stare.

Roger, one of the Lost Kids, interrupted us. He felt free to saunter over now that Liv was absent, and he started ribbing Angus about her in spite of my presence, which was doubly insulting. I thought the boys had assumed Angus and I were together.

"Shut up," said Angus simply and seriously enough that Roger backed off immediately.

"Hey, we're going in." Roger stalked off, duly chastened and out of favor.

Angus made the move to stand up and leave me. I could sense he was antsy, and also feeling protective of Liv, who was in the water alone. My answer was to lash out.

Forever, I'd look back and wonder why, after all the years of mastering my emotions, I'd lost control so easily. I wanted to scare Liv away from Angus. I wanted to tempt him away with something I thought would trump his feelings for her. I wanted to hurt Liv for growing up and becoming like the rest of them.

But what if Roger had stayed, or what if Liv hadn't gone to Barton Springs that day and jealousy hadn't gotten the best of me? What if I'd left moments before instead of sitting back down? So many things could have changed the course of what happened next. One question turned my life upside down.

"Angus?"

He raised his eyebrows, as if to say, *What now?*

"Have you ever tried to drown?"

Chapter Four

It was like you could see the wheels turning in Angus's head. Then he wordlessly descended the hill to the water.

For a moment I felt nothing except self-satisfaction. Angus would choose the dare over Liv. That's where his focus would go for the rest of the afternoon while she stood by, disgusted.

I took off my tank top and lay back on the blanket, feeling like I'd put everything back in order.

I sensed him behind me, and I tried not to care. I knew he needed to meet his brother. Any time now he would leave Barton Springs, and I'd never have to think about him, and what happened, again. But with my eyes closed, I realized I was listening for his movements.

Perhaps fifteen minutes passed, and I wondered if he'd left and I'd missed it completely. At the thought I sat up quickly, surprised by my disappointment.

He was reading his book again, but as soon as I sat up he looked over, his eyes scanning my body for a split second. Sweat trickled continuously down my back. I felt far too naked. Trying to cover his interest, he threw his book aside and felt for his phone. But now it was to check for the time, not for texts from his girlfriend. I felt it—he wasn't thinking about his girlfriend now.

He stared at his phone, annoyed. Before I could turn away, he looked directly at me, making eye contact. "Excuse me, do you know what time it is?"

He obviously knew I'd heard him, but for a moment it seemed not answering would be the best thing to do, making it clear I didn't want any contact.

But I couldn't leave him hanging like that, I told myself. Without consulting a phone or a watch, I said, "Just after two." My voice sounded a little huskier than I would have liked.

I was about to face forward again when he said, "I'm John." And then to my pure mortification, I blushed.

I wasn't sure what I was about to say in return when, without warning, I felt all the blood drain from my face. The feeling was like a connection had been severed, like a light had been switched off. I wasn't sure how, but I suddenly knew Liv was gone.

I didn't think about concealing anything. I ran so fast down the hill, I knew I was a blur, maneuvering too precisely between the groupings of people camped out on the now-jam-packed hillside.

Once I got through the people and leapt down to the sidewalk next to the springs, I ran directly to the far end of the pool, which was marked by a chain-link fence. Behind and below it was the runoff, a rocky pool a steep drop down where people took their dogs and swam for free. The Lost Kids were there at the entrance to the runoff. You could see the group of them diving and popping up like fish before going under again. It looked like they were taking turns trying to see something at the bottom of the pool, laughing and shouting to each other whenever they'd come up.

I heard myself scream, "She's trapped!" I dove into the water, leaving behind me a crowd of people who'd risen to their feet.

The shock of the cold knocked the wind out of me. I swam hard over to the general area of the boys. It would seem suspicious that I hadn't come up for air yet, but I was close now. I opened my eyes underwater. There were plants floating everywhere, and rays of sunlight were shining through the brown water in dusty beams. The stillness was in complete contrast to the chaos on the surface.

Between the bodies of the boys treading water, I saw Liv flattened against the runoff grate, sucked hard against it, long hair fanned eerily out around her. She wasn't moving. I could hear the group shouting above the surface, yelling, "What are you doing? Leave her!" I heard Angus scream, "Shut the fuck up!"

Then I felt the intensifying suction of the water drawing me. I suddenly flew toward Liv, landing my feet against the metal bars to stop myself. I grasped at one of her arms, which floated lifelessly out from her side. Using all my strength, I tried to break away from the water's pull and swim us to the surface. Her body didn't follow. Through the haze, I saw her leg caught from the knee down in one of the slats of the grate, pinning her. I began desperately trying to free it. Her body was motionless, and I realized I was staring point-blank at someone who had drowned. I felt my own body begin to go into shock just as someone swiped at me underwater, trying to get my attention.

Like it was happening on a movie screen, I saw Angus

angrily make a banging motion against the runoff grate. When he did it, a rusty slat bent outward, freeing Liv. Her body slammed against the grate again, the suction reclaiming her, and I struggled to grab hold of her.

Someone reached out to take her from me. Angus tried to stop him, lashing out with one long arm. I remembered his name was John. In the midst of the complete chaos, it came to me very clearly. He was the one who used his strength to haul Liv to the surface.

Everything happened in slow motion. John pulled Liv to the side of the pool, some of the Lost Kids right behind them. Hands of strangers reached out and helped move Liv's body so that it was lying flat on the pavement. I flew up the silver ladder and rushed to Liv, Angus a second behind me. Somehow the group of us edged out the bystanders and circled Liv, trying to protect her from prying eyes.

"Livvy, come on." I put my hands on her cheeks, until Angus pulled them away and started slapping Liv not so gently on the face.

"Come *on*, Liv." This was lasting too long now. For a second Angus's eyes met mine. "Are you kidding me?" I snarled at him. "She's not like us."

Angus couldn't look at me and turned his attention back to Liv, determined to somehow make this okay.

"Liv!" I shouted at her, rubbing her arms. In my peripheral vision I saw George attempt to remove Angus.

"What did you do, you asshole? Get the fuck away from her."

Within one second of George laying a hand on Angus, the Lost Kids jumped him. Marko, Daniel, and Max from Liv's group descended upon our group to defend George. Suddenly I was surrounded by a nasty brawl, the Lost Kids choosing this moment to release months of repressed rage on Novak's chosen ones.

"CPR?" It was John. Somehow he had remained in the inner circle, right there at Liv's side.

"Not yet," I answered.

I was vaguely aware of the shrieks of lifeguard whistles and sirens in the background. I bent low and started whispering in Liv's ear, "It's over. You've got this." Before I could stop him, John moved fully over Liv and began using his hands to try to warm both her arms, undoubtedly the first stranger who had ever touched her.

In a blink Liv came to. She sat up, twisted her body, and exhaled all the water that had filled her lungs. She took one look at John, who moved aside, and then, in full view of the crowd who had just seen her all but dead on the pavement, Liv simply stood up to her full five feet ten inches.

I let out a ragged breath, as if I'd been hyperventilating this whole time. "What were you *thinking*?" I yelled. It was pure instinct, I was so scared. I had never yelled before in my life, and most definitely not at her.

Startled, Liv looked at me, and I watched the expression in her blue eyes cloud. I realized my mistake immediately. Lowering my voice, I asked, "Are you okay?" I stood and reached out protectively.

"Jesus. I'm fine." She shook my hand off her arm.

Angus appeared, a gash under his eye and blood seeping

from a cut on his head. He placed his hand gently on Liv's back. Liv looked from me to Angus as if we were her parents, hovering. I could see she was deeply embarrassed, and I knew she suddenly felt like an inept little girl.

Liv took in the crowd around her. Things had suddenly grown very quiet.

"Thanks, Julia," she said nastily, gesturing around her.

John sat back on his heels, trying to catch his breath, a long, raw scratch on his cheek from Angus. He looked up at me. His eyes told me he'd seen everything. He'd seen more than any other person had.

Excess adrenaline coursed through my body, and I felt like I was going to vomit as the enormity of what had just happened began to sink in. How had I known from halfway across the park that Liv was trapped underwater? And I had created a spectacle. We all had.

After being hyperfocused on Liv, I was fully coming out of a daze. With tunnel vision I saw lifeguards leading a pack of EMTs, all of them running toward us.

Moments before, the two groups had been beating each other to a pulp. Now, in what looked like a choreographed wave, the Lost Kids and Liv's friends turned on the descending EMTs and lifeguards, forming a wall to block them from examining Liv. I saw Angus take hold of John's arm to push him from us, but John jerked away. Everyone was yelling and shoving.

A police officer grabbed me roughly from behind, dragging me backward to make way for the medical workers. Angus lunged forward to stop him, his fingertips gouging the cop's shoulder. The policeman was thrown backward as if electrocuted.

I stumbled forward and John caught me. I heard a sickening crack as the cop's head smacked the pavement. Whipping around in John's arms, I saw Angus standing over the cop he'd rendered unconscious.

It was like time stood still as we all accepted the inevitability of what would happen next. Seconds later Angus allowed himself to be tackled to the ground.

Chapter Five

The heavy door opened, letting fresh air wash into the humid, stale room. In with a youngish cop came Angus, looking no worse for the wear, behaving like it was no big deal that he had just assaulted a police officer. They had taken Angus separately in a police car. The rest of us were driven in a white corrections van, a police chaperone riding in the back to make sure we didn't talk and change our stories. After a fifteen-minute ride, we'd pulled into an underground parking garage. They'd taken us in and questioned us individually before leading us to this large room with a concrete floor and benches lining the walls.

Angus's smile disappeared when he saw why we weren't talking. There were twelve of us in the room, and one stranger.

I'd heard him give his full name and date of birth to a cop when they had us sit on the low concrete wall, out on display for all of Barton Springs to see, some people even taking photos. *John Ford.* Four months older than me. Already eighteen. I knew that was going to make things worse for him.

I couldn't believe they'd slapped handcuffs on him as well.

The only thing he'd done was pull Liv out of the water. But happily it worked in our favor. There was no need to even discuss it; we automatically knew to coordinate our statements and point the finger at him for the damaged public property. We'd completely screw him over.

Everyone waited for the cop to call the next name. Liv's friends Emma, Serena, and Kate had escaped the roundup at Barton Springs, so we knew support would arrive soon. Until then we waited. A couple of the boys were vibrating with anger but were barely moving—just knees bouncing up and down and sudden shifts from upright to elbows on knees. Whenever they made eye contact with John, they simply looked bored and unimpressed, the standard reset face when dealing with the public. Then their gaze would slide away as if they had already moved on.

John sat directly across from me on a bench by himself, long legs crossed at the ankle in front of him. Once in a while he'd subtly roll his left shoulder, like he was testing out an injury. I saw him scratch the back of one of his hands, and I suddenly remembered seeing his hands on Liv, how they'd been unexpectedly scaly and raw. It was eczema. His hands were a crazy contrast to his otherwise tan, smooth skin. Like he knew I was thinking about it, he shoved his hands deep in his pockets to hide them from view.

It was impressive how contained he was in light of the fact that he was essentially trapped in a jar with a different species. He didn't know, but subconsciously it had to unnerve him. I knew it was eerie to be in such close quarters with this many people who looked so much alike and pretended you didn't exist.

I tried to avoid eye contact, which was difficult. I found myself continuously looking sidelong at him, wanting to know what he was thinking. Maddeningly, whatever that had been—reading his mind—was gone. It was like I'd imagined it.

He knew exactly what had really happened: I had predicted an emergency from hundreds of feet away, and he'd seen Angus bend steel. He must have known I'd stayed underwater a little too long. And he may have been the only other person besides Angus and myself to see what happened to the cop when Angus touched him.

No one would believe him, I told myself. Or if they did, they couldn't do anything about it. Everything that had occurred sounded right out of a ridiculous urban myth, no matter what any bystanders or even police claimed they saw. We could cover our tracks somehow. We always did. I wasn't sure we had ever had an incident on this scale, though. And the police had taken our fingerprints.

Everyone I knew had instantaneously iced me out while we were at Barton Springs. I began to realize that among our people, this was on me. It seemed lost on them that Liv could have died while they watched. I was being blamed for doing the one thing we weren't allowed to do.

I turned my gaze to the dirty floor, shocked at my friends' coldness. It was terrifying, like being completely separated from a lifeline.

The walls were so glaringly white, they hurt my eyes. I stared at the fluorescent tube lights that lined the ceiling and decided to put three of them out with a glance. When the room dimmed, I expected some sort of acknowledgment—a half smile—something to let me know we were going to be okay. I felt the Lost Kids refuse to even look over, though they obviously knew it had been me.

And so I sat by myself at the end of my bench, isolated just like him. Angus and Liv now sat together. Liv whispered in his ear.

John caught me watching the exchange. This time I didn't turn away from him. He looked back at me, openly questioning. Even though he appeared calm at first glance, I could see in his eyes that he was exhausted and stressed. I wasn't sure if he was trying to figure out the ramifications of being arrested or if he was mentally ticking through all the unbelievable things he'd witnessed today, wanting to grasp a plausible explanation.

I stared deep into his eyes, silently asking him to never talk about what happened. I experienced a glimmer of the feeling I'd had at Barton Springs when we looked at each other for the first time. He looked straight back at me, and I realized he wouldn't say a word. He was smart enough to know no one would believe him anyway. Still, he wanted answers. I couldn't give him what he wanted, so I dropped my eyes from his and cordoned myself off. He didn't exist. Again.

The young cop entered. "Julia and Olivia Jaynes," he called out. I felt John recognize my last name from the Jaynes Pavilion sports arena. I wondered if he now realized me and Liv were sisters.

Things had changed at the police station since the last time I'd been out of the room. Now it was dominated by suits—a combination of our parents and their lawyers. They were here to fix this thing. In a matter of hours, wheels had been set in motion. You would have thought a celebrity or political figure had been caught breaking the law, not that a group of kids had been merely detained.

"Wait here." The police officer gestured to some chairs. I could wait all day. I wasn't ready to face what was coming next.

Liv stared straight ahead. I rested the back of my head against the wall behind me, settling in for another wait, my eyes burning, covered in a film of grime from both sunscreen and sitting for hours in that warm, airless room.

"He's not even supposed to be here. He was supposed to be safely on scholarship at that goddamn academy." The woman's voice sounded angry and teary at the same time.

"We'll figure it out. There's no way he would vandalize some runoff grate. They just want to hold someone accountable for shutting down the pool and costing the city money."

I realized I could faintly hear what was going on directly behind me through the wall. It was obviously John's parents talking.

"No matter what, we're going to have to pay for a lawyer." The way his mother said this made it clear this was going to be a financial hardship. "What the hell kind of charge is 'criminal mischief'?"

"Let's talk to him first, before he feels this enormous disappointment coming from you. It's been hard enough on him this summer."

"That's not fair. I'm sorry, but how did we get here? He was on this great track, and now it feels like everything has gone completely off the rails."

"He got injured. He came home."

"But he was going to get a great scholarship to a top university. Have this tennis career if he wanted it. And now? He seems like he doesn't give a shit about anything since he came back."

"Stop, Kathleen. Okay? Let's just get him home."

"How are you not worried about this?" Her voice sounded incredulous.

"I'm very worried." When the calm voice said that, it was worse than Kathleen's outburst.

Just then a door clicked open and the hallway hushed. Victoria, hair in a tight bun, stalked out of an office across the hallway. She was wearing sky-high heels, making her six feet tall, and she looked made of ice.

"Dr. Jaynes, I'm sorry you had to come all the way down here." An older police officer approached, holding out his hand. They obviously knew each other, since he didn't introduce himself. She eyed him but didn't say a word and didn't take his hand, then turned abruptly to one of the lawyers. She whispered something to the lawyer, who looked up and said, "They go through the back door. Understood?"

"I didn't see any media. . . ." The cop stopped talking at their expressions and changed direction. "Of course."

The apologies were beginning. This was exactly why Novak donated millions of dollars to campaigns, to the university, to other powerful people's causes. He needed to have this kind of influence just in case something like this happened.

I watched Victoria dismiss herself from the conversation and wander farther down the hall. At first her mind was elsewhere, but then she focused on something. And she smirked. I leaned forward to see what she was looking at. Victoria had heard about the stranger in our midst and was checking him out.

John sat on a chair across from where Victoria was standing. He had the balls to confidently lock eyes with her, which probably accounted for her smirk. I'd never seen anyone stand up to her like that, let alone an eighteen-year-old boy. Or maybe that was exactly the type of person who was unafraid: someone like Angus.

I saw John had been given his phone back. He looked down at it and then up at Victoria again, as if reconciling what he was reading with the live version of her. I guessed what he was reading. Victoria probably did too. I understood why he was questioning his sanity right now, wanting to know more, trying to justify what he'd seen. John actually succeeded in making Victoria uncomfortable. She pivoted on her heel and stalked back down the hallway toward us.

"Let's go," Victoria rasped at Liv and me, exposing the fact that she wasn't totally in control. The police officers snapped into motion, ready to provide us with an escort. Liv stood up, and I reluctantly followed. We had to pass John on the way to the exit. His was a front-row seat to this Kennedy-like show of power—the rich people getting their kids off, the regular person completely screwed. I kept my eyes down, not liking at all that I felt ashamed.

I saw him slide his feet back in anticipation of our passage, either to be polite and make room for us to pass, or because he didn't want us near him. As I drew closer, I strained to see out of the corner of my eye if I'd been right about what was on his phone, but I couldn't quite see.

John loosely cradled his phone in one hand and then put

it in his pocket. His ratty beach towel and *All the King's Men* had been returned as well and sat in a pile on the bench beside him. With a look I forced the paperback book to fall from the bench and skid under Liv's feet as she walked by. She tripped and stumbled forward. John reflexively half stood up and grasped her arm to steady her. I was one step behind them and deftly removed the phone from his pocket during the diversion.

Liv recovered from the rare stumble and shot John a look of death for touching her. She replaced the flip-flop she had lost, and our procession continued toward the exit, his phone now plastered to my side. I looked straight ahead and kept walking, feeling his eyes on my back.

Chapter Six

Victoria put the G-Wagen in reverse and tore out of the parking lot, not speaking to either of us. From the blacked-out window of her Mercedes-AMG G65, I saw a Honda Accord in the parking lot, a Patagonia LIVE SIMPLY sticker on the bumper. I guessed it belonged to John's family, since it was the only other civilian car in the lot.

No one spoke. The atmosphere was so glacial, even Liv knew better than to say a word. I sat in the backseat, which gave me a small amount of privacy. I took out John's phone to look at it. It was strange holding something that had just been in his hand.

The phone wasn't passcoded. It was as easy as sliding the power on, and the screen came alive with exactly what I thought would be there.

It wasn't the more generic profile of my father featured in the billionaire's issue of *Vanity Fair*. It was the story that came out shortly after from a semitrashy online news source. Entitled "Novak Jaynes, the Luckiest Man Alive," it was the one that had made all the rounds on social media, my school being ground zero. I was a little surprised it hadn't been scrubbed from the internet, given Novak's resources. I knew it by heart, but I found myself reading what was on his screen, wanting to see it from John's perspective.

We've all heard the phrase "born lucky." But how many times can you get lucky before people start to wonder if something more is at play? At first glance Novak Jaynes is an accomplished hedge fund manager with movie-star looks, living a dream life of wealth and power in Austin, Texas. This began as a straightforward look at a man whose hedge fund has achieved outsize success and who had the good fortune to miraculously survive a near-death incident. But the profile took an unexpected turn.

In the summer of 2001, just before the events of September 11, a twenty-four-year-old named Novak Jaynes started a hedge fund in a home office with $100,000. He predicted and profited handsomely from the market swing in 2001, single-handedly building the fund to one hundred million dollars in a breathtakingly short amount of time. He profited again during the market crash of 2008–2009. Today Novak Jaynes has an estimated net worth of over 1.2 billion dollars and has presumably made his investors millionaires several times over.

Jaynes came to the attention of outside financial circles when he was profiled without his permission in a best-selling book about the profiteers from these two events. The book dubbed him "the Oracle of Austin." From there, like it or not, he was on the map. And things got stranger as people began to look more closely at the man himself.

In early 2013 Jaynes, a rumored adrenaline junkie, went

skydiving in Monterey, California. When his chute deployed at fourteen thousand feet, Jaynes cut it loose, prepared to deploy his backup chute at six thousand feet. In a one-in-a-million chance, however, the backup didn't deploy properly. Jaynes plummeted to the ground, outside the drop zone. When the instructors found him, he was reportedly sitting on the side of the road with only facial lacerations. He stunned bystanders by refusing emergency medical care, citing his preference for his own physician. He then walked away from what should have been an unsurvivable incident.

There is no record of a Novak Jaynes before the year 2001, when he registered his fund with the SEC. Jaynes has declined to be interviewed for this article, and all the research tools available in this day and age yielded no results. Witness protection is one theory, though Jaynes would never live such a public life if this were the case.

Over the past two years, Novak Jaynes himself seems to have broken with his strictly private nature by becoming a major philanthropist—donating to the University of Texas at Austin's athletic facilities and medical school, Austin's New Central Library, and countless other civic projects in and around the city. As a by-product of his celebrity, Jaynes's family has been put in the spotlight as well, and very quickly it has become clear that Novak Jaynes's family warrants as much scrutiny as the man himself. Jaynes has two daughters in his immediate family. But then there's the extended family.

Ten families seemingly related to Jaynes live on the same street in a winding, exclusive neighborhood. All of this is notable, certainly, but things grow odder when you hear that this group keeps almost exclusively to itself. Those who have seen them together speak in hushed tones about their pure beauty—"a band of angels" was one vivid description—and how there are so many of them who look so stunningly alike.

Who are these kids who routinely receive national recognition in the various arenas in which they compete? They all attend the same exclusive private academy, St. Philip, a school that prides itself on sending students to the Ivies, which strangely none of these children attend, opting instead to stay local. When speaking to former and current students about the presence of Jaynes's group at the school, it's clear there is endless fascination and speculation where this group of children is concerned. There was both admiring and disparaging talk of the immense talent these children seem to possess—their incredible athleticism, their photographic memories. But then there were the stranger observations and rumors most likely born of envy: the eerie calm of the group, their seeming ability to communicate with just their eyes, and, most persistent, the conviction that if you watched them on the fringes long enough and hard enough, you would eventually catch them doing something out of the ordinary—making the impossible catch, jumping a little too high, each of them avoiding the cafeteria salad bar on just the days of the E. coli breakout.

Regardless of the rumors, we all like to study the shiny people, the powerful and talented, to see how they differ from us. But there is something uncanny about a mysterious group of so many similar people, as if they are their own island, living among us but also apart from us.

In the years since Jaynes's outrageous windfalls, his fund has performed steadily, yielding only slightly better than average returns. Could this be an attempt to stay off the radar? If so, he is lying low for now.

You can't see the Jayneses' home from the road, but from the water you get an unobstructed view. Staring at the architectural wonder of glass, rock, and steel, you have to wonder what takes place inside and what the Oracle's next act will be.

Jesus. But it was what was in the comments section that elevated us to the status of urban myth. Everyone and their brother claimed to have seen us do extraordinary things. More than one person said they'd seen us off to one side, mastering a professional-level gymnastics move or skateboard trick before simply dropping it to move on to the next thing. Others commented on ESP-level powers of anticipation—turning to the exact page in a book before we were told, opening a door before someone knocked. It was all true. Those were moments when we had been sloppy.

The article had surprised us when it appeared out of nowhere a little over a year ago. No one spoke about how much it had gotten right. Suddenly anyone who hadn't heard about our presence in Austin was aware of us. That's when Novak began to make changes and segmented us into smaller groups. After a bit the conversation died down, but from there on out you could feel people's excitement when they thought they had identified one of us around town.

I wondered if John had made his way to the one comment that unnerved us most of all, the one that named us. After reading this, John would feel both better and worse. He'd know he wasn't making things up, but he would also be scared. Even if you thought you were an open-minded person, it had to be different when you saw something so strange with your own eyes.

I exited the article and went through his open tabs. The first tab was a search for "Julia Jaynes."

"Hand it over." Victoria's voice cut through the car.

Dammit. She'd seen exactly what I'd done at the police station. I quickly looked for one more second, wanting to see his emails, his photos.

"Now."

I handed the phone over to Victoria. We were close to the house, but she made a detour farther down the road to a dock landing. Pulling right up to the water's edge, she stopped the car and looked down at the phone in her hand. Victoria also looked through his searches quickly, the only indication we had of what might be on a potential witness's mind. Regardless of what he might say, it was obvious that what had happened today would reignite the fire this article started a year ago. I couldn't overestimate how much trouble I was in.

Victoria handed the phone back to me like it was something disgusting. "Get rid of it."

I opened the car door and walked in the dark to the water's edge, throwing the phone as far as I could out into the lake.

Chapter Seven

I sensed Novak before I saw him, my eyes coming to rest on a shadow in the corner of the dark living room when we entered. He appeared to be lounging lazily in a soft, upholstered chair. Just sitting and waiting, which struck me as odd. Then I realized I never saw him not in motion or without his phone.

Crossing the room, Victoria stood before Novak, and I could sense the change in her attitude.

"Didn't know," Victoria said, so softly, most of her words dropping away.

"Not to try," Novak said.

"Private. Please."

She was pleading with him. And most definitely not for me. Her golden child had screwed up, and Victoria didn't want to discuss it in front of me. He would never send our future leader down to our group, the Lost Kids, if that was what Victoria was worried about.

Liv and I stood in the foyer, the waiting making it worse. We were not together in this. Until this summer I'd never felt apart from my sister. Even when we were small, we didn't fight—I didn't dare, and Liv was too kind to and wanted to please me. She had broken our dynamic first by taking one step too deep into my territory.

My dad stood up, light on his feet. He was dressed in jeans and a T-shirt from a local club, his feet bare. I still saw him through a little girl's eyes and could perfectly recall him tossing me into the air, me practically weightless and laughing uncontrollably.

"Liv, come with me." Novak turned to walk toward his large office at the top of the stairs. I watched Liv, spine curved, flip-flops slapping on the limestone, following him at a snail's pace. "Vic, come on," he tossed out. Victoria snapped into motion and trailed them up the staircase, not sparing a backward glance for me.

I didn't bother to sit down. Chewing a nail nervously, I walked over to the wall of glass and looked out at the water. At night, the house felt like a houseboat sitting on the silvery lake, the moon glinting off the water's surface. Most of the lights were off in the houses across the lake. My stomach ached. How much should I tell Novak about what happened?

Should I tell him everything the stranger may have seen? There were so many things, all because I'd paid him far too much attention. If we hadn't been speaking, he wouldn't have followed me.

And then there was the other question: what I should tell Novak about myself. In the space of a couple of hours, I'd read someone's mind and I'd known with certainty from a football field away that Liv was drowning. I'd suddenly seen all of Barton Springs in total clarity, like a scene laid out in

front of me, and known exactly where to run. I didn't understand it—was this what all the adults were capable of? This
kind of power didn't seem inconsequential the way Novak
had said when I came to him after the ski trip. I didn't know
what to do, because after that meeting I was no longer cer-
tain what Novak's reaction would be.

I heard a door open, and voices poured out into the hallway, echoing off the high ceilings. "Julia," my dad called. His
voice sounded so nonthreatening. Numb, I walked over to
the stairs and looked up. Liv and Victoria stood in front of
the display of family photos, watching me. When I reached
the top, I edged past them, keeping my gaze averted.

I hadn't been inside my dad's office in years. To me this
office felt like the nexus of power—where the secrets and the
future were managed by my dad, "the Chosen One," as Angus
had once mockingly called him. It was only over the course of
this last summer when I heard some snide comments about
my dad slip out from the Lost Kids that I realized not everyone admired him. They especially loved talking about
"Novak's girls"—the revolving door of assistants he chose from
an elite-seeming pool of predominantly female outsiders.
Eventually, each and every one of them was dismissed and cut
off when they'd inevitably become too infatuated with Novak.
There'd been more than one restraining order. Novak knew we
had that effect on the select few chosen to get that close to us,
so it was a mystery why he continued to court trouble.

I could see how it would be easy for the other Lost Kids
to resent Novak. Still, no one would ever dispute his leadership. For our own safety, no one mentioned the immediate
past, but from the time we could speak we were introduced

to our culture with stories of our ancestors and the diaspora of our people. As children we heard tales of the great ones—those who lived to one hundred and thirty, who could levitate, who could heal with their touch, and who could, most important, see the future. And we came to understand that Novak was like the great ones, the first in many generations, and he received guiding visions.

Novak had foreseen our inability to have children in spite of all attempts. He knew Liv would be our future leader, and for reasons that weren't clear to me a vision had brought us to Austin. These foresights were also what enabled Novak to see three steps ahead on the chessboard of our lives and know just how to manipulate and outrun an increasingly volatile world.

I was sure there were other billionaires hiring top minds, figuring out how to protect their direct descendants as the planet grew warmer and the world more unstable. But it made members of the group nervous that Novak was out front and center, influencing political leaders and CEOs, ensuring they made decisions that landed in his favor. As he smiled in public, behind the scenes he was using the wealth he'd accumulated to secure resources for our future by any means necessary, within an inch of the law.

The office seemed smaller to me now that I was older, but by entering the room I still felt that shift in perspective, as though you were walking into the presence of something larger than yourself. The door closed behind me, and for a second I wondered if my father had closed it from several feet away or if I had imagined that. Just like outsiders watched us, the kids in our group grew up vigilantly watching the adults, trying to catch them doing things they didn't yet trust us to know they could do.

My father sat behind his marble-topped desk that I always thought looked like a cloud. Floor-to-ceiling windows on two sides made it look like we were sitting directly atop the lake. Wood built-ins with a series of locks on them like safety deposit boxes lined the wall. The vault was disguised by the built-ins. I wondered if Liv and the others had seen inside.

Usually all surfaces in the home were clear, but today his desk was covered with photographs. Pictures of what looked like nature scenes straight out of storybooks—streams, mountains, forests. I scanned a piece of paper with a census of game that must be in the area, such as fish, elk, deer, and fowl.

"It's perfect, isn't it?" Novak asked me. "It will be like going home," he said more quietly.

I nodded wholeheartedly in agreement. In a flash, Novak gathered up the photos and they were out of sight. There was no point in asking where it was. He wouldn't tell me.

I didn't know if I should take a seat, so I stood waiting. His energy was calm and neutral. Any trace of that morning's loving father—or his version of how an average loving father behaved—was wiped away. Not being able to read any emotion made interactions disorienting.

"This will be quick," my dad began. "You need to tell me what that boy saw."

It was my chance for full disclosure and sparing myself months of worry, wondering if any lies would come back to haunt me. Still, I chose to lie. I couldn't risk what might happen if Novak knew how bad it was.

"He helped pull Liv to the side. He only saw what everyone

else did. It was too cloudy under the water to see much of anything."

"Why was he arrested?" I'm sure my father already knew the details but wanted to hear it from me.

"He was in the middle of everything. Just wrong place, wrong time. It was a mistake. Can you get him out of it?" I knew he wasn't my responsibility, so I surprised myself by asking.

Novak narrowed his eyes and said ruefully, "Really, Julia? More damage control?"

"Can you fix it?"

"You know I don't like to interfere with them." But I sensed an agreement that he would take care of it. He wouldn't risk someone going to court.

Suddenly Novak stood up, crossed to the other side of the desk, and perched on the edge, directly across from me. He rubbed his face and then slid his hand into his hair. All at once I realized he was about to break some bad news. Oh shit. He was purposely giving me time to steel myself.

"Sit down, J," Novak said. I sat on the edge of a nearby chair, which brought me even closer to him. Now I had to crane my neck to look up at him.

"Dad . . . ," I began.

"Let me start." That put me back on my heels. "You let randomness in today." He leveled his eyes on mine. I wanted nothing more than to break eye contact and look down. "That makes it much harder for me to do my job, to keep everyone safe and to see clearly. Do you know what it took to get everyone's fingerprints back? Not to mention getting Angus off those charges? If anyone had been badly hurt today, if someone had gone to the hospital, if our blood had been taken . . ."

Novak lithely stood up and circled back behind the desk, quietly sitting down in his chair across from me. He then looked at his watch, as though he didn't have much time left for this conversation. It was the longest I'd been alone with him in so long I couldn't remember. But I was relieved we were almost done. Maybe this talk was the extent of any punishment.

Before continuing, Novak seemed to take me in, pausing to study my features closely for a moment, like he was trying to recognize something, or someone, in me. I may have been wrong, but I thought I saw some kind of recognition pass over his expression. This time, he broke eye contact first. I wondered how often he thought about my mother when he looked at me.

"Julia, I need to put some distance between you and the other kids. I'm aware you've been showing the boys your tricks. This is after I specifically warned you never to do that. You're going to have to leave the group for a bit." Novak looked at the ceiling while he said this, before turning his once-again-impassive expression back to me.

I didn't think I'd heard him correctly. "Excuse me?"

"As we get close to Relocation, I assess everyone," Novak continued. "For our protection and longevity, individuals who aren't committed don't move on with us."

"You're saying I'm not coming?" I felt jolted into a hyper-reality, scared out of my mind.

"No," Novak said hastily, "for now, you're simply going to a different school—a public school. You need to comprehend exactly what you did, Julia. Feel how it is to be on your own in their world and show me you can earn your way back. Prove to me that you listen to rules, that you won't influence others. In December you'll be eighteen, an adult. Show me you can be an asset to the group, that you would never threaten everyone's safety."

"What about everyone else from today? Is anyone coming with me?"

"No," he said simply. In our culture, isolation was the biggest insult there was.

How had I become the scapegoat? What about Angus, who assaulted a cop? Novak stood, finished with our conversation. I didn't move. Here was my chance to tell him what an asset I could potentially be, that I wasn't the juvenile delinquent everyone seemed to think I was. I knew Victoria was standing outside the door listening. I wasn't sure when or if I would ever get this audience with my father again.

"So—"

"No, Julia." He stopped me. "You know I have to put the group first. Even above my own daughter. This is about you putting your ego in check."

What ego? I wondered angrily. I hadn't been showing off when I jumped in the water to rescue Liv. His accusation gave me pause. It wasn't the right time, and I was almost relieved not to have to tell him. It was safer to take the punishment than to risk him reacting unpredictably.

I found my voice again. "Where am I going?"

"Kendra will get in touch with you with the details," he said, referring to his latest assistant. Novak's eyes rested on my wild ones. "Think of yourself as our ambassador. Show them we are just like them, no differences. You'll learn self-control. Before you know it, it will be June and everyone will be appeased and assured you belong with us."

So he was delivering this punishment to make other people happy as well. Everyone hated me, apparently.

"Julia, I have faith in you. Show me you want this."

The funny thing was, no one wanted it more. I had rebelled over the past year, but there was never any question in my mind that I wanted to be a member of this group. That's all I'd ever wanted, since it had never seemed like a given for me. Since I was a little girl, I'd wished I was exactly like them.

I thought we were done, so I wasn't prepared for the last insult. "Also, Victoria wants you to give Liv some space. I don't know if it was hanging out with your friends today or a first rebellion, but Liv needs to refocus."

I was incredulous. "You're asking me to stay away from my sister? We live in the same house."

"More like telling you to. Obviously, you will sleep here, but we'd like you to spend less time at the house. For Liv's sake. We know you invited her to go with you today."

I didn't bother to correct that misinformation, because I was stunned he was asking me to stay away from my own home. That must have been Victoria's request.

"But I'm one of you." It came out pathetic and bold at the same time. "Novak"—his eyes snapped to mine at my use of his name—"I saved Liv today."

He shifted his position again and looked out the window. "You broke rules by going out in public as a group, you were the one who started these challenges that could have killed your sister, and then you made a scene. People who were there believe they witnessed a miracle when Liv came to. That endangers all of us."

The finality and horror of what was taking place hit me. I had to do everything he asked. I had to stay away from my sister and from my de facto family of the Lost Kids. I had to become the outcast. I couldn't give them a single excuse to leave me.

My dad stood up. "So we're clear? I want you to start the school year at your new school. No discussion about this with anyone. I'll be the one to explain what's happening."

Victoria walked into the office, cutting off the conversation. She crossed the room to perch next to my father. She looked more beautiful without makeup, but also more worn and tired.

I stood up, my legs visibly quaking as I turned to leave the room. To my shame, tears filled my eyes, and both Victoria and Novak saw. Another flaw, another failure.

When the office door shut behind me, I had the physical sensation of being kicked out of their world. I was headed to the one that lay outside the gates—ugly and a complete unknown.

SEPTEMBER

Chapter Eight

～・∘・＜

I turned off the car and sat stock-still, the hair on the back of my neck raised, my breath ragged. I was in the west parking lot of Austin High after getting briefly lost, even though Novak's assistant had provided me with a folder containing everything I needed to know: a map of campus with the parking lot and my classrooms highlighted on it, the list of my classes, how after-school sports worked. My tennis gear sat in the trunk—playing tennis was my way of getting out of PE. I wondered what Kendra thought about all of this. Ironically Kendra, the regular person, was now less of an outsider than I was.

I had intentionally arrived early so I could adjust. I hadn't slept at all last night, going over the rules again and again, telling myself I would be able to mask all my differences. Don't speak in whispers, listen closely while shutting out surrounding noise, don't act on what hasn't yet happened. Tamp down my reflexes in sports, my hyperfocus in class. Essentially, quash all my natural instincts. Most important to maintaining the plan: keep that imaginary wall firmly in place between them and me. If I got overwhelmed, I would be less in control, and unexpected things could happen like they had at Barton Springs.

Since that night, there seemed to be a sanction placed on me. Angus hadn't called. I had imaginary conversations with him. I would tell him what was going on and he would reassure me that I could do this, that it would be fine, that I'd come back for Relocation. Within the confines of my pale bedroom, I could barely breathe—my chest hurt so much with shock. I wrote him several texts, then deleted them.

Liv ignored me. Honestly, I was relieved that she never knocked. I'd only have to shove her away. I tortured myself by replaying events again and again, hating myself that I'd let this happen.

My eyes flitted from my lap to the bodies passing by the car. Hopefully my white Prius blended in fine. Already I could tell the student body was one hundred times more diverse than at my almost-all-white private school. From the few girls I saw, I knew my clothes wouldn't fit in. I wore my usual uniform—black and more black Alexander Wang. They wore athletic shorts and baggy T-shirts with flip-flops—the official shoe of Austin, Victoria had once scoffed. More cars poured into the parking lot. I needed to walk to class before there was a crowd.

The sooner I started, the sooner I could come back. Relocation was set for June, so at the very most I had a school year in front of me. I'd just go on autopilot and this would be easy.

As soon as I set foot outside the car, it was like a dam

broke. A tide of noise and smells overwhelmed me. There were too many people, and I was too nervous.

I felt the onset of the rash on my arms. *Just keep your head down and walk.* I tried to ground my senses by taking in small details of my physical surroundings: the broken pavement, LOYAL FOREVER written on the face of the school. To me the high school was depressing in its austerity, a decades-old facility composed of concrete-block buildings.

I found my first-period classroom. I was the first student there. An African American woman around my parents' age looked up from her desk and smiled at me automatically, then did a bit of a double take before hiding her reaction. It was obvious she was expecting me, and I wondered what she'd been told.

She walked only partway over to me, as if she didn't know whether I minded being approached. "Hello! You're Julia? I'm Mrs. Bartell."

"Hi. Yes, I'm Julia." I nodded. I practiced not looking at her too long or too intently even though I needed to concentrate on what she was saying and how to make my reply sound normal. After a summer away from school, this type of playacting and slowed-down conversation was taxing.

Mrs. Bartell had short hair and wore dangling chandelier earrings that almost dwarfed her small shoulders. Her eyes were friendly, and I decided to be open-minded as long as she wasn't nosy. The main energy coming off her was motherly and sincere, and thankfully my heartbeat responded by slowing. I was safe for the moment.

"Welcome! You can have a seat wherever you'd like." It felt to me like she was making a concerted effort to behave normally. I wondered how all the kids were going to act if even the teacher was anxious around me. I looked different from the rest of my family so that bought me some time, but soon enough the kids would know who I was. I felt my cheeks redden and then reminded myself it didn't matter what these people thought of me. I just needed to try to blend in as best I could, all while not breaking into the rash. And maybe I was being paranoid. There was no way everyone in Austin had heard of us.

Kids began to walk in, loud and in throngs. This atmosphere felt much more laid-back than at St. Philip's. I could feel the myriad emotions that came into the classroom with the students, and I tried to hold their noise and feelings at arm's length. I bent down to my bag to check my phone for no reason other than it kept me from looking at anyone. I noticed conversations halting as the students saw me. At this point they saw only an expensively dressed new girl who had some exposed tattoos.

"I heard there were a ton of them." Without looking in their direction, I picked up on the conversation of the two girls across the classroom.

"No, I heard there weren't that many. But he told her they all looked exactly alike."

"I heard he was in a prison cell with them. Oh, and that he got hurt."

They shut up abruptly. The moment I realized who they were talking about, my gaze landed on the doorway. And there he was.

I'd been told it was called the oddball effect—an evolutionary advantage, the ability to slow things down in order to make decisions in critical moments. It felt like everything in my view came to a standstill. And then inched slowly forward.

John was flanked by two big guys, but he was the tallest and leanest. They had been laughing, but John stopped in his tracks when he saw me. He recovered quickly, though, and kept walking. To my surprise it appeared he was going to be the one to pretend we'd never met. He took a desk in the back row. His friends kept talking and placed themselves in front of and next to him.

After Novak seemed to promise to take care of the legal issue, I'd willingly forgotten about John. I hadn't even considered he might go to school here as a remote possibility.

He didn't look at me again, and I felt smug at the thought that he was intimidated by me.

"John Ford?"

He raised his hand when his name was called for attendance. I could sense the buzz that went around the room at the announcement of his name, especially from the girls in the classroom—as if it gave them permission to look over at him, which they'd wanted to do since he walked in. One blond girl in particular stared. It was obvious to me that she and John had a history. Thankfully Mrs. Bartell just called out "Julia" when she reached my name on the roster and checked it off without fanfare.

The class officially started and the first-day-of-school housekeeping—attendance, general syllabus for the year, grading—took up a good portion of the period. As long as I didn't need to participate in a conversation, I only had to half-listen to get all the information. For most of class, I tried to act unaware that everyone's eyes were on me, while at the same time trying to tell if John Ford in particular was staring. I wondered which part of the article had bothered him most. Best-case scenario, he thought, like everyone else, I was a member of a cult. I felt embarrassed by the thought.

"So, *All the King's Men* was your summer reading. What'd y'all think?" Mrs. Bartell asked, pretending class was going to have substance on the first day of school. I glanced at the wall clock, surprised to find the period was almost over. John's presence had distracted me for almost the entire class and at some point I'd begun to calm down.

Mrs. Bartell was only killing time and there was total reluctance in the air, everyone's brain still clinging to thoughts of summer. Before she said his name, I felt Mrs. Bartell's attention shift to John, and I knew she was going to call on him. "John?"

Startled, John sat up straighter, moving his hands under the desk to hide his eczema from view. I realized I was nervous for him, assuming he was unprepared on the first day. But he surprised me.

"It was good. Actually, it was great. And that's the way it works—only a select group of people call the shots and pull the levers. Some we elect—others just use their money." Ouch. So he did have something to say to me.

"Was there a scene or chapter that stood out for you?" Mrs. Bartell asked, opening the question to the rest of the class.

But John answered. "When Jack finds out about Anne and drives nonstop from Baton Rouge to Long Beach and then sleeps for days." You could tell this had great self-destructive appeal to John. I'd loved that part too.

Against my earlier resolve, I turned to watch him. You

could see remnants of the long scratch from Barton Springs on his cheek. I noticed his full lips, the top lip slightly bigger than the bottom. What struck me were his eyes. He would probably be considered classically handsome, though his almond-shaped eyes were unexpected in a way I couldn't pinpoint.

He was not my type. With his brown eyes and his dark-brown hair, he was so different from the more exotic-looking boys in our group. He wore jeans and Vans. His T-shirt wasn't tight but fit him well, in a way that showed he had a hard, well-defined chest, which I'd noticed at the pool. Everything about him was just . . . not what I was used to. I took all of this in, every detail of him, over the course of one second. When my attention turned back to the whole class again, I was surprised that most of the kids were listening to what John had to say.

Suddenly John snapped his head to look directly at me, sensing I had been staring. Fortunately that's when the bell rang.

I looked away and began to pack up my bag. I needed to fly out of there to my next class in case he attempted to speak to me. I didn't even want to acknowledge we'd met before. I needed to be very clear. What happened the other day had never happened.

Walking out of the classroom, I had to cross his path. I picked up on a huge dose of resentment.

During the first week of school, I watched him try not to watch me. I knew he must be mad at me. So mad, he was pretending I didn't exist. In addition to being angry that I'd lied to the police, he was probably also angry and confused about what he'd seen.

I should have thought it was funny that he ignored me, given that everyone else in the school stared at me and whispered now that they'd heard who I was. I couldn't believe I was bothered by John's anger. His parents sweating the expense of a lawyer stuck in my head. My family would consider it a major flaw that I had any concern about an outsider. I was letting it distract me, when my job here was to feel nothing at all.

Every day at school, time ticked by slowly since I had to be vigilant, staying in an almost meditative state so as to remain composed and not fuel the rumors.

I took long, hard runs the first week to see if that helped to relieve stress. Then I told myself I'd just do a few small tricks in my bathroom, that the release was what I needed in order to manage myself at school. That small release turned into more than a few tricks—exploding bottles of shampoo and soap in my shower, sitting on the bathroom floor while moving my phone hypnotically back and forth across the tiles. It helped me stay rash-free.

The few times I couldn't resist, I tried to read John's mind again by focusing only on him, shutting out everything else around me, wanting to relive that feeling of oneness I couldn't forget. I tried multiple times, but nothing. After each failure I told myself I'd stop trying.

It shouldn't have felt like some major achievement or ego boost when I caught him looking at me once. So he wasn't totally oblivious. It almost made me smile outright. I loved that I knew how he initially felt about me at Barton Springs.

He had been fascinated by me, not Liv. And not fascinated like I was a spectacle, but actually attracted to me. I'd never felt that before. I had hoped Angus was attracted to me, but even if he or any of the boys in our group had felt that way, they were too hard to read.

Every English class, John would saunter in with just his binder, and he always sat with his same two friends. They were soccer players; I knew this because one of them wouldn't stop talking about being a soccer player. The other always wore cowboy boots.

"Ford! Next weekend," one of them said. "I heard there's a party at Robertson's. Are you allowed to go out, or are you grounded?" He laughed mockingly, a total shit-talker.

Unfortunately I'd been early to class that day, not knowing if it was easier to slip in with less attention that way or to come later. But John and his friends were five minutes early too. They usually walked in from the parking lot together just as the bell rang. I felt off-balance, since it was just the four of us in the classroom.

"Shut up" was all John said, though not unpleasantly. It was awkward; the boys sat at desks too close to me even though the entire classroom was empty. I'd seen John pause when he first saw me and then reluctantly follow his friends to their chairs. Now he was doing his best to ignore everyone, looking at his new iPhone intently.

As I studied John's two friends, I was happy to feel something close to the revulsion I was supposed to. After a week of being at the school, I was now comfortable enough to look up and observe the dynamics. These were the male athletes who were at the top of the food chain. In the parking lot they were magnets for everyone—the cool kids, the high-functioning stoners, other athletes of both sexes. I saw John with them, but he always seemed to keep himself a bit apart.

"Dude, when you were gone last year, Robertson had a party"—inside-joke laughter—"and Hannah took our friend here to the bathroom, and they—"

"Tom!" John interrupted sharply and looked over at me as in, *Not in front of her*. I'd looked up at his sharp tone and our eyes met involuntarily. Again, that electricity. Those placid, hard-to-read eyes looked away quickly, his resolve to ignore me back in place.

"What? Jesus, Ford. God knows what *they* do for fun. I'm sure all this is nothing to her." Was Tom really talking about me as if I weren't right there? Then he was cocky enough to do the thing no one had done yet—address me directly. He made a dramatic show of slowly turning in his seat to face me. It was easy for me to channel Victoria after all these years and look at him with complete lack of interest. Besides our obvious differences, there was something I didn't like about this guy.

"Sorry. It's rude to talk about parties in front of people without inviting them. Do you want to come to a party with us this weekend?" He looked at me with pretend ease, giving out his fake invitation.

I couldn't figure out if he thought he was being daring by talking to me or if he was disrespecting me. "No, thank you," I said, hoping my cold attitude would put him in his place and he'd turn back around. I felt John look up from his phone and watch our exchange.

"So, what's your deal?" I have to admit I was taken aback when Tom continued.

"Excuse me?"

"Why are you at this school?" Tom was trying not to smile, so now I knew he was holding back nervous laughter. Knowing this made me relax and so, Angus-like, I toyed with him.

"I scared people at my old school." I crossed my legs, stretched my arms over my head, and yawned. I kept my gaze direct and dead.

"How?" chimed in the other boy, Hudson, but I continued to look only at Tom.

"Because I knew about bad things they'd done." I'd said it just to sound scary so they would leave me alone, but I saw real paranoia in Tom's eyes, and he backed off and turned around. He had something to hide.

Hudson reluctantly turned around too, as people began walking into the classroom. My gaze slid back to John's.

Just then a girl with luxurious glossy black hair dashed into the room. Her clothes were casual and messy, but she had some style. She looked around for a second, and her eyes landed on the boys and then me. The bell was about to ring, and she wasn't in our class. As she beelined in our direction, John sat up straighter in his seat and held out his hand like he was going to touch her when she reached us. When she squeezed between the desks, John put his arm around her waist, but she looked past him and, with wide eyes, quickly passed a phone to Tom. Because her tank top hung long and loose, you could see the sides of her black bra.

"Megan said you left it in her car. I've got to go." She

turned from Tom and squeezed John's hand while she untangled his arm from her waist, and I saw she wouldn't meet his eyes. Hudson looked over at Tom with ill-concealed worry. John missed it all as he watched her walk out. John's girlfriend.

Immediately John was back to wearing his normal impassive, prove-it-to-me expression. Because he always seemed so detached, I was pretty floored by his affectionate gesture.

My impression of him shifted. What was he like with her? What was he like when he let down his guard? I should have known right then that it was competitiveness that led to my fascination with him. That, and my desire for him to discover his girlfriend was cheating on him with his friend.

Chapter Nine

The court was scorching, and it was my serve. I was good enough after years of playing sporadically that I had already kicked ass—too much ass—so now I had to start missing shots and throwing matches, which was exhausting. The black outfit of the day had been exchanged for white tennis clothes. Needless to say, I didn't feel like myself.

The tennis-team girls weren't friendly. They were a close-knit clique who resented my displacing people at the top of the ladder. They didn't speak to me but they did watch me closely, trying to catch me doing something odd they could gossip about. The freshmen on the JV team seemed to be ostracized too.

My second week at the new school was coming to a close. I had my feet under me and was beginning to trust that I could handle most situations being thrown at me. I could self-regulate a whole lot better than I'd been able to the first couple of days.

My life was almost unrecognizable now. It was as if I'd been in this routine for ages: wake up early, run for an hour, and then get out of the house to avoid watching Liv live her same life while not quite meeting my eyes. I'd barely seen Victoria, and nothing of my dad, for two weeks now. I'd spend the early morning at the same coffee shop, filling up on food I could never get at home, finishing my homework in minutes and still getting to school early.

English class was my favorite because of John. Trying to figure him out was the only thing that was interesting in the least. I finally admitted it to myself. Covertly, I watched his every move, attempting to reconcile two different people I had seen—the one from Barton Springs who had some depth, and the one who appeared to be a distant, popular, one-dimensional jock, however smart. But I couldn't glimpse the John I'd seen at Barton Springs or even at the police station—the one who was curious, intent on me. Whenever he did look in my general direction, his eyes revealed nothing—not any sign that he found me attractive or even interesting.

Our only interaction had been when I struggled with my assigned locker one day outside the English classroom. I hadn't used it yet and was fumbling with the completely foreign mechanics of the handle. Passing by, he reached out, opened it, and kept right on walking before I could say a word.

Every day, I kept my head down while progressing from one period to another, skipping lunch to read in the library, sitting through two more classes, then going to tennis practice. After tennis I'd find dinner somewhere, linger, and then go home. When I arrived, people in the house made themselves scarce.

I could go a full day without having one conversation. After spending hours in my room, waiting in vain for Liv to come apologize or at least check on me, I'd fall asleep, sometimes before dark, the exhaustion a result of the sheer amount of effort it took to manage the sensory overload of the day. And then I'd wake up and hit repeat.

If I had felt alone a year ago when the separation into groups had happened, that didn't come close to this. I still had friends then, and I had maintained a close relationship with my sister.

Not one of my friends tried to contact me. Why did they all hate me? I was playing into it by steering clear, acting like I wasn't one of them, as if I had done something very, very wrong. I was being a good girl and doing everything Novak asked.

I bounced the ball a couple of times and served to my teammate, who hit it into the net. I had to be careful not to laugh. Grace Ellen was one of the bitchiest players—and also a senior and one of the captains. I had to hand it to her: she didn't act as if she was in awe of me at all. Grace Ellen wanted to bring me down.

"Okay, ladies. Five minutes for a water break," said Coach Kim, a youngish woman who had played for UT. She was easily steamrollered by the girls, and there was a general sense that the inmates ran the asylum.

Like a spoiled brat, my opponent walked away without a word and didn't bother returning the shot I'd just fired off. Reluctantly I left the court, not wanting to deal with the inevitably social water break, which was always more like ten minutes.

"What is he doing here?" one of the girls asked in surprise, and gestured with her chin. Everyone was grabbing their water bottles from the bleachers, crowding into the small slice of shade. I stood alone, twenty feet away from the group, but I could hear them clearly.

"No way," someone said dramatically. "He's not playing on the boys' tennis team?" Toweling off, I couldn't help but look in the direction the girls were staring.

"His brother said he has an injury, so maybe he can't play at his level anymore or whatever."

"Alex told me that's why John left that Florida academy. Something's wrong with his shoulder."

"Who is he?" A freshman girl on the JV team dared to speak and then instantly looked like she regretted it.

One of the seniors filled her in. "John Ford. He's a senior. He was at a tennis academy in Florida, and I think he was maybe hoping to go pro? But he wasn't good enough or he got injured. So he's back this year." I noticed an unusual silence in the group as everyone watched him serve. You could barely see the ball, he slammed it so hard.

"He's got a cannon," someone said in awe. "I heard he hit one thirty-five." That meant nothing to me, but, watching, I couldn't help but be impressed.

"Damn. How do you get two kids from the same family who are that hot and that good at tennis?" someone wondered aloud. Funny—they were words I'd heard people say about my family forever. *How do you get people who are so wealthy and smart and athletic and attractive?* I definitely did not consider myself included when I'd heard that last speculation.

"Sarah said John's parents are stressed about him getting a tennis scholarship after being kicked out of the academy.

And then he was just arrested. . . ." The air became uncomfortable when, paranoid, they looked over at me, wondering if there was a remote possibility I could hear what they were saying.

I stared back impassively, and anyone who turned in my direction looked away quickly. I knew I must look jarring— heavily made-up smoky eyes and tattoos in contrast with my pristine, sporty tennis outfit. It was fun standing up to these people in a way that was harder to do with my friends. But I was annoyed by the interruption in the conversation. I found myself wanting to know more details about John.

"Come on, y'all! Back with your partners. Let's go!" *Clap clap.* Everyone reluctantly unwound themselves, took a last drink, and stood up. I watched John hit another shot. I couldn't tell he was injured at first, but then I saw him favor one shoulder. That's why he'd been testing it when we sat in the police station. Wow, I'd ruined his tennis career too. He must have reinjured it when he pulled Liv from the water.

"Pretty impressive, huh?" I looked up in surprise when one of the tennis-team girls spoke to me. She was a senior at the bottom of the ladder but firmly held a place in the clique. I remembered her name was Meredith.

"Especially if he's injured. He doesn't play with the team?" I asked in spite of myself. Luckily everyone was suddenly more focused on John than on me for once.

"No. Never. He and his younger brother have always had private coaches. And then John was gone last year. . . ." She trailed off and looked past my shoulder. "Is that . . . person . . . waiting for you?"

I glanced around, uninterested. "Grace Ellen?" I asked.

My tennis partner was dragging herself back to our court. It was hot and humid, but Jesus she was dramatic.

"No. That guy. In the BMW? Over there."

I whirled around to look. Unbelievably I recognized the familiar BMW, a new car that looked like it had been through a war. I was so relieved, I could have cried. It felt like someone had decided to come get me out of jail. Angus rolled down the window and stared straight at me, dark sunglasses on and loud music trailing out of the car. I remembered I was mad at him, but in spite of myself I had to admit he looked like a handsome badass.

"He is." Heads turned to watch me as I jogged over to the car.

When I reached it, I slowed and crossed my arms across my chest. "What are you doing here?" I asked.

"Get in." He looked all around.

"I can't!" I gestured around me.

"Look," he said, frustrated now. "Just get in for a second." He took off his sunglasses, revealing those electric eyes, and reached over with a long arm and opened the passenger door. He looked different. More conservative. There were no uniforms in the upper school, so Angus usually wore jeans and whatever band T-shirt he felt like wearing. But today his curls were brushed and he was wearing an untucked button-down. This was something one of Liv's A-group boyfriends would wear.

I felt all eyes on my back as I reluctantly climbed into the car. "I have about one minute." As pissed as I was, it was so good to see him. It made my stomach ache with longing to know he got to drive away from here and go back to my old life. Like a child, I wouldn't look at him. I made the mistake of glancing out the window, though, and I already saw a few people pointing.

"Nice outfit," he said, laughing at me. "What is this look? Goth tennis-Barbie?"

"Shut up."

"Do they stare at you all the time?" I could feel Angus trying to get me to look at him.

"I think they're getting used to me maybe."

"How are you?" He made his voice buttery-soft and gentle, like he used to when we were alone.

"Fine."

"Really?" he scoffed. Silence. Then, "We miss you."

I looked over at him. I snapped. "If that's true, then why haven't any of you said a word to me? What happened to family coming first?"

"At first we were mad at you. What were you thinking, Julia? Wow. And you really humiliated Liv."

"I don't know. I was off my game." Angus saw my face burn red and lifted the back of his hand to my cheek. He seemed thrown for a moment when our eyes met.

Angus dropped his hand and dragged his gaze away to stare straight ahead. He continued, "When Liv was fine and the whole thing with the cops blew over, we tried. You know we all went to Novak to ask for you to come back, right?" When he saw my look, he said, "No one told you? Yeah, we—most of the group from Barton Springs and even George—went to Novak."

"What happened?" I suddenly felt one hundred percent better knowing my friends had fought for me. It was the first thing that had made sense since that day.

"Novak shut us down. We aren't supposed to communicate with you. Which is bullshit. So that's why I'm here. To check on you. I also need to talk to you." He angled his body so he was facing me now, arm going around the back of my seat.

"Wait, what do you mean you're not supposed to communicate with me?"

"We aren't supposed to go near you," Angus stated matter-of-factly.

"What did he say exactly?" Now I looked Angus full in the face. I had been surprised he would come here, but now I realized it was safer than him being seen with me in front of our own people. The thought enraged me.

"Novak laid down the law. We aren't allowed to go near you. He said you're being punished for stepping out of line and we should all be careful or the same will happen to us." Angus waited for my reaction.

I had been happy one second ago for the first time in weeks. Now I felt humiliated. And scared.

"Julia, it was a fuckup—not the rescue, but the rest of it. He's making an example of you to show that even his own daughter needs to follow the rules. It probably also helps him for you to blend in here to make us look normal. It buys us some time."

"And of course it's easiest for me to do," I said bitterly. I was slipping; I never brought up that I looked different. And it was an unspoken rule that no one else was allowed to bring it up either.

He was quiet for a moment. "Don't worry—you're coming back. I think it's a bullshit scare tactic. What would he really do? Leave his own daughter behind? I mean, how can any of us go from that to this?" He gestured out the window at the school beyond. "Alone, trying all the time not to get caught."

Angus changed the subject. "Look, Liv's been telling me things she shouldn't—about stuff they're learning."

"She what?" While of course I wanted to know anything about what Liv and the other kids were learning, I couldn't believe she would talk out of turn and break the rules. And Angus was right there to take advantage.

"Actually, Liv's worried about us. You know how we start to have abilities at the beginning of adolescence and they come into full expression by early adulthood—eighteen or nineteen? We all kind of guessed that. But then the freaky part . . . Liv might have overheard that if we don't use our abilities during this growth period, they just never develop."

I was already shaking my head. "That's not what we were told. She misunderstood. She 'might have' heard. They just said they'd delay our training."

Angus wasn't finished. "Do you know what else Liv told me? Novak's teaching them how to move objects. Liv was so excited that she moved a pencil a quarter of an inch. And I'm not sure the others in her group are much better."

He paused. "Julia, I'm beginning to wonder . . . I don't know, what if Novak didn't pick our groups at random? You and me . . . we were incredible at Barton Springs. And the boys—they aren't like us, but they're getting better. It's like Liv's group's on training wheels while we're competing at the X Games." Angus stared blankly into the parking lot. "What if we're the talented ones and he wants to take it away from us? Make what we have go away?"

"Why would he do that?" I was ready to blow him off.

"I don't know. Maybe he thinks we're harder to control and we'll get everyone caught. And he's right. Look what happened at Barton Springs. But, still, you fucking saved Liv's life and now look where you are."

I studied Angus. It was true that no one had ever acknowledged that fact.

"We both had something happen that day," Angus said shortly. "I've never had that kind of strength. It felt like an electrical charge went through my body to those bars and then to that cop. You can't tell me that wasn't high-level shit. Maybe Novak doesn't want us to have what he has. Maybe it's a power play disguised as covering our tracks. He's practically worshipped because he's been the only one for years."

"No, Novak put us in groups because he wants to keep us safe, Angus." I sounded like I was trying to convince myself.

"Has anything happened to you since Barton Springs?"

"Not since I've been here." Just my little tricks to keep me calm, but I wasn't going to admit to that. "You?" I asked, almost jealously.

"No, I've been . . . distracted."

"I'm sure Liv and the others are being shown things we can only imagine," I said.

"I don't know. Maybe Liv isn't the next leader like Novak says. We choose based on ability, and if Liv's really only moving a pencil, she's not looking so good. Anyway, I don't know about you, but if there's any truth to what Liv said, I want to know what I have and I don't want to lose it. If we're the last, why shouldn't we go out with a bang?"

"Well, I think your theory is wrong. Novak is too busy to know what each kid is capable of."

"He knows everything," Angus said shortly.

"And he wouldn't undermine his own daughter."

Angus looked at me almost kindly, and with some pity in his voice said, "Yeah, but you're the wrong daughter."

That sat between us like a bomb.

Angus indolently lit a cigarette. "I'm supposed to meet your sister," he said vaguely, as if remembering that part of his life.

So they were together. I had been afraid to know for sure. It really was the final blow. "He's letting you near the princess?" I said snidely, getting him back by reminding him of his status as well.

Angus looked at me hard, growing cold. "He doesn't know."

"He knows everything," I said, using Angus's own words right back at him.

For a second Angus looked at me like he wanted to explain or even apologize. For what? The mixed signals he had sent all summer and even today? That he'd chosen my beautiful younger sister? Then his mood shifted. "Your coach is going to yell for you in five seconds."

I hated myself for asking, but I needed to know one more thing before I lost him. "Did Liv go with you to my dad? To try to get me out of here?"

Angus paused before giving a small shake of his head, knowing he was delivering bad news. Then he reached across me and opened the door, signaling he was done. I turned to get out, annoyed he had dismissed me but also scared to cut off contact. I stepped out of the car and numbly closed the door behind me.

The coach had her hands cupped to her mouth and was yelling to me. I didn't say good-bye or look back. I kept walking. I began to process what he'd told me—that I was an official outcast, that my sister, the one person I had always loved, no longer wanted me around. And then he'd planted seeds of doubt about my father's noble intentions where we were concerned. I could feel myself edging toward panic.

"Julia!" Angus called out from behind me. "I'm sorry." I heard him rev his engine, and then he was gone.

❧❦❧

Left with nothing, I walked back to Coach Kim, who was gesturing at me to follow her to a set of bleachers closer to where the boys were playing. I complied, walking over dead patchy grass and litter, not up for my first talking-to from an outsider.

"You can't just get in some boy's car in the middle of practice," she began. To my total humiliation I saw John standing within earshot, bouncing a ball with his racket, looking like he was waiting to be told what to do next.

"Ford. What's up, man?" A stocky, sandy-haired boy walked up to him. "What are you doing here?"

"Hey, man. Rehabbing my shoulder. How's it going?" I pretended to give the coach my attention and I did listen to her, but I could follow the two conversations simultaneously.

"All good. Have you heard from the big schools? UT, Duke?" The boy scratched his nose and tried to act nonchalant.

John lowered his voice as if he didn't want me to hear. "No, you?"

"Nah, just Michigan and Princeton."

"Damn. That's awesome."

"They've been circling you forever. They'll be all over you as soon as you kick ass again on Saturday," the other boy said.

"Hopefully," John said noncommittally.

"How's Alex playing?"

"Great." John sounded proud and amazed. "He really likes his new coach. Well, he's my coach too, but he wants me to practice out here for now while I'm in PT."

"Do you like the new coach?"

"No," John said flatly. The other kid laughed, and I sensed John's smile.

"John!" The boys' high school coach came over and slapped John's sweaty back. "Why don't you and Pete play for a bit?"

John's whole demeanor instantly changed to business-like.

"John?" Pete looked at him warily, his demeanor also changing since they were about to be opponents.

"Yeah. Sure. Let me just get a drink real quick and lace up my shoes." He sounded resigned, like he was a soldier going into battle. He'd clearly stopped feeling any kind of joy for the game.

John turned and realized his water bottle was in my vicinity, but he couldn't change course now.

"Got it?" Thankfully Coach Kim had finished her lecture.

"Yes." I nodded, reassuring her. She walked back to the girls, expecting me to follow, but I needed a second to catch my breath and sort through what Angus had unloaded. I looked down at my arms and legs, which were now entirely covered with the rash. I was surprised the coach hadn't said anything. And of course now John was the closest he'd been since Barton Springs.

"Excuse me," he said, his first words to me since that day. He reached right next to my side and swept up a scratched pink water bottle.

"Oh, I'm sorry," I said. Why was I apologizing? Ever since I got out of Angus's car I'd felt shell-shocked, and here I sat out in the open with a full-blown rash. It was bad—blisters with whiteheads all over. No one else besides me had ever seen it this bad before.

John didn't walk away. He took a long drink from his water bottle and stood next to me, almost like he sensed my panic and didn't want to leave. I looked up at him and began rubbing my arms, mostly to hide them.

"Don't touch it. It will just make it worse," he said.

I felt my cheeks turn bright red. I realized he knew all about stress-induced rashes. I rested my eyes on his as I tried to slow my breathing.

"Thanks," I said sincerely, surprising both John and myself. It felt good to look him full in the face for once instead of the usual sidelong glances. I leaned forward to rest my elbows on my knees, trying to disguise the extent of the problem.

Oh my God. That's hot. She is so . . .

I blinked. It took a moment to realize what had just happened. He hadn't said it out loud, but I had heard him clearly. I sat up, realizing I had inadvertently given him a view of cleavage. I looked in his eyes, and again I knew we felt that connection to each other. All the panic I felt a moment ago moved to the background.

 98

Talk to her. Just talk to her.

"Ford! You coming or what?" Pete yelled. Left with no other choice, John turned and walked to the court.

What the hell had happened? Why could I read his mind again? I didn't want it to be over so quickly.

Just like that, John began to play. I stood up and walked over to his court, wanting to be close to him.

He knew I was watching. I went right up to the sidelines, rash forgotten. It was his serve and he slammed it. I could tell he was showing off for me. But Pete seemed more motivated, running harder and making some crazy shots. John double-faulted and then double-faulted again.

First I saw the coach come over to watch the match, and then a few other players from the boys' team. When Pete began to win games, the girls drifted over and were allowed to watch. The coach shushed his team when they clapped and yelled "Go, Pete!" at their number one player. When Pete took every game of the first set, you could tell something momentous was happening.

At the break John toweled off and caught his breath, keeping his eyes to the ground. I saw him look for me out of the corner of his eye when he lifted his water bottle to take a short drink. And then, like a floodgate, he was completely open to me.

One more set like this, and that will officially be rock bottom. And in front of her. Definition of a shit show. I should be handing out toilet paper.

I half laughed out loud at that.

Did she just laugh? At me?

John walked back to the baseline. *Okay. Now. Turn it on.*

Put her out of your mind. But there's no way in hell she's going to see me lose.

He served, Pete returned, and John slammed it into the net. It didn't look like things were going to change. John's head was slowly being taken over by the game, though, and I became just another nagging problem in his headspace.

Probably 50k invested in my game by my hardworking parents and this guy will probably get a better scholarship than me. I've got to stop the chatter. I've got to stop caring so much about tennis, about this girl, about every stupid thing. Just play like I give a shit.

It was fascinating. John appeared completely calm on the outside. I couldn't believe he was tearing himself up inside and the only evidence was the awful game he was playing.

This shoulder is fucking up my swing, fucking up my rhythm. I should just take a year off. Better yet, I should quit. The schools think I'm damaged goods anyway. Dammit.

"Wasn't he supposed to be the next Texas Regional champion?" one asshole muttered jokingly for everyone to hear.

I couldn't take it anymore. I'd never done it with something that was already in motion, but it was worth a try. It took a few more lost points for John, but I finally felt the rhythm of the game and connected with the energy of the ball.

Pete returned John's serve and it was a solid shot, but at the last second I veered it into the net. I had done it. And then I did it again.

Pete began to teeter out of his zone, shaking his head, hitting the racket on the tops of his feet. The coach didn't say a word. It seemed like everyone was holding their breath. Pete served and it looked like it was good, but I angled it low and the ball grazed the top of the net. I felt everyone around me blink.

Ten thousand hours of tennis and I've never seen a ball do that.

John won the game on the next shot, and Pete's confidence took a hit. There was a major momentum shift after that and John got his head together. His mind was beautifully blank.

I pushed off the chain-link fence and straightened, now knowing he would win. I left before the match was over, my rash completely gone and a gigantic smile on my face.

Chapter Ten

The impact jolted me off my high, putting my consciousness squarely back on Cesar Chavez Street. The car that had rear-ended mine reversed and, tires squealing, peeled around me, taking off into the distance. The light turned green and I drove, pulling over at a point where the street quieted. I got out of my car and was walking back to inspect the damage when a white SUV pulled up behind me and stopped. *Dammit.*

"You okay, miss?" A man maybe in his thirties, suit jacket missing and sleeves rolled up, jumped out and walked right up next to me to look at the back of my car.

"I'm fine." I tried to keep annoyance out of my voice since I didn't want him to call the police.

"Looks good. No visible damage." He said this officially, like he was reporting it.

He turned to me and sized me up as if checking that I was unhurt, and then he began to back away, returning to his car. "Glad you're okay." With that, he got back in his car, and I noticed another man sitting in the passenger seat. The car pulled out, expertly made a U-turn on the busy street, and disappeared as fast as it had shown up.

Relieved they were gone, I stood on the side of the road and looked at the back of my car, grateful that pecan trees were shading me. I was surprised to see there was visible damage. The back wasn't level anymore.

It dawned on me that I now had an excuse to go where I'd thought about going. I wanted to see my dad. Kendra handled stuff like this, or at least she had someone she could delegate to. I could drive downtown—it wasn't quite five o'clock, and everyone at my dad's office stayed until late. While I dropped in to see Kendra, I could talk to Novak, away from the house. If I felt the usual comfort and affection, it would assure me there was no need to let any of what Angus had said get under my skin.

My hands shook slightly from the aftershocks of the minor accident as I drove. For a moment I fantasized about telling Novak what had just happened at the tennis court. It was the second time now. At best he'd probably say I needed to do a better job keeping it under control—that these spurts were dangerous without any guidance. Worst case, my punishment would be more severe.

But what if it wasn't a run-of-the-mill ability? Of all the rumors and stories I'd heard about our people since childhood, hearing someone else's thoughts was never mentioned. Novak obviously didn't want me cultivating abilities right now, but what if I told him and it turned out it was unusual or even special?

But there was a problem—it was only with one person, and I didn't understand why it happened when it did. The high I'd just had—oh my God. Minutes before, I'd felt lost, and then it happened out of nowhere, as though reading his mind was something important I needed to know I could do. I'd entered into such a state of clarity.

I wasn't stupid—it was terrible timing to confide in Novak. Allegations of insider trading had tarnished his image, and now he had our arrests to contend with. Novak himself had escaped any official charges so far, but it had put the wheels of Relocation in motion. Though everything had really started when that magazine article came out.

Mostly though, Angus's comment that I wasn't the right daughter played in the back of my mind. Still, I wanted to see my dad, even if now wasn't the time to tell him what had happened.

I drove up Congress toward the Capitol, finally making it to his grand building. I handed my car keys to a valet and saw my dad's Aston Martin in his spot. I was in luck—he was in town. There was no name marking his parking place, just a plaque with the company name: Sovereign Venture Partners.

A visitor's badge stuck to my chest, the elevator transported me to the world of Sovereign. Their offices were located in the penthouse on the fifty-sixth floor. I was nervous. I rarely saw my dad, but I didn't think I should feel like I was trying to get an audience with the pope.

The reception-area furnishings were stark white on a gray concrete floor, and the room had floor-to-ceiling windows with city views. No one was seated at reception. I perched on a leather chair and waited for someone to walk out, not sure what to do. The office was quiet, like my dad preferred. Phones didn't even ring here—they just blinked. I stared at my dad's collection of six Gursky photographs he'd bought at auction, beating out the Museum of Modern Art in New York.

"Excuse me? Julia?" Paul's mother, who worked closely with my father, entered the room.

I stood up, smoothing my tennis skirt, feeling grossly out of place. "I'm here to see Kendra?" Why did my voice sound apologetic?

"She's occupied at the moment," Anne said curtly. She stood looking at me like she wasn't going to encourage me to come into her house. It was a blank-faced *Yes?* like you'd give to a stranger.

I was annoyed. I'd have to use my trump card. I caught myself before I said, *Is my Dad in?* I knew he was in. "I'd like to see my dad." Anne's eyes flared. She had always been cordial—everyone had—so why was she acting like I was a trespasser? I hoped I was just being paranoid to think that somehow Novak's punishment opened the door for everyone to show their true feelings about me.

"I'll be back," was all Anne said, and she pivoted in three-inch heels and disappeared beyond the reception area.

I waited for another fifteen minutes, growing more agitated. After playing with my phone for a bit, I got up and walked to the edge of the agarwood reception desk. I could see a bit beyond and down a hallway. A door opened, and I took half a step back.

"What do you want for dinner?"

"Let's get Jim to pick up something around seven. No more barbecue."

"Ha!"

I edged closer and watched a man walk down the hallway,

leaving the door open behind him. I saw a group of about ten people—a mix of men and women I'd never seen before—working at a long conference table. Boxes were scattered around the room, laptops out.

Remembering the probability of security cameras, I quickly sat down on the closest chair. A woman walked out into the hallway with her phone.

"Hi. This is Helen Jacks from Pricewaterhouse Coopers, returning your call."

There was an outside firm here. Auditors. I had no idea the SEC was this far along with their investigation. That had to be it, because outsiders didn't get involved in Sovereign operations.

I realized I should leave. The moment I stood, people swept into the room in a sudden burst, rushing past me toward the elevator. It was security dragging an agitated young man. They practically lifted him off the floor as they walked on either side of him. It all happened so fast. Kendra walked behind them, her face blank.

The man was shouting back to Kendra as security hauled him to the elevator. "Whatever this is and whoever they are, you need to get away from them. You have to call your parents right now!" The doors to the elevator closed, and the office was startlingly silent.

The auditors had come out of the conference room to see what was happening. It took me a second to register Novak at the edge of the room. Everyone watched as Novak walked calmly over to Kendra.

In the lowest voice imaginable, he said next to her ear, "You ever bring that in here again, it's over. This won't work."

He leaned back to look at her and placed a finger under her chin to force her to look at him. Novak's eyes practically glowed, and you could see every vein standing out in his neck. Kendra looked into Novak's eyes and gave a very small nod. I noticed for the first time that her features looked uncannily similar to those of my family. She turned and left the reception area, everyone watching her.

Novak saw me. His face registered what looked like annoyance for a millisecond before he covered it. He walked over to me and gave me a quick greeting, kissing me on both cheeks. I was so unsettled, I forgot to kiss him in return.

"I hear you came by for Kendra. Should I be jealous?" he teased.

"I got into an accident." He looked at me quizzically. "It was minor, but since I was close by I thought I would talk to Kendra about what to do with my car." I felt relieved that I had an excuse for why I was here. Clearly I was anything but welcome, and Novak couldn't be happy about what I'd just witnessed.

"I'm glad you're all right." Had I said I was all right? "Now is not the time, but why don't you email her and she'll take care of things? I have a plane to catch."

Suddenly there were voices in the hall—presumably from the conference room—and before I knew it I was being whisked out of the office and put in front of an elevator. My dad pushed the button, but I realized it was Anne's hand on my back, guiding me out. *What the hell?*

The elevator arrived. I automatically stepped in and had the presence of mind to arrange my face into calm. I turned and faced my dad's beautiful, easygoing grin.

"Bye, princess," he said just as the doors closed. My stomach dropped as the elevator made its sudden descent.

All night I was convinced Novak wore a mask and I'd seen it slip, and that at heart I was insignificant to him. I pictured him delivering the bad news that I wasn't invited on Relocation.

I hadn't thought I'd be able to get to sleep, but I must have nodded off at some point. My alarm went off and I had one blissful moment of not knowing who or where I was.

I couldn't help but be disturbed by everything that had happened at the office, especially the scene with the man who was presumably Kendra's former friend. I knew I shouldn't feel one way or the other about him or Kendra's family. . . . It was just that these things always played out the same way. One by one, the outsiders Novak let in would immerse themselves in Novak's world. They'd cut off their family and friends. Eventually they'd lose their sense of boundaries with Novak, he'd fire them, and they'd be left devastated. From the gossip I'd heard, they had trouble recovering, as if Novak were a drug and nothing ever felt quite that good again.

Novak called them lost souls—the people bold enough to try to insert themselves in our world. He believed they were reincarnated family members who wanted to make their way back to us but couldn't. None of us really believed that. It was just sad what regular people would do to be near him.

In the shower I realized that in the light of day things didn't seem as bad as they had last night. I was being self-centered—the terrible vibe in the office could have been attributed to the scene with Kendra, not to mention the auditors. It had nothing to do with Novak disliking me. I knew him. It was bad timing when I showed up. Clearly.

I knew my number one priority should be to obey Novak's rules so I could make my way back to the safety of the group. I would tell him what had happened at the tennis courts once we left Austin.

All I wanted was that feeling again. I kept thinking about what Angus said—that if he had gifts, he wanted to know what they were. But if I wanted to be careful, I needed to stop even the smallest things I was doing. It was getting difficult to hide all the broken and bent objects in the trash. I definitely needed that release, though, and I was confident I could hide those small transgressions. But it was a slippery slope. I had to stop, I decided.

When I was ready to go downstairs, I experienced the familiar nervousness. The last couple of weeks, I'd run into Victoria only once. This morning, however, she was in the kitchen. I slowed, thinking maybe I could leave through the front door instead. But it would look worse if she caught me avoiding her. And she obviously knew I was there.

When I entered the kitchen, Victoria looked over her shoulder at me. "Would you like some breakfast? I was trying to find juice." She turned back to the mammoth Sub-Zero.

"No, thank you. Thank you, though." I hovered, unsure of whether I should try to make conversation.

"How is your new school?" she asked.

"It's fine. Strange." I hated these polite conversations. I felt my cheeks turn bright red—my stupid tell. I turned, about to head to the garage. I would just take my damaged car. I hadn't bothered to contact Kendra.

Both Victoria and I felt Liv coming at the same moment. I sensed that Victoria wanted me to leave before Liv and I crossed paths. But I didn't move. It was a minor rebellion, but a rebellion just the same.

Liv rounded the corner into the kitchen. She stopped short when she saw me and asked in a way that wasn't quite natural, "Are you okay? I heard you were in a car accident."

I avoided looking at Victoria, who must have been the one to tell Liv. So at least Novak thought it significant enough to mention to Victoria.

"I'm fine. It was minor." I could barely bring myself to answer Liv or even look at her. It killed me to know she hadn't stood up for me along with Angus and the boys. I realized she appeared different somehow. Messier. Happier. Prettier, if that was possible. Since Angus mentioned it yesterday, I was aware she'd been with him last night, so I knew exactly why Liv looked that way. She needed to do a better job of hiding it from her mother. The thought of Liv and Angus being together physically—I couldn't even let myself go there.

"Do you need a ride to school?" Liv asked, surprising me. This whole interaction was her first overture since Barton Springs. I could actually feel the bad vibes coming off Victoria when Liv offered.

I knew I had to say no, per my agreement with Novak. And I wanted to say no. I was upset with Liv, and I was altogether ashamed of my feelings where she was concerned. Still, I wasn't allowed in a car with my own sister?

I answered before Liv was forced to rescind her offer.

"Actually, I have to deal with my car today. Thank you, though," I said, sounding distant. Liv looked surprised.

As I drove to school, I was pissed, for the first time since everything happened. In the confines of my car, where no one could know what I was feeling, I indulged in waves of resentment aimed at Novak and Victoria. It was followed by anger at the entire group for blocking me out. I had willingly taken on the dishonor they all seemed to think I should feel, but what had I really done to deserve being cut out and told to sink or swim?

After weeks of being a ghost, I recognized myself again. Defiance felt so much better than shame.

Chapter Eleven

"John?"

The group of boys turned in unison. John looked surprised by my use of his name. It felt strange to say it out loud for the first time.

"Hi," he said after a brief pause. I could feel his friends looking back and forth between us.

"I was . . ." I felt my cheeks turn flame red. "Can you possibly give me a ride home?"

"Of course," he said without any hesitation. It must have been fairly obvious to everyone present that I had a million other options for a ride home.

"Thank you. I'll meet you here after practice." For one microsecond we paused the way you do when you have either a crush on someone or something unspoken between you. I turned and began to walk away slowly, tuned into his thoughts, knowing he was thinking how startlingly blue my eyes were. He liked all my contrasts—bright blue eyes against black hair, tattoos and tennis outfit. He even loved my voice. I heard him remind himself not to stare like everyone else did.

I felt John turn back to his group, waiting for the coach, trying to act casual, like this happened every day—an untouchable Jaynes asking for a ride home. He steeled himself, ready to catch shit, hoping they would have the decency to be quiet so I wouldn't overhear, which of course I did.

I stole a glance behind me. Their faces were surprised and full of admiration. It took a second for someone to go first. Then, "What's Sarah going to think?"

I heard him blow it off. "She just needs a ride."

"You talk to her?" This was said in an incredulous tone.

I could tell he didn't know how to answer. We knew each other, but we'd barely spoken. He was thinking about how I hadn't been in class that morning and how he didn't like that he felt disappointed when I didn't show. He'd wanted to see me after what happened at the courts yesterday—to see if my rash was gone, to see if we were now on speaking terms. He told himself he only wanted to see me to get answers and be reassured, that while I may have been a billionaire's daughter, I was a regular person in all the ways that mattered and he could let go of what had been nagging at him.

"We have English together," he said, as if this explained things.

"Damn. I didn't know she'd even lower herself to talk to the masses."

"Looks like she's into Ford."

"She's not," he said.

"Was she arrested when you were?"

He must have nodded.

"They shared a love of breaking the law . . . ," someone started in.

John laughed. "I have a girlfriend." I couldn't believe I felt annoyed when he said that.

I knew John had feelings for his girlfriend. I'd stumbled on them today, sitting with their friends in front of the library. When I saw her—Sarah Navarro, I'd discovered—sitting in his lap, John playing with her hair unconsciously, I knew she had to go. It wasn't because I was jealous. It was because I felt she shouldn't get away with cheating on him anymore while lying to his face. This morning Liv had given me an idea of how to take care of John's problem when she asked if I needed a ride.

After practice I stood apart from everyone else while I waited for him, absentmindedly twirling my racket, making it spin magically on its own for just a few seconds before anyone noticed. The other girls hung out on the bleachers, always aware of me but of course not speaking to me.

"Hey." John's voice was soft when he approached.

"Hi." I looked up and our eyes met. "Thank you again for driving me," I said. "I was in an accident yesterday and my car is more messed up than I thought. Anyway . . ."

"Was it after tennis?" he asked. I nodded. "Are you okay?"

That was kind. "Fine. Just got rear-ended. Are you ready?" We were on a timeline.

"Sorry it took so long, I had to shower real quick." He looked at me still in my tennis clothes.

Besides the front of my white tank top being damp, I'd fared okay despite playing hard on a concrete court in full sun. I hadn't bothered to change. It was convenient having a higher tolerance for heat. And pollution. And toxins. "I'm ready."

Oh God. In her tennis outfit, in my car.

It took me a second to recover. I wasn't used to knowing John was attracted to me. I felt shy about it, but it was also the first time in my life I'd felt that kind of power.

We walked silently next to each other to the parking lot. I was petite next to him, the top of my head coming to just above his shoulder. I knew he was gearing up to confront me about Barton Springs but he didn't feel he could just blurt it out. I used that to my advantage, doing my best to act like we were past that and I was just a girl from school who needed a ride. I knew he was less wary of me now. The stranger details from that day had faded for him. He wanted me to explain it all away.

I felt him checking out my gear—bag, racket, top-of-the-line shoes. I could tell his stuff was decent as well—it had to be, since he played so much—but it was worn.

"Can I carry anything?" he asked.

"Oh, no, I've got it."

Stop acting like you're going on a first date.

I laughed under my breath. "What?" he asked, suddenly paranoid that his nervousness was apparent.

"Oh, nothing. I was just thinking I should have showered. I'm sorry I'm going to get your seat all wet."

"No one should shower in the locker rooms unless they absolutely have to." He smiled.

"I know. It's really disgusting. So, you just joined the team?" I felt his surprise that I was capable of casual conversation.

"I did. It's supposed to be temporary. To work on my shoulder. We'll see," he said.

"You were at a tennis academy in Florida," I stated. He looked over at me.

"People talk." I shrugged.

"I was there last year."

"Only for one year?"

We had reached his car. Now I felt his anxiety about how old and beat up his car would seem to me.

"Here—your door—I have to open it from the inside, and then the hinge is kind of broken, so you have to lift it up as you close it." He managed to sound matter-of-fact.

"Okay," I said. He let me in, and I took the big step up into the Explorer and did exactly what he'd instructed with the door like it was no big deal.

John started the car and turned the blaring radio way down. He was praying his car didn't smell like sweat and that the air conditioner worked.

"Your car smells like shampoo," I said, accidentally in answer.

"Good. I was worrying it smelled like sweat."

"Like your friends in English?" I laughed. He just looked at me for a moment.

That's when you can tell she's one of them—that glow.

Wow. I was so relieved we were in a car and we could mostly look straight ahead instead of at each other. It took the pressure off.

"Yeah, exactly like those guys." *Breathe, jackass.*

"So, the academy . . . ?" I prompted.

"Oh. It was . . . crazy. I didn't perform as well as expected, and then I got injured, so . . . " *Jesus, why am I telling her this? Nobody asks me about last year.*

"Were a lot of people better than you?"

He laughed in surprise. I hadn't meant to be mean.

"Sorry, that came out wrong." I laughed too, and our eyes met for a second. We both looked away quickly.

"No, that's okay. Most of them were better. I ended up playing with the best girls a lot."

"You make that sound like such a terrible thing," I teased, and brushed my hair away from my face. That sounded a little too flirty. I was surprised how easy I was finding it to talk to him.

I hope I haven't offended her. "I know, it sounds bad, but I don't mean it like that. It's just when you have an odd number, the weakest player has to play matches, so I ended up playing the number one girl, who was great, but . . ." *Shut up, John.*

"Uh-huh" was all I said, to make him squirm.

"I think it has something to do with muscle mass. . . ."

"Are you digging yourself into a hole?" I laughed again.

"Yes!" He stared straight ahead, but now he was smiling, looking so much more relaxed than he had a second ago. I studied his strong profile a moment too long.

"How's your shoulder?"

"Ninety percent."

"So what's next?"

"Getting into college," he answered.

"What about tennis?" I realized I was sitting ramrod straight in his car and I should at least try to look relaxed. I leaned back and looked over at him, my cheek resting against the seat.

He suddenly started talking. "We've always played tennis to help us get into the best college possible, then for a brief moment it was about potentially going pro—which is why I went to Florida. Now it's just to get into college."

"But why would that be a problem? You're in AP English. You're smart." I couldn't quite figure out what he was saying.

"I have to go where I can get the best financial aid."

"Oh." I hadn't meant to make him embarrassed. The silence hung awkwardly between us. He glanced at me quickly, like he was trying to put his finger on something.

"What about you?" he asked. "Where am I going, by the way?"

"Just drive me to Mozart's, please. You know, the coffee shop on the lake? I can walk home from there."

"I can drive you."

"No, I'm going to do some homework there." I knew I sounded like I didn't want him to know where I lived.

He was a fast driver and we were almost there. This time alone together would be over soon. In spite of myself I wanted to know more about him while I had the chance.

"So, what about you?" he persisted. I looked at him, confused. *That's what's odd. She doesn't blink.*

I blinked.

Okay, so maybe I'm wrong.

"I want to get into UT," I said automatically.

"Have you ever wanted to go out of state?" he asked, genuinely curious. He was thinking about how the article said the group all stayed in Austin, always remaining near each other.

"No. We're big UT supporters." You could say that again, if it meant donating millions of dollars.

He looked at me curiously. He surprised me by starting to laugh.

"What?" I asked, confused.

"Nothing. It's funny this is the first time we've talked since Barton Springs."

I didn't laugh. I put up the armor immediately.

Am I supposed to pretend it never happened? That feels ridiculous.

"It's just a bad memory," I said, surprising myself.

"How did you know about your sister?" he finally asked.

I folded my hands in my lap and stared out the window, trying to work out what I was going to say.

"Haven't you ever had a premonition?" I asked. "It was like that. I felt like . . . I don't know. Anyway, I shouldn't have behaved so erratically." All that was true.

It seemed like a hell of a lot more than a premonition. "Erratically? You saved her life," he stated.

"Thank you. No one else saw it that way." That was too much information.

"What about what happened with the metal? How did he do that?"

"I don't know. It must have been old. What ended up happening with the police?" I asked, and then regretted it. It was the wrong thing to ask when we were in such close quarters, but I'd been wanting to know if it had been taken care of.

"They dismissed the charges. Now I'm working on getting my record expunged so legally I can say it never happened." The tone shifted in the car again.

He was remembering how I'd allowed him to be arrested and charged.

Thankfully we'd arrived at our destination. "Can you pull up to the back parking lot?" I asked as we turned toward Mozart's. It was steaming hot, so it was hard to explain why I would want to be that far from the entrance.

"I can drop you in front," he said.

"Actually, how about right over there?" I pointed to the back corner of the lot.

He thought I was meeting someone I didn't want him to see, and he suddenly felt like an idiot and thought I should have called my BMW boyfriend for a ride. I hadn't realized he'd seen Angus at the tennis courts.

I know my family's not rich, but I've never had a girl be ashamed to be seen with me.

He parked in an available spot as directed. *Crap.* I didn't see them. I was sure they'd be here. I very slowly and deliberately began to gather my things. He watched my every movement, not quite believing I was in his space, knowing I'd be gone for good in a second and we'd probably never be alone like this again. I put my hand on the car door, pensive and frustrated. He waited for me to say something first, beginning to pick up on my odd behavior and wondering why I was suddenly so reluctant to leave the car.

I couldn't stall anymore. "Thank you for the ride."

"No problem."

Dammit. He would be gone in one second, and he wouldn't see them.

I opened the door, and a car next to us pulled out. I saw them, parked right in view of us. I paused and stared, knowing John would look over.

It took a second for him to grasp that we were looking at Sarah and Tom. They were in Sarah's car, their lips locked. I felt him put all the pieces together. Everything made sense—why the whole school seemed to be talking behind his back. Everyone knew about his girlfriend and his good friend except for him.

Sarah and Tom looked up, sensing they were being watched. I had the pleasure of seeing their faces register that they were caught. And that John and I were in a car together.

Again I had the urge to rescue him and help him save face. Out of nowhere I moved closer and took the sides of his face in both my hands—the first time I'd voluntarily touched an outsider. I made him look at me, staring into his brown eyes, which I saw were flecked with gold.

"Forget them. They aren't worth it. You're so much better than they are." My words were forceful and honest, but I kept my touch soft because I wanted to act for Sarah and Tom's benefit. I felt a sudden surge of attraction.

"Let's go," I coaxed. I backed off, not believing I'd just done that and not liking what I'd felt. I needed to catch my breath. Without sparing another look at Sarah and Tom, John reversed and exited the parking lot.

"Take a right. Here, on Scenic." Mansions lined the tree-shrouded, winding road, all of it passing by in a blur. This wasn't part of my plan. I didn't know what I was doing.

"Um, here is fine." I couldn't help that I seemed nervous. John pulled over where I gestured—a small, manicured dirt parking space at the side of the road, near the front entrance gate. It was a service person's spot.

"Thank you for the ride. I just figured you wanted to get out of there. . . ."

I didn't ask if he was okay. It would have been the final straw if he thought I felt sorry for him.

I opened the door, feeling a little sick. My face turned bright red. "I just wanted to say, I'm sorry I lied about Barton Springs." As soon as I said it, I shook my head, knowing I needed to stop. "Anyway . . . bye."

I waited for an appropriate response from him, but all he did was nod, and I was left feeling like I was on uneven footing. As I got out of the car and closed the door behind me, I tried to read his mind. Nothing happened.

Chapter Twelve

The next morning I walked to English class later than usual, wanting to dodge John in case he decided to question me about how I'd led him to Tom and Sarah. As I approached the classroom, I realized someone inside was talking about me.

"She was in his car?"

"That's what I heard. God, she's so pretty, but scary pretty. I bet she could eat Sarah."

That made me laugh. How the hell had I ended up embroiled in gossip with one of the kings of the school? And just when people had stopped staring so much.

"Do you think they'll get together?"

"I don't know. . . ."

"Why the hell is she even here?"

I stopped listening when I realized John and his brother were walking right behind me. I had learned John's brother's name was Alex, and I knew he was just a year younger—similar to the age difference between Liv and me. I'd seen him from afar and knew exactly who he was after hearing talk about the Fords.

"Dude, you have to deal with her at some point," Alex was saying. "Do you even care?"

"I care that she lied to me. And that she didn't break up with me because it made her life exciting. Maybe if I had known about this last year when I was away and so into her, I would have been crushed. Now, though, it's not going to be hard to forget about her."

"Damn, you're cold. So now the way is clear for Julia Jaynes. . . ." Quickly I realized Alex was joking.

Sarah was waiting by the entrance to our classroom. Face-to-face, she had the nerve to give me a dirty look. She couldn't be serious.

"John." Sarah looked past me, her eyes red and puffy.

"You don't need to say anything." John passed me and looked like he was going to head straight into the classroom, but Sarah blocked his way.

Tom was coming toward us from the other direction and then slowed, wanting to avoid the scene. Alex kept walking to class and shoulder-checked Tom on his way. "You're a piece of shit," Alex called over his shoulder. Tom didn't bother to respond.

I had planned on going back to pretending John and I were strangers. I could read his mind from afar. But now I couldn't resist.

It was a risk, since I wasn't sure how John felt about me now. I walked up to him and put my hand on his arm.

"Ready?" I asked him.

If he was surprised, he didn't show it. He nodded and we walked into English, leaving Sarah in our wake, everyone looking at us as we entered together.

When we took our seats, I expected to be able to read his mind.

Nothing. *Dammit.* I didn't understand why it happened when it did.

Tom walked in and, eyes glued to the floor, took a seat near the front. I felt everyone look from him to John.

Was he upset that his whole group of friends would be forced to pick sides? I realized I was even more frustrated that I couldn't read his mind because I was curious. I also wanted to know if John hated me now.

Class started, and Mrs. Bartell announced a pop quiz on *Beloved*, the book we'd been assigned to start last week. John probably wasn't prepared. He seemed tired.

Tom was the one chosen to hand out the list of questions we could write about. I wouldn't reach out to help him, so he had to place the papers on my desk. I peeled one off the stack and handed the rest to John.

He reached out, but I let go too soon and papers started to fall. We reached out to catch them at the same time, and our hands touched accidentally.

"Sorry. Thanks," he mumbled. I was surprised to see him blush.

"No problem. Did you read the book?" I whispered, and he leaned his head closer to mine to hear what I was saying. People were passing out the papers and hadn't settled down to write yet.

"Not all of it."

"Okay. Just write about the first chapter and introducing character and how it's done." He gave me a strange look. "This is the last thing I would want to do if I were you," I said by way of explanation. So much for ignoring him.

"Time is starting now," Mrs. Bartell said officially from the front of the classroom. Everyone dug into the assignment, including John.

I turned my attention to it, dreading having to pretend this would really take forty minutes of my time. I don't know why I decided to write what I wanted to write. I'd just have to replace it with a dumbed-down essay ten minutes before the end of class.

"Five more minutes," Mrs. Bartell eventually chimed. I crumpled up my dissertation and switched over to start the new essay. Out of the corner of my eye, I noticed John was finished with his essay and watching me. Shit. I quickly wrote the dumbed-down version.

Fuck Tom. He'd turned into an asshole anyway. Fuck Sarah. This is fucked up, but at least it's a fresh start. It's just me now.

I was excited I could hear him and his nihilistic thoughts again.

"Okay, everyone. Thank you! Have a great weekend!" Mrs. Bartell acted like she hadn't just tormented everyone on a Friday morning.

John held out his hand, offering to turn in my paper. I paused and then handed it to him. I suddenly felt a wave of relief. Then I realized it wasn't mine.

It was John who mostly felt liberated, like he no longer had to play a part he'd grown out of. His old life was finally gone and he could freely admit how things really were. He had no idea which direction he was headed in, and I sensed I was somehow part of that.

He walked our two papers up to Mrs. Bartell. "Thanks, John." She gave him a maternal smile.

I left before we could walk out together, elated that I'd figured it out. He needed to be open to it, to me. When he was scared or mad, I couldn't read his mind.

When I'd almost reached my next class, I realized I'd left my first essay in a ball on the floor. I ran back to Mrs. Bartell's classroom, but it was nowhere to be found.

"What are you doing here?"

His tone was surprisingly sharp. I'd found Angus and the Lost Kids on the sheer cliffs by the Pennybacker Bridge. Curiously, Ellis and Roger weren't there. Before I left, this had been the Lost Kids' hangout—usually boys-only. From this vantage point, you had views of the Colorado River, the downtown skyline, and the Hill Country to the north. The boys had put up some crappy barbed wire and an unconvincing-looking Private Property sign along the trail, at least temporarily claiming this spot so they could do whatever bad things they wanted in private.

"I need to talk to you," I said. The Lost Kids stopped their balance-beam walk along the edge of the cliff to stare, surprised by my appearance. I focused on the spot where they were standing until a few rocks gave way under Paul's feet. He instinctively grabbed on to Angus to catch himself as the ground crumbled down the side of the cliff. Paul recovered and gave me the finger.

"What?" I shrugged and hid my smile. It felt good to mess with them like the old days. Angus grabbed my elbow and led me from the edge of the cliff, farther away from the group. Angus turned his back on them, blocking me from sight with his height. I took a step back when I realized he was annoyed.

He squinted at me. "You're supposed to be at school."

"So are you." I'd raced here after English, deciding to skip out. Regardless of how I felt about him and my sister, I needed to see him. I was on such a high now that I was getting it—what it was and how to use it. I wanted to describe it to Angus: how I knew John's thoughts, what he was going to do, this incredible control I suddenly had. Angus was the one person I knew who would understand the risk I was taking. But now, based on his reaction, I could see coming here seemed desperate.

"What's going on?" he asked impatiently.

Over his shoulder I could see the Lost Kids stripping off their shirts and egging each other on. It was about a million degrees and they'd done this before—jumped off these cliffs to the water below. They were idiots. Anyone driving on the bridge or in a nearby boat could see tiny figures falling through the air.

I changed tactics and slowed way down. "After our conversation, I wanted to see how you're doing. What you're doing—"

Angus stole a glance over his shoulder again, clearly uncomfortable being alone with me.

"Julia, forget everything we talked about. I never should have gone to that piece-of-shit school. It wasn't fair to you." He ran a hand through his hair, messing it up and making him look less preppy and more like I was used to seeing him.

He knew me. He couldn't suddenly pretend we weren't on the same wavelength. Why was he acting like this?

"Angus, shut up. I can handle that you lowered yourself to come visit me."

He spoke quickly, trying to extricate himself. "Look, it's best for both of us to lie low."

"What is going *on*?"

After a moment he relented. "Curfews, school, and then home every day. We're not supposed to hang out in a group anymore."

"Who's not allowed to hang out?"

"All of us—our group. Ellis and Roger stay away now."

"Novak decided this?" It sounded like a military state.

"Yeah, he's cracking down. Something about cutting away any individual who puts themself before the group. Clearly he's worried about us getting caught before we manage to leave. Looks like the party here is over."

"Then what are you guys doing here?" I asked, skepticism more than apparent in my voice.

"By three p.m. we'll be back at school and no one will have missed us."

"Yeah, right," I scoffed. Leave it to Angus to think he could get around my father by dating his daughter and pointedly ignoring his rules. It was a problem that he thought he could get away with it. Angus's ego would be his undoing. I realized the same could be said for me. It's what brought me here today. I'd wanted a friend, but I'd also wanted to brag.

"So besides hanging out together secretly, you guys aren't breaking any rules?" Just then I heard whoops and glanced around Angus. Paul took the plunge that would break any regular person's body. For a second both Angus and I were quiet, vicariously enjoying what must have felt like a second of pure freedom.

"Let me rephrase that," I said. "You're not doing anything new?"

"No." He shifted. I couldn't resist, but Angus could? He was far too competitive with me to let it go.

"Yeah, right, Angus. I know you too well. All you want is to be recognized as one of a kind."

"We have a good thing going on. Why would I want to lose it over using this strength I seem to have? Especially when lying low for now is the one consistent thing I've been asked to do." Angus looked in the direction of the boys behind him, wanting to get back to them. "Look, I'm sorry, but I don't want to end up at that school. And there is no fucking way I'm living away from my own kind. You need to get out of here before it gets back to your dad. It could get us all in trouble."

"So if you don't use it and it never comes back, you're fine with that? You're okay with being mediocre?" I knew I could get him with that.

"I'm not mediocre." Angus's nostrils flared.

"Tell that to my dad."

I began to walk away, but not before he got in his parting blow. "Julia!" I turned back to him. "I can't see you anymore," Angus said. Then, lackadaisically, like he hadn't a care in the world, he walked back to the boys.

I made it down the rocky trail and back to the parking lot before I lost it.

Angus didn't matter. I had to remind myself that only Novak mattered. I just had to weather this until he let me back in. And then I would make sure I never forgot who had prematurely written me off.

Not knowing where else to go, I drove back to school. Fifteen minutes later I was walking to class. I passed a trash can swarming with flies, and it couldn't have smelled worse. Graffiti was all over lockers that no one seemed to use. A total hellhole. How had this become my life? Did I really have nowhere better to be than this godforsaken school?

"Hi." I looked up at the passing voice and saw John walking in the opposite direction. I turned my head, looking at him over my shoulder, and he did the same. Unwittingly we both smiled.

Sad that a smile from the boy I was using was the best part of my day.

Chapter Thirteen

He thought I was sexy and beautiful. That was the first thing I knew John thought when we had our initial encounter at Barton Springs. It was strange knowing what someone thought. It began to feel wrong. Especially since I was growing to actually like him, in spite of myself. I didn't know anyone from our group who would admit to feeling fond of an outsider.

He was like a radio frequency, and his thoughts were now a constant stream playing in the back of my head. The more I listened to him, the more impressed and surprised I was. He had a fascinating mind. I highly doubted anyone would still like me if they knew the inner workings of my mind.

He was funny, although that could get annoying. For instance, he wouldn't stop rhyming the name Regina with the word *vagina*. Every time he saw Regina in class, same thing. So I chose when to focus and when to tune out, depending on when it became interesting. Typically that was when it had something to do with me.

I would hear him in class, thinking about me. Thankfully

he'd decided our differences had to do with my family's limited exposure to the real world. Other than that, I was the same as him in all the ways that mattered. Besides, anyone searching the internet could read about strange things that occurred in emergency situations. I had to constantly be on guard, making sure I didn't do anything out of the ordinary, but he no longer watched me closely to see if I was a strange phenomenon. Now he watched me because he liked me.

When our English class was hijacked so we could discuss college applications, the class gathered in a counselor's room. I sat down at a table, John taking the seat next to me. Midway through the lecture, he shifted and stretched out his legs. The side of one leg was suddenly against mine. He was wearing jeans, so I wasn't sure he knew. I tried to read his mind, but I couldn't focus—I was too aware of him and wrapped up in the fact that we were touching. I let it happen, sitting with it for a full twenty minutes.

For a couple of days after that, I backed off, wanting to discourage his attention. He quickly got the message and looked the other way. But I found I missed it when it stopped. I began talking to him again. I was aware of how, when I'd sit low in my seat, he would always look at my legs. It was harmless and one-sided and definitely made English class less boring. In one of my few interactions with Victoria, she commented that my shorts seemed to be getting shorter.

The overall dread I'd picked up from John was decreasing. His parents watched him with eagle eyes, wondering how his every move was affecting his future. This weighed on him, but it was like he'd already quit trying, believing he would inevitably disappoint them.

I felt accountable for his bad fortune to some extent. I was directly responsible for his being arrested, not to mention his shoulder getting reinjured, which put potential scholarships at stake. No wonder he was freezing up. I got it. I was in the same position. We were both stumbling at the moment when it mattered most.

My priority was getting back to the group, but I did want to see where this skill was going. It was in the back of my mind that if my ability was special, it could earn me some long-awaited respect from the group. At the very least I needed the distraction and it would keep me from falling too far behind Liv, George, Emma. . . . And, honestly, how could Novak catch me reading someone's mind?

Reading John's mind did feel invasive and manipulative, but I told myself not to feel bad. I wasn't hurting him. It would have been so much easier, though, if this ability worked on someone besides John. I was still disturbed by the fact that I could put a mental barrier between myself and outsiders so I wouldn't be distracted by them, but John always broke through, like he did the first day I met him. Either he broke through or I let him in. Neither was a comforting thought.

It was taking him longer today than usual. I looked at the time on my phone and then threw it back in my bag. I was going to have to leave pretty soon if he didn't show. We'd silently fallen into a routine. Every day we met up after practice and talked, lingering until we had no excuse and had to start walking to the parking lot together, our teammates' eyes on us.

I heard steps and turned around, trying to hold back my smile. *Jesus, Julia.* But it wasn't him. It was his brother.

"Hey." Alex nodded at me and then looked over at the locker room, like he was waiting with me for John.

"Hello." I wasn't sure what to say.

"I'm Alex." He turned to me and looked at me hard. Oh my God, he was protecting his brother. That was funny. Alex looked almost identical to John, but he had light-brown hair. The kind of light brown that only lasts through childhood and eventually turns dark. He was cute, but his good looks didn't have the depth that John's had. Alex's were simple, easy, what you see is what you get. John's were layered and deceptive. At first he looked almost plain, but when you studied him more closely, he became even better looking . . . especially with the way he would look at me, the expression on his face so completely calm and totally in contrast with what he was really thinking.

Alex was staring at me expectantly, which snapped me out of my reverie.

"I'm Julia," I said. I was glad when John walked up just then.

"Sorry," he apologized to me, acknowledging for the first time that we did have some kind of standing date. "What are you doing here?" he asked his brother.

"I blew off the workout today," Alex said.

John was annoyed and shrugged. I felt all of his irritation. He thought he was being spied on, that his parents had asked his brother to see how he was doing at practice. And I assumed Alex was here because he thought John was going down the tubes hanging out with me. *Nice.*

"I have an appointment," I blurted out. I needed to get out of there. These two had a major bond. Best friends. I hadn't known that. I didn't want to get in the way. That's what I used to have with Liv, and I knew their parents' crap was interfering. I didn't want to be one more thing.

But it made John even more pissed at his brother, thinking Alex was chasing me away.

"No, really, I have an appointment at five thirty." No one said anything, but they were staring at my hand.

"What happened?" John took a step closer and reached out as if he was going to examine my hand. But he seemed to remember himself and didn't try to touch me.

"What?" I glanced down, surprised to see I had blood on my hand. The glass water bottle I'd been holding had shattered, the shards contained in the perforated rubber casing. I'd crushed it with my hand and hadn't even noticed. Maybe Alex had made me nervous. It was extremely hard to break one of those bottles with your hands, but I was more concerned about my blood being everywhere than the boys being suspicious of my strength. It was my paranoia. They didn't know it was a big deal for me to leave behind traces of my blood.

I walked the remains of the water bottle to a nearby trash can and saw there was an ugly gash on my palm. We all started looking around for something to stop the bleeding. John quickly rifled through his bag and came up with a clean T-shirt.

"No, I can't," I said when he tried to hand it to me.

"Take it," he said.

I did, reluctantly, knowing he wouldn't be getting the shirt back. "Thanks. It's fine. I'd better go."

"Are you sure? It looks bad."

"No, it looks worse than it is. Really."

"Okay," John said gently, "I'll call you tonight?"

He froze the second after he said it. It had just slipped out. John looked completely nonchalant—I thought he really should be an actor—but he was absolutely freaking out inside.

I needed to respond.

"Of course," I said, not knowing what else to do. In spite of everything I knew was smart, I stood next to him, his shoulder close to my cheek, and watched him put my number in his contacts while his brother looked on.

I felt John's mood change to pure happiness. It was nice to know what that felt like.

As I walked away I heard his brother ask, "What was that?"

John said, "Nothing."

"You like her."

"She's from a whole different world."

"Well, now she's in ours."

I stood by and watched my phone buzz, the unfamiliar number lighting up the screen. Right before it was about to go to voice mail, I grabbed it.

"Hi," I said in a completely normal voice, as if he called me all the time.

"Hi," John said.

"What are you doing?" I asked.

"Nothing. Well, not nothing. I just finished dinner with my family. I have a lot of reading to do. What are you doing?"

"Supposed to be reading, but I'm staring out the window."

I looked at my bare feet, trying to get a grip. I couldn't believe I was nervous. I realized too late that not being able to read his mind from this distance put me squarely in the same position as any other girl on the phone with John Ford.

"What are you looking at?" he asked. John didn't sound nervous in the least. It made me want to know what he was thinking even more.

"The lake."

"Nice. Are you in your room?"

"Yes. I practically live up here." I didn't mean to make that sound like a bad thing.

"I hear you. I walk out, and I have to answer thirty questions." John laughed, a little humorlessly.

"It's nice they ask you." God, I didn't want to sound like I felt sorry for myself. "Where do you live?" I sounded pleasant, like I wanted to get to know more about him. If he only knew.

"I live in Zilker. Right by the elementary school. Actually you probably never come south of the river," he teased. We always seemed to fall into easy flirting.

I laughed. I wasn't expecting the playful shit-talking to start already. "What are you saying? I go south all the time!" I realized I was winding my hair around a finger and smiling. I dropped my hand to my lap. "I spent many a night at the train tracks."

"What were you doing there?"

I was sure he had visions of rich kids buying drugs. "I'd watch my friends try to jump on the passing trains. It was pretty frightening actually, but safer than watching them play chicken with their cars."

I had to be careful, I realized. The only people I was used to talking to and spending time with were my family. It was too easy to get sloppy with him. "You're leaving the tennis team, aren't you?"

"How'd you know?" John asked.

"That's why your brother was there today, right?" I lowered my voice in case anyone was in the hallway outside my door.

"Yeah, it's time to go back to my real coach." He sounded like he actually regretted having to leave.

"I'll still see you in English." I realized I'd just admitted there was something between us.

"True. But I'll miss seeing you after tennis." I couldn't believe he just said that.

"I know." *What was I doing?*

"Are you seeing that guy? The one who punched the cop?" John sounded like he wanted to know once and for all if he was wasting his time. I'd caught him in class thinking about the way I'd looked at Angus at Barton Springs. He hated Angus. It bothered me how much he still thought about Angus touching the police officer and what he thought he saw.

"No," I said quickly. Maybe too quickly.

"It's weird. I don't know why I went to Barton Springs that day. I never go there."

What if I hadn't met you? My own thought flashed by and took me by surprise.

I decided to ask, "What about you? Do you miss . . . what's her name?" He knew I knew her name.

"You mean Sarah? No, I don't miss her. I miss believing she's a good person. And that Tom is my friend. Whatever."

"Not whatever. Maybe they're basically good but they made a mistake."

"Mistakes are one thing. But I think you can't consider someone good when they hurt other people. On purpose. Repeatedly." He was definitely cold to the people who crossed him. It looked like he never thought about Sarah or Tom anymore.

I needed to change the subject. "What are you doing this weekend?" Oh no, now he was going to think I wanted him to ask me out.

He sounded resigned. "I have to play a tournament this weekend."

"Where?"

"In town, actually. At UT. It's a big one."

"Maybe I'll come by."

"No, don't."

"Why?" I was curious.

"Because I'll want to impress you." Wow.

"Can I come?" I persisted, suddenly realizing what I wanted to do. I was sick of feeling bad about Barton Springs and about reading his mind. It wasn't appropriate to care. If I helped him win his match—one more time—I'd absolve myself and be able to move on.

"It's open to the public."

Oh, now I had to be at this tournament.

"No, of course you can come," he finally said.

"Okay," I said, as though we'd reached an agreement. We had a moment of warm silence. I felt myself begin to blush. "I gotta go."

"Good night." I heard the smile in his voice.

"Good night." I lowered my voice to almost a whisper.

I placed my phone down on the bed and stared out my window, telling myself I had this thing under control.

Chapter Fourteen

The night before the tournament, I wandered downstairs after talking to John. I was looking for something to eat, deliberately waiting until late so I wouldn't run into Victoria or my sister.

I was replaying our phone conversation—which, this time, had lasted for hours—enviously thinking about all the cool concerts he'd been to, and laughing to myself about his unexpected devotion to both Run the Jewels and Taylor Swift.

Unwittingly I stumbled onto a scene. As soon as I set foot in the living room, I saw Victoria and three other group members, including Paul's mother, Anne, standing stock-still across the room. Victoria quickly got my attention and held up her hand, halting me from taking another step. It was like they were all watching a dangerous animal, no one making any sudden movements.

Novak sat on a plush white sofa in the middle of the living room, Kendra tucked in at his side. He had his arm around her and was murmuring in her ear. Kendra had her face turned into his neck, and she was sobbing.

After what felt like minutes, she lifted her head, looked up at him, and, in a tiny little-girl voice, said, "But I don't understand where I am."

Novak couldn't have been more loving. "You're okay, sweetheart. You're Kendra, right? Can you say it?" Novak spoke so soothingly. Kendra just nodded. "I'm going to have Anne sit with you, and then she's going to take you home, now that you've seen me. You know Anne."

"But I want you to stay with me." Kendra sounded about four years old. She seemed so lost.

Novak very gently untangled himself and stood up. As soon as his back was to Kendra, disgust played over his features.

The abrupt change in demeanor was chilling. He lifted his chin to Anne, and she immediately walked over to Kendra and took Novak's place.

I wanted to go back to my room, shut the door, and take a shower. Anything to wipe what I'd just seen from my memory. Kendra had finally gone the way of the other assistants. She had just been helping me, arranging my transition to Austin High. It was different seeing it in person instead of hearing about it secondhand—seeing someone lose all sense of who they were and their life before they met Novak. Kendra had lasted much longer than anyone else. Maybe that made the comedown even worse.

For the first time in my life, I hoped Novak wouldn't acknowledge my presence. I hadn't seen him since that day at his downtown office. I hadn't known he was home. Usually I could tell because the air felt supercharged, like everything in the house changed focus and turned uniformly in his direction.

Novak crossed the white room to where I stood, rooted. He kissed both my cheeks. Victoria and the rest of the party nodded at me as they passed on their way to the dining room, where presumably they'd been interrupted during a late dinner. No one seemed concerned by what had just happened. Novak was the one who seemed most bothered. I tried to look like I wasn't shaken either, even though Kendra sat in plain view in the middle of the living room with Anne.

"Julia." He held me at arm's length to really look at me. Then he dropped his hands from my shoulders and took my hand, as if he instinctively knew I had a nasty cut on my palm. Novak turned it over and then clasped it between his hands while he began to talk.

"How are you finding your new school?"

It was hard to switch gears and suddenly have an important conversation with Novak. What was the right thing to say? I settled on "Very different. But I'm handling it."

"Ah" was all he said as he studied my eyes. Then, "Is there anything I need to know?"

What did he mean? He couldn't know about what I was doing, could he? He had never concerned himself with the details of my life.

"No," I said, hoping nothing in my voice gave him pause. "I'm staying under the radar."

He nodded slowly. "Be careful at that school. Obviously these people can become addicted to us."

He squeezed my arm before turning his back on me to return to the long, orchid-covered table beyond. I was not invited.

"Julia, one more thing," Novak said, as if he had just remembered something.

"Yes?"

"Be on guard if anyone approaches you. It seems the Department of Justice has sent the FBI to town." Novak said this almost laughingly, and I knew he wasn't worried. This case against Novak was an annoyance, if even that, before Relocation. Novak would never get caught.

"I would never speak to someone about us," I said sincerely.

⤜ତ⤛

The next morning I felt off the second I woke up, my mind preoccupied after my face-to-face encounter with Novak. I wanted to withdraw, not potentially fix a tennis match.

I hadn't really thought out going to John's tournament. I didn't have a plan for what I was going to do, and I hadn't given enough thought to what it meant that I was showing up. I arrived at the tennis complex late, not in the mood for the task.

I'd thrown on the wrong clothes, I hadn't had time to put on sunscreen, and I'd forgotten my sunglasses.

Of course I found him. I always knew exactly where he was, even in this impressively large space.

"Hi," John said when I walked up.

"Hi." Damn, the sun was bright. John was looking in my eyes. For a second I got caught up looking in his. It grounded me somehow, like I remembered him again. I felt the excitement begin to come back.

"I'm playing on court three, so why don't you go sit anywhere else."

I smiled. "No."

"I can't believe you're here. Don't you have anything better to do on a Saturday morning?" He was joking, but he also wasn't. My being here was a lot of pressure. His breathing was too shallow.

"Sadly, I don't. No, seriously, you'll play better if I'm here. You won't want me to see you lose." I smiled, torturing him.

"Stop. You're killing me." His smile lit up his eyes, even in a moment when I knew he was stressed. Then both of us were silent, unsure of what to say next.

Somehow it had been easier on the phone. Now it was like we were too blinded by the reality of each other to behave normally. Over the phone my senses weren't overloading me with an outpouring of information about him—the way he moved, his scent, his expressions.

At school this week we'd had our same routine. We'd sit next to each other in English, where I would think about him thinking about me. Next we'd see each other at the end of the school day, when we had a little more time to talk. So much of what we communicated was silent, though. Like how he carried my tennis bag yesterday. And how I'd grabbed his arm when I was laughing earlier this week. He'd nearly jumped out of his skin. I didn't know why I did it. Because I could. Because I wanted to, and I liked what it did to him.

"Okay, I'll see you afterward. But feel free to leave if you get bored. Or if it goes long." He looked serious.

"Stop! Don't worry." And because I couldn't resist, I reached over and grabbed his hand. "You're going to do great." He surprised me by snatching his hand back.

"What? Sorry, I didn't mean to . . ." Then I realized. I reached out for his hand again. Reluctantly he let me take it.

It was pretty bad. So scaly and irritated. I grazed it with the fingers of my other hand.

"John!" We both jumped. His mom was standing a few feet away. I knew that's who she was. She was tall—really tall—wearing khaki shorts and a polo shirt. She dangled a baseball hat in one hand. John had told me she was a middle school principal, and you could tell. I dropped his hand immediately. She knew who I was and she wasn't happy I was here.

"They're ready for you." I watched her turn and walk away, not even bothering to introduce herself. She was mad at John. *Crap.* He didn't need this.

"That was my mom. Sorry—she's pissed at me. It's not like her to be unfriendly." He blew it off gracefully.

"You don't want to meet my stepmother," I joked, although that really wasn't very funny. When John had asked about my family, I'd shut down, making it clear I wouldn't talk about them. He had actually stopped wondering about them as often. He was too caught up in us.

"Okay. Good luck," I said, about to walk away, but at the last second John caught my hand and kissed my cheek. He smelled like really nice sunscreen. He was gone before I had a chance to say anything. *Very smooth, Ford.* I actually hadn't seen that coming at all. That should have been a sign I wasn't paying attention.

I was a little rude and squeezed myself onto a bleacher next to a family where there really wasn't any room. But I needed to be close, in the front row, so I could see what was going on. I felt John noting his family's presence, and I quickly glanced over my shoulder. His mom was watching Alex on a different court, so I guessed the man sitting two rows behind me who bore a striking resemblance to John was his father. He looked like he was of Asian descent, which explained where John got those dark eyes.

I watched John cross the court, tense, then gracefully serve the ball like it was nothing. It was rare for us to be impressed, but John had skill and a quiet confidence to go with it that even I found enviable.

Seeing him on his stage, I finally admitted to myself how deeply attracted I was to him. And how not okay that was.

What was wrong with me? This made me different. He was supposed to be nothing to me, just an experiment. I would be abandoned here if anyone ever found out about him. It had to stop.

I realized John was losing badly. And that was when I made several technical errors at once. John was panicking, and it was intermingling with my own panic. I felt the pressure overwhelming him. His mother had now joined his father in the stands, his brother had probably won his match, I was here, and his shoulder was hurting.

I watched John's opponent, a much higher seed, slam the ball back at John, and I decided it was time to intervene. It wasn't hard—it only took a second until I could actually see the traces of light coming from the ball. I focused just ahead of where I wanted the light to go, and I began to manipulate the trajectory of the path. Out. I did it again and again, also moving John's shots in.

But no one was playing along. John's confidence didn't change, and neither did his opponent's. The opponent kept questioning calls, which annoyed me, so I broke the strings of two of his rackets and cracked the frame of a third. Unfortunately it threw off the rhythm of the match even more.

I had to handle the majority of John's points. He won, but the match had a terrible energy. Something felt not right.

I was ready to brush off the match. It was over. I didn't feel okay about it, but I hadn't figured out why yet. My plan was to watch the last match and then be done with him completely. Just set John up and then he would be on his own from here on out. I stood up to leave. It was hot, and I decided to seek out some water, hoping that would make my sudden nausea disappear.

"Julia." Dripping sweat, John was standing discreetly just outside the exit. Why hadn't I known he was there? "I need to talk to you."

I realized I couldn't feel anything because he was so pissed.

"Where are you parked?"

"I don't know—over there somewhere. Why? Are you okay? Congratulations, by the way." It was starting to dawn on me what this was about, and my mind scrambled to figure out how I could cover my tracks. I realized it was hard to build a defense when I wasn't sure exactly what I'd done in front of him today that was so obvious.

"Not really. Let's go."

"Sure," I said slowly, and reluctantly turned in the direction of the parking lot.

"John!" his mother called after him. Of course.

He turned around and said loudly, "I'll be right back!" He didn't wait for her reaction. He just kept walking.

We got to my car. Stalling, I turned it on and toyed with

the air-conditioning. The music was on, and I only turned it down, not off. "So . . ."

"I know what you did with the match," he said, his voice sounding raw.

I took a deep breath, "I don't know what you're talking about."

"Why are you fucking with me?"

"I'm not! Why would you say that?" I found it hard to look him in the eye.

"You think I'm an idiot? You don't play tennis your whole life and not notice when something's that off." He shook his head, like he didn't understand why I was blowing up his world like this. "You didn't have a random premonition at Barton Springs. And what about Sarah? How did you know she was going to be there that day and that she was cheating on me? And that paper on *Beloved* you wrote . . ."

I looked straight ahead. I knew I had to launch into an explanation, but for some reason I didn't speak, almost like I didn't want to insult him with lies.

We were silent for a second.

"Your hand is completely healed." Inadvertently I glanced down at my palm, surprised to see he was right. That had happened even faster than usual. John's voice sounded calmer now, but I knew he was scared. "What else can you do?" he asked me.

With sudden terror I realized he was completely past the point of needing confirmation. Now he wanted details.

"God, John, nothing!" I looked at him for a second and knew my eyes, pleading with him to drop it, must have been brighter than usual.

John abruptly opened the car door. He got out and walked back to the stadium. I knew he was wondering why he'd ever convinced himself he was wrong in the first place. He'd always known what he'd seen.

Chapter Fifteen

I spent the next day and a half in sheer panic. I went over and over every ability I could have used in his presence. I had been so sure of myself and oblivious that he might be picking up on the things I was doing. I'd completely underestimated him.

I rotated through different coffee shops the rest of the weekend. I sat thinking for hours, trying to be methodical and figure out next steps. Would he tell people? Did I need to tell Novak?

The last time any suspicions were out in the open was when the online article came out. I knew it got under everyone's skin—how close it got. Especially the one comment buried so deep, I wondered if John had read that far. It was the most information I had on where we'd lived in the past. Scared, I had only read it once before. I searched through the comments until I found it again.

I'm convinced this group is the same as the one that was living in Lima, Peru, where I studied in the '70s. They had the same characteristics—blue eyes, light-brown hair, phenomenally gifted, eerily alike. At the time I became fascinated, reading everything I could about these mysterious people. There was widespread hope that they were descendants of a lost tribe called the Chachapuris, whose ancestors were thought to have traveled, pre-Columbus, by sea from Europe to South America. The Chachapuris resided in the Peruvian Amazon for centuries, in complete isolation until miners happened upon them in the late 1800s.

According to lore, the Chachapuris astonished the miners with their unusual beauty, healing prowess, and mystical abilities. Descriptions included intricately-braided hair and height that surpassed that of nearby indigenous people. The tribe was reportedly decimated shortly after it was discovered. Gold prospectors killed the people for their land, and the remaining members who didn't die from disease were taken as wives and slaves.

From what I remember, at the peak of national scrutiny and a frenzy to establish a connection, the group living in Lima simply vanished.

I cleared my phone.

I remembered how soon it had been after the article came out that we'd been gathered, the group of sixteen teenagers.

Again we heard the lecture from Victoria's father on the dangers of differences and how a society can be dismantled—first by criminalizing a behavior, then by segregating, confiscating property, and incarcerating. After that Novak divided us into two categories: kids who could keep doing what they were doing, and kids who needed to stifle their instincts.

Novak said we needed to police ourselves before we were policed. This would only last the couple of years it would take to get Relocation in order. Aside from being crushed that I'd been assigned to the wrong group, it had seemed doable for the short term. None of us chosen to take a step back had had any idea how hard it would be.

I now realized Victoria's father might be right. Novak was being pressured legally. We'd been arrested. Were these the first steps in rooting us out?

Maybe it was childish, but I didn't believe Novak would let that happen. Even if some frightening powers-that-be focused on bringing him down, Novak had an edge. He'd see it coming and we would leave in time. I could feel Relocation coming. This year was beginning to feel like the last lap.

God, I missed the days when all I had to worry about was feeling like the black sheep in my own family. If I could go back to the hours before Barton Springs, to that morning, I'd do it in a heartbeat. Maybe I would wake up and realize this was a dream—that I was back at my old school, with my family, that I hadn't exposed us.

Monday morning came around. I sat in first period, on pins and needles, pretending I wasn't watching the door. John only suspected, I kept telling myself. He didn't have confirmation. And that wasn't a problem, because he would never get it.

Just when I thought he wasn't coming, John walked in, almost late. He wore a gray T-shirt and a pair of madras shorts. It was preppy for him, but was balanced out by the almost-ratty shirt. He looked like he'd had a lot of sun over the weekend, his hair a little lighter. The funny thing was, he walked in wearing Ray-Bans. He didn't want me to see his eyes, I guessed.

I tried to look impassive as he walked to the back of the classroom, navigating between desks to take his seat near mine in the back row. As soon as John was in close proximity, my plan to act and feel like everything was his problem was obliterated. It was going to be impossible to ignore him.

I tried to hear his thoughts and feel his emotions but couldn't. He'd closed himself off from me. Unexpectedly my eyes began to burn, and I quickly busied myself with my phone. What the hell was my problem? I told myself I was just tearing up because I was frustrated I couldn't read him, not because I gave a shit that he was ignoring me.

It didn't help that all eyes in the class were on John and me. Something had changed, since it was clear our little bubble in the back of the classroom had burst. We'd never done more than exchange hellos and the tiniest bit of chitchat in class, but post-Sarah, John had always stuck a leg out awfully near my desk and leaned his body as close to me as he could get.

Last week, in the middle of class, he'd rested his cheek on his palm and slid his gaze to my face. It was the kind of look you only gave someone you were with. He had been bored and half-asleep and his guard had dropped. Of course, I had known what he was feeling, and it had been overwhelming. How could I not feel something for him when I was immersed in his intimate thoughts?

But all that lightness and excitement was gone. Now I

knew school would be even worse than the first day, when at least I'd felt more Jaynes than not. Now I felt like a fuckup. I was back to being on an island all my own.

On Wednesday I arrived at English class a little later than I usually did. I hadn't slept well—I never did anymore—and I felt like a zombie. I was surprised to see John already there. Although I'd fully expected to be ignored as usual, my heart involuntarily skipped as I thought maybe he'd come early to talk to me. If that was the case, I was too late. A girl from our class with red hair was standing next to his desk, and he was looking up at her, laughing. Was he flirting with her?

"Your name, please?" I whipped around at the nasal voice. It belonged to a middle-aged man with a potbelly, his short-sleeved shirt straining, and a pointy little brown beard and greasy ponytail. Mrs. Bartell was nowhere in sight.

"I'm Julia."

"Julia what?"

"Jaynes." The substitute nodded and, without introducing himself, crossed my name off a class list. I cautiously edged away and headed to my seat. The redheaded girl saw me coming and began to back away, but not before saying to John, "Are you going to Brandon's on Friday?"

"He lives right by my house. Sure, I'll probably see you there." John smiled at her. That was when I got jealous for real.

John glanced at me as I sat down, acting indifferent overall. I internally rolled my eyes.

Even if he was making me miserable, the best part of my

day was being next to him. I must have sighed out loud, because I felt John turn his attention to me. I looked up when I felt him continue to watch me, and, just as he seemed about to say something to me for the first time since Saturday, class started. He shifted his eyes to the front of the classroom. *Dammit.* I could feel the redhead watching us.

I tried to remind myself that it was good. We needed to stay separated. But then, as the substitute announced that Mrs. Bartell's son was ill and then droned on about short stories, I felt the first trickle of John's thoughts coming to me since the tournament. It took a second to recognize, and it was small, like a crack had opened and I could just barely squeeze through.

I expected more from her, even a half-assed explanation. Is this how it's going to go from now on? We both pretend I don't know?

I didn't have time to delve further, because suddenly the class grew quiet and began to work on something.

"Thirty minutes. Go," the sub said pompously. The dry erase board read "Mr. Cantugli."

What? I wasn't usually so out of it. Since that overwhelming first day of school, I had come a long way toward developing a system. It was like having multiple plates spinning and I could focus on each one just enough: listen to the teacher, monitor the goings-on in the classroom, and, since the second week of school, pay attention to John's thoughts as well. But today I couldn't manage anything correctly.

Looking around, I realized I had no idea what everyone was writing about. *Shit.* I looked over at John's handsome profile, with his straight nose and full lips, his dark head bent as he wrote. He suddenly stopped and swiped a hand down his entire face and leaned back, looking at the ceiling before glancing over at me. I noticed his eczema was pretty bad. I was just about to whisper to him when the sub scrawled, *Write a short story: 30 minutes* on the overhead projector.

Okay, I could do that. I got busy, relieved to have something to focus on. I immersed myself and wrote for longer than I should have. When the sub called "time," I hadn't done my typical second round of work—writing something average that wouldn't stand out.

"All right," the sub intoned in a nasal voice, "who's going to read their short story out loud?" Then to my complete horror, the teacher pointed his finger at the class as in "Who's going to be the lucky contestant?" But I knew he was about to pick me.

"Miss Jaynes. You come up here and read, please."

I realized the substitute had no idea who I was. If he had, he would have had one of two reactions to me—deference or polite avoidance. Now I saw that it had been a gross mistake to stare out the window during his lecture.

I sat for a moment longer than I should have trying to figure out if there was a way to defy him. I stood and walked slowly to the podium.

"No hiding behind the podium. Come out in front of the class for the reading," the sub said.

What an asshole. He just wants to check her out.

John didn't like that everyone was looking at me or that my outfit was more revealing than usual. I'd dressed haphazardly, never thinking I'd be standing up in front of everyone.

She's panicking.

John was worried for me, knowing I didn't like drawing extra attention to myself.

I stared down at the words I had written and paused, not believing I was really going to have to do this. What I'd written was too good. I looked down and pretended to read. In reality I recited a Hemingway short story from memory.

I didn't know why I did it. We'd read the story earlier that week in class with Mrs. Bartell, and maybe I wanted to exhibit how clueless the substitute was. It was a way to communicate with John. To have him laugh with me.

I knew exactly when the story began to sound familiar to John.

But he wasn't impressed. He couldn't believe I was taking a risk like this—throwing an assignment in the teacher's face, letting other students know I had memorized an entire short story verbatim. I felt my rash begin to creep up my wrists.

When I finished, it was quiet, everyone spellbound.

The bell rang seemingly out of nowhere. The class sat there for a moment before remembering themselves and packing up.

I went to gather my things. As I passed him, the sub touched the bare skin on my arm, and it took everything I had not to jerk away. "Well done, Ms. Jaynes," he said in a smug tone of voice. He had no idea it wasn't my story.

Fucking pervert.

John was watching. I nodded to the sub and walked over to my desk, not wanting to look at John. Now I felt foolish.

John ignored Reese, the redhead, who seemed to be waiting for him near the front of the classroom by our aisle. She got the hint when he waited while I put all my things together. I felt the substitute's eyes on us as we left the classroom.

"Can I talk to you for a minute?" he said.

"I don't know. Don't you have to get to class?" I didn't want to do this.

"It doesn't matter. It'll be quick." He gestured for me to follow him through the rush of students making their way to class. To my surprise he stopped in front of an elevator and stabbed at the button. When it arrived it was empty. John entered, then turned to give me a challenging look.

I stepped in. The doors closed behind us and we stood on opposite sides, locking eyes. We didn't say a word. Every second ticked slowly as the elevator whirred endlessly to the second floor.

The elevator settled and opened. "This way." John led me to a door that let out onto a deck. The bell rang, and all at once a hush fell over the school. We were the only two people outside.

I leaned indolently against the building and raised an eyebrow, trying to gain the upper hand from the start.

"You've got to be more careful."

"What are you talking about?"

"The short story. The whole class recognized it. What, do you have a photographic memory?" Then he laughed derisively. "Of course you do."

"Sure, I have a photographic memory." I shrugged.

"I'm not an idiot, even if you want to pretend I am. I can see it all, Julia. It was right in front of my face at Barton Springs. I see all the things that make you . . . you. I just wanted to let you know you're getting bad at hiding it. Who knows? You may not care."

"Seriously, John, what are you talking about?" My tone was sarcastic: *You're crazy, I'm not.*

"Everyone in there was trying to figure out what seemed off. You don't blink often enough, your hair is different—like it got longer overnight—and you suddenly have freckles. A lot of freckles. Your skin is . . . your skin is perfect. You're perfect. But you're going to be on everyone's radar if you keep doing what you just did. It's the opposite of blending in."

I couldn't believe he was trying to help me. I had no idea what to say.

He shrugged and held up his hands in an *I tried* gesture. "Maybe you don't care. Maybe you want everyone to know that every rumor about your family is true. I just wanted to warn you." He started to walk away.

"John!" He turned back. "I'm just like you," I said softly, but it was a weak effort.

"No, you're not. I've seen it with my own eyes, and I'm sick of you pretending I don't know. I just don't want you to get caught if you don't want to be. It would make my staying quiet about Barton Springs and being dragged to jail all for nothing." He turned away, done.

She's not mine to protect. She's not my girlfriend or even my friend.

I was so overwhelmed by his response. How he'd accepted it. I didn't think—I just walked after him and stopped him, putting my hand on his back. He turned and we were face-to-face.

"Why do you care?" I finally asked.

"You know I've been aware of you since I first saw you. You felt it too." He sounded annoyed and frustrated that he'd bothered to reach out to me, breaking his resolve to cut me off completely. But it also felt like he couldn't fight it anymore.

He was exhausted from holding his feelings in. This week had been hellish for both of us.

I backed against the building again, taking in what he'd just said. He moved closer. I reached out, as if to touch his arm, but then lowered my hand. It was the opening he needed. The energy between us completely changed.

John put his hands on either side of me, touching the wall, his arms enclosing me. Our bodies were now just inches apart, the air between us charged. I didn't move, I just watched him and knew he finally saw my attraction to him in my eyes. It was like everything I'd been struggling to keep inside rushed out. He bent his head and kissed me. It was soft and long, his lips on mine. For a moment I allowed myself to rest an arm on his shoulder, and my whole body softened into the kiss. I pulled away first. We both took a breath, his heart pounding in his chest, dying at the slowness. He wanted to intensify everything.

I put my hand on his chest, my touch giving him a heart attack. But as he pressed forward to kiss me again, I gently pushed him back.

"John—" I took a huge step to the side.

He shook his head, as in *Don't say it.*

"I can't, John."

"Yes, you can."

"I can't be with you. It's . . . It doesn't work like that."

"What do you mean it doesn't work like that? You can't be with someone off the approved list, or because you don't want to?" He shook his head in disgust. "Look, I'm just going to say it. In spite of everything, everything I've seen, I want to be with you. I know who you really are, Julia, and it scares the shit out of me, but I can't help it and I'm sick of trying to stop it."

For a second I wavered. Then I said, "I won't be here forever." It just popped out.

He ignored that entirely. "Go out with me. Just hang out."

"It would only lead you on, John. There's someone else," I lied.

"Who? That asshole in the BMW?" He made a disbelieving sound. "You're better than that, Julia."

"I'm sorry." I was slowly coming back into my persona, knowing this had to be over. I could never let him in.

"You know I know everything. Just be honest with me. Why are you fucking this up?" John backed away, now completely regretting he'd even tried. He knew I was bad for him, so he didn't understand why he'd lost all reason and kissed me.

Because I'm so attracted to her. Because I'll never meet some-one like her again.

But to me he just said, "Whatever." Leaving me outside, he walked back into the deserted hallway, preparing himself to forget what he'd just done.

Chapter Sixteen

It was fine. It wasn't natural anyway. I sat cross-legged on my bed, attempting to absorb myself in a book I'd once been excited to read. I had skipped school the last two days, pretending I was sick. Like a coward, I hadn't been ready to face John.

I couldn't believe I'd kissed him back.

Going forward I was going to be singularly focused on following the rules so I could come home, so to speak. I never should have done anything else, and I knew I should be grateful nothing worse had happened. I needed to remember what was at the end of this. I'd be back with my family and, soon, in a new place where we could all be ourselves again. For a few years at least.

I stared at the same sentence until I gave up, allowing my inner voice to take center stage since it wouldn't shut up. I put my face in both hands and closed my eyes, my brain wanting to replay what had happened one more time. Who was that person? I couldn't be her.

How could he kiss like that?

I had hated the guardedness of his face after I said no.

That was how he looked at other people, but not me. When I said no, I could feel what he felt for a moment—embarrassment followed by emptiness.

Maybe because I knew John was, presumably, at that big party, it was even harder to stop thinking about him. . . .

No. It was done. It had kept me occupied and I'd killed a whole six weeks of the semester. Not only that, I would always have the knowledge that I had read someone's mind, even if it never came back or I could never use it again. In some ways it had been the most interesting six weeks of my life. I picked at a thread on my bedspread before reaching for my book again.

Friday nights were tough, since I knew I'd be holed up in my room for a two-day jail sentence until school on Monday. I picked up my phone and checked the time. It was nine o'clock. I was thinking about whether I could go to bed that early when I heard voices outside. I crawled to the end of my bed, snapped off the lights, and stepped silently over to the bank of windows. Lifting a shade with two fingers, I gazed out at the glowing expanse of the backyard.

I could see five people in the black-bottomed pool, illuminated by underwater lights. They were splashing, talking loudly, and laughing. I was about to lower the shade when the moonlight caught a large tattoo on one back. Lost Kids. The lake in the background glittered. I dropped the shade back in place.

Something broke inside me. It was one thing to be excluded by the people who had been my best friends. I'd grown accustomed to that these past several weeks. It was another thing for them to be right outside my window. Had they given me a second thought? No, they didn't seem to care. They were here for my sister.

I had to get out of here. Even I had a threshold.

Since no one was going to see me tonight, I didn't bother to change. I had on what I'd worn in my room today—not clothes for being in public. I bent to grab a pair of flip-flops in one hand and softly left my bedroom, clicking the door shut behind me.

At the far end of the long hallway, Liv kneeled on a window seat, calling out the open window to the pool below, her back to me. There was quite a bit of distance between us, but I honed in on what was different: through her sheer white shirt I could see the outline of a large tattoo on her right shoulder blade.

"I'm coming!"

The Lost Kids must have snuck into the backyard and jumped in the pool. Victoria and Novak had to be out of town and no one had bothered to tell me.

Of course Liv felt my presence, but she didn't turn around. Both of us chose to pretend the other person wasn't there.

As quietly as possible I wound down the back staircase.

I drew to a stop on the last step. Angus. He was in the next room. I had assumed he was in the pool.

When I entered the kitchen, he stood alone, almost like he was waiting for me. We were both silent, eyeing each other for a moment. I was wary, but I realized how much I had missed him. I'm sure I was wrong, but it seemed like he was feeling the same thing—that I was a sight for sore eyes. I had never gone this long without seeing him.

He was standing at the counter, looking bored, picking up forks from a stack he'd made. Without looking up, he imperceptibly flicked his wrist, piercing the ceiling with each one, waiting for a reaction from me. He'd made them spell out *hi*.

"Victoria's going to love that," I said. *Asshole. Do that in your own house.*

"You look different," he said. He pushed off the counter and sauntered over to me. He lifted a hand to touch my hair but then thought better of it.

I cleared my throat. "I look different?"

"Your hair is longer, and what's up with the freckles? You don't look as much like us as you used to."

I'd noticed the same thing, and it really bothered me. It was as if my physical appearance was affected by my proximity, or lack thereof, to my family. I'd been hoping no one else would notice, and I'd go back to normal as soon as I was with them again.

"You've gained weight."

"Great. Thanks, Angus."

"No, you look good."

I was unsure of what to say. I hadn't seen him since that day on the cliffs. I was surprised I didn't feel the same attraction I used to. Now it was more that I wanted to talk to him. Badly. I knew that if I stayed, I'd make an ass of myself to my sister's new boyfriend. I had to remember the last words he'd said to me at the cliffs and how much they hurt. I couldn't fall back on him. He'd made that clear.

"Hey," he said, conspiratorially, "I found out what's going to be different about this Relocation." He leaned in to share a secret, like the old days. When I remained stone-faced, he continued anyway. "This is the last place we'll be going. No more moving around."

"That's impossible. People get suspicious, and then we move," I said.

"I know, I know, we can only stay in one place for so long. I'm just telling you what I heard. My source is pretty good." My sister.

"And you want to hear the latest thing that's helping fund it? It's genius. Novak bought a nearby utility and sold water to a city that was getting sick from their own tainted supply. For some ridiculous profit. What a hero." Angus laughed. "Suckers!"

I knew Novak had been pumping vast quantities of groundwater from the aquifer located beneath land we owned in West Texas. Our whole group, me included, had laughed that Texas's most precious natural resource was available to whoever pumped first and fastest, waiting to profit off the inevitable shortages. Somehow now it all seemed despicable.

"Where are you going?"

"On a drive." I didn't bother saying good-bye. I was so angry at him for suddenly acting like it was the old days, expecting me to play along after he had humiliated me.

Alone in the dark car, it all came up. Six weeks' worth of hell.

My sister wouldn't even acknowledge my presence now? What reason did she have to ignore me? She'd taken my almost-boyfriend and my group of friends on top of everything else I'd handed over. Was it because she felt guilty? Or maybe the new Liv was so self-centered, she wasn't thinking about me at all.

But I felt sick knowing that what was bothering me more than my sister or Angus was John. I had lost my mind. I kept coming back to thoughts of him. And now, in the safety of the car, I was crying over him. I was such an idiot and so weak. I finally indulged in images of John. When he asked me to hang out with him, he'd had his hands behind his back, which meant he'd been really nervous. And then I thought about how it had felt when he kissed me and how I'd backed away when he tried to kiss me again.

I drove the winding roads of Scenic too fast. I hit Lake Austin Boulevard, driving farther away from the neighborhood. At the last possible second, I swerved into the right lane and got on the freeway. A short stretch took me over the lake, and I exited almost immediately, curving around Zilker Park. I drove the flat, fluorescent-lit streets, pretending to myself that I didn't know exactly where I was going.

The car whirred to a stop fairly close to the party. I watched dozens of teenagers with red Solo cups gathered on the small front lawn of a two-story house. I couldn't believe neighbors hadn't called the police yet.

He was probably here. For a second I closed my eyes, searching for him.

A sudden smack against my window, inches from my face, made me jump. I turned and there was some drunken idiot cupping his hands around his eyes, smudging the glass with his forehead as he looked in my car. I sent a powerful, direct signal—*Walk the hell away from here.* Whoever he was, he was gone in seconds.

What was I doing here? If it was to somehow test myself, I could check that off the list. This was repellent. I realized I could go, and I wanted to, but something was keeping me here. Was it that I didn't want anyone else to have him? Did I need to see him with another girl so I could let go? He'd have so many takers, with his dumb door-holding and the way he listened so intently and asked the right questions. And the way he could kiss.

I had to leave. What was I thinking, that I'd secretly date an outsider and then disappear on him one day?

Starting the car angrily, I glanced at my side-view mirror, scanning for him for one last time. In the mirror, an upstairs window caught my attention. Just like at Barton Springs, it felt like the scene in front of me was suddenly framed, individual features leaping to the forefront in extreme focus.

Maybe it was nothing. I watched it for a moment. Then I sensed a temperature change in that room. Even if someone was in peril, Novak had ordered us to turn our backs on the urge to intervene. But a sick, pressing feeling curled in my stomach. If I got out of this car, I was crossing to the other side. I couldn't have it both ways and manage it all.

But I couldn't leave it alone, not with John possibly in there. I turned off the car, got out, and jogged across the street. I kept my head down, though I could feel the stares as a few people picked me out of the crowd.

When I entered the house, a wave of stuffiness and the smell of beer hit me. The ceilings were low and the sounds of wall-to-wall people and pounding music hurt my ears.

I immediately saw Alex in the shadows near the staircase with a boy I recognized vaguely from the parking lot at school.

I made my way to them, navigating through the crowd. Alex looked like he was about to kiss the boy when I shouted to him above the din.

"Where's John?"

Alex looked annoyed until he saw it was me. Then he looked surprised.

"Um, I don't know. Upstairs, I think." They watched me as I bolted up the carpeted stairs.

Upstairs there was a short hallway with several closed doors. Even though I could have stopped and figured out which room belonged to that window, I started indiscriminately opening doors.

"What?" shouted a small group of people passing a bong around. I shut the door. I opened another, and a couple was sitting on a bed making out. I moved to another one. It was locked.

Smoke began to curl out from under the door. Without thinking, I slammed my shoulder into the hollow core door until it gave in.

A huge cloud of black smoke billowed from an area near the bed. A couple I couldn't see well was trying to bat at the flames with a quilt, making it worse. I got closer and saw them, my eyes burning. It wasn't John.

"It's too late. Call 911." I shoved the girl out. I saw that the idiots had put a scarf over the bedside lamp to create mood lighting. The scarf had shriveled, dancing with flames. The fire had quickly spread to the curtains behind the lamp. It had obviously happened fast, in the last minute or so, just as I got out of the car.

"Go!" I shouted at the boy, who was still in the room.

I'd stayed in the room past the point of what was tolerable. Coughing, I backed out.

"Julia!" It was Alex. He pulled me in the direction of the stairs, getting me away from the smoke.

"Wait! John?" I suddenly panicked.

"He's outside." I couldn't tell if Alex was positive. He looked scared he might be wrong. The crowd at the party had mostly run outside.

I decided to trust Alex. We made it out into the front yard, and he yelled frantically, "I'll check here! You go to the backyard!"

Running along the side of the house, I followed the din of the kids in the backyard. My eyes adjusted to the darkness, and I scanned the large group on the patchy grass. They had no idea what was happening since they were farthest from the smoke, but I could hear the news of the fire starting to spread through the crowd. Jesus, where was he? I was starting to get frantic.

There. I felt total relief. For the first time since Wednesday, I felt like I could breathe again. He was talking to Hudson and Reese from English class. She leaned against him as she laughed at something he was saying.

"John!" I yelled hoarsely. Totally inappropriate, and I was too far away. I just wanted him to see me right now.

He turned around at the sound of his name and looked expectantly for whoever called it. When his eyes landed on mine, there was no description for the look on his face. There was so much there—surprise, anger, relief.

I practically knocked him over, I hugged him so tight. I couldn't remember the last time I hugged anyone. Besides what had happened two days ago, we had barely touched each other. And here I was. . . .

"Hey." He kissed the top of my head. Suddenly we were both acting like we were at this level. He started to let go so he could pull back to see me. I kept my hold for a second longer, and he tightened his grip on me again. Then I heard the sirens. I moved away and saw Hudson and Reese staring at us with looks of amazement. I looked down and saw the red cup in John's hand. I grabbed it and tossed it as far from him as possible.

"Whoa!" John said, like *What the hell?*

"The police are coming. There's a fire upstairs. We have to go. Now." It took a beat for this to register.

"My brother . . ." He started searching the yard, suddenly alert.

"He's outside. In front."

Hearing that, John took the lead, pulling me out the side of the backyard and into the shadows of the neighbor's front yard. It looked like a mass exodus had started. Black smoke now poured out of the upstairs window. A cluster of teens had gathered on the front lawn.

We saw Alex immediately, and John pointed in the direction of down the street. Alex nodded. I realized John was leading me to his house.

"Wait! My car is here." I felt foggy. The adrenaline surge was over, and I was getting a hungover feeling.

"Give me the keys." He held out his hand.

I started lamely searching my pockets. A fire truck pulled up in front of the house. John said something to me, but I couldn't hear over the shrieking sirens.

When I kept fumbling, John pulled my hands to the side and started searching my pockets himself, immediately finding the keys. He opened the car doors, and I numbly let myself in the passenger side.

John pulled out. Behind us I saw more flashing lights. We had just made it out. Undoubtedly they wouldn't be letting more people leave the scene until they'd been questioned. With the smoke, it had been hard to see in the upstairs bedroom. I just had to hope the couple would seem dazed and unreliable.

Chapter Seventeen

John parked my car in front of a small ranch house. Lights were on inside, but I could tell no one was home.

I suddenly felt so relieved and just better than I had in days, now that he was with me. I also felt completely spent.

John turned off the ignition but didn't make a move to get out. The glimmer of the interior light went out, making the inside almost pitch-black. I knew what was coming. He'd digested the oddness of the past few minutes.

"Were you there because you knew there was going to be a fire?"

I didn't answer, just stared out the window, looking at the telephone wires lining the streets. Now I needed to begin the lying.

"Julia!"

I reluctantly looked over at him and then wanted to look anywhere but. All he wanted was for me to admit it.

"Just say it."

"Why do you need me to?"

That hung between us, suspended. I hadn't known I was going to say it. That one sentence began the unraveling of everything I'd been told to guard as tightly as I could.

"Because I do." John's voice was soft, wary.

I started to open my car door to get out and away, the rush of what I'd admitted hitting me.

"No, stay." John's voice was urgent. I was so relieved he wanted me to stay that I didn't resist. When I leaned back into my seat, he said, "Explain. I think I know part of it."

If I said the words out loud, I could never take them back, and it wasn't just me I was supposed to protect.

Frustrated, John spoke. "You can predict things and . . . I don't know . . . tamper with things. There's truth to that exposé written about your"—he searched for a word—"people."

I could sense he was waiting for me to deny it. When it became clear that my long silence was all the confirmation he needed, John said under his breath, "Thank you," as in, *Thank you, I knew I wasn't crazy.*

I put my hand to my face to rub away my total confusion at what the hell I was doing, and I felt a layer of grit. I pulled my hand away to look at what came off, but I couldn't see in the dark.

"I need to go." Two seconds after my silent acknowledgment, I was already starting to worry. But the thought of going back to my glass cage made me want to be sick.

"No! Look—let's at least go inside. No one is home. You can get cleaned up."

John surprised me by getting out of the car in one swift move, striding to my side, and opening the door for me. He offered me his hand, which he usually hid from me. Like a robot, I undid my seat belt, took his hand, and stood up next to him. He closed the car door and started to lead me to his house.

"I have to get home." If I went inside, I was agreeing to talk. I dropped his hand and stopped where I was on the sidewalk. John took a step onto his property.

He turned to face me. "Come inside. Just for a little while. You know I've known for weeks, Julia."

I hesitated. At that last moment of decision, I felt suspended in time. I looked at him waiting, wanting me to say yes. The moment slid into the next, and I watched myself step toward him.

❧◦❧

"We forgot to turn off the lights," John murmured as we walked into the small front room. The crisp air conditioning was a relief after the sticky October humidity outside. I looked around at the living room and the open kitchen beyond. I could see dirty dishes on the counter. I looked everywhere but at him.

Eventually, I glanced over at John. He averted his eyes.

"What?" I turned toward the mirror hanging by the front door. "Oh." I had streaks of ash on my face and arms. My black sleeveless shirt was basically see-through, displaying the black bra I was wearing underneath.

"Don't laugh," I said to him.

"Who's laughing?" he asked, looking like he was trying hard not to smile. "Look, do you want to shower? You probably don't want to go home looking like you were just in a fire." John put it out there like it was no big deal, but I could tell he was trying too hard to sound casual.

❧ 177 ❧

I realized he was freaking out in his own quiet way. He was procrastinating, suddenly unsure of how much he actually wanted to know. I needed a moment too, before I committed myself to doing something stupid. And he had a point—I couldn't go home like this. I was doing everything I could not to draw attention to myself.

"Okay," I said slowly, trying to calculate what to do with my clothes, which were just as telltale as my ashy face.

Like he'd read my mind, John said, "I can take your clothes and wash them if you want."

I nodded. "Thank you." We'd barely spent any time alone together, and now I was showering at his house. Both of us were trying to act normal when all of this was anything but.

"Come on." He led me down a short hallway to the first open door. John snapped on the light.

I entered the small bedroom, now feeling extremely shy that I was in his room. It was overstimulating being surrounded by everything John—the person I had been fixated on, like it or not, for weeks now. A queen-size bed was pushed to one corner of the room, no headboard, dark-blue sheets on the unmade bed. The room had a wood floor like the rest of the house, and there was a hefty desk taking up too much space under the one window. French doors led to the backyard.

While John gathered clothes from the floor as fast as he could and tossed them in his closet, I peered closely at the photo on his desk next to a wireless speaker. It was of John and his brother, a huge fish dangling in front of them for the camera, mountains in the background. They looked quite a bit younger—maybe thirteen or fourteen—but even back then, in their sunglasses and trucker hats, they appeared overconfident and cute. I'm sure girls—and boys, I now knew—had been chasing the Ford boys forever.

Then I noticed a pink wristband on the desk scattered amid the ChapStick, school papers, and spare change.

"Is this mine?" I held it up for John to see. He momentarily stopped his cleaning frenzy.

"I've been meaning to give that back to you, and then I kept forgetting." He shrugged, trying to sound offhand.

"This was from the first match. I remember because I didn't want to wear team swag. Did I drop it?"

"You left it where you were sitting."

I dropped the pink wristband back on his desk. For some reason I wanted it to stay there. John was done cleaning and he scanned the room, as if looking at it from my perspective. There was no escaping that we were in his bedroom by ourselves.

In spite of how reckless I was being, or maybe because of it, I had the feeling of being exactly where I wanted to be. It had been a long time since I felt this peace and thrill at the same time. Maybe since before I'd become a Lost Kid.

"Do you have something I can wear while my clothes are in the washing machine?" Both of us blushed at that. Damn. I wanted to look like this didn't faze me.

"Of course." This sent John into another small tailspin, and he started opening and closing drawers to find me something. "Here. Take this—" He quickly began unbuttoning his shirt. "It'll be long enough." He was still blushing. I took the shirt but probably didn't look away fast enough. His body was even nicer than I remembered.

"What?" he asked. I couldn't help it. I started laughing.

"What are we doing?" I grinned. "You're standing there half-naked."

"I'm handing you my shirt! And I'm not naked." But he quickly went to his drawer, threw it open, and grabbed a T-shirt, pulling it over his head. "Better? I didn't mean to offend your delicate sensibilities. Wait, before you go in, let me make sure the bathroom's clean." He put his hand on the doorjamb of the connecting bathroom and leaned in, quickly taking a look. It was clear my presence was making him crazy.

❧⟨⟩☙

The bathroom smelled like a boy, but in a good way, like a bar of green soap. It was actually decently clean. The tile looked vintage, an aqua blue. John's total of three products lined the side of the bathtub. I was surprised to see contact solution on the sink counter. I opened his glasses case, curious to see what his frames looked like.

While in the shower, I wondered what I was doing. I couldn't live with the anxiety of John knowing. It wasn't too late to backtrack, put on my clothes, and leave.

When I was done, I pulled the shower curtain aside and realized I'd forgotten to ask for a towel. I stretched my arm out to reach for John's. Fluffy and tan-colored, it was slightly damp but felt fairly clean. Something was seriously wrong with me if I didn't at all mind drying myself with John's used towel.

I stepped into my underwear and regretfully put my smoky bra back on, not feeling quite so clean anymore.

I grabbed his shirt and buttoned it up, making a concerted effort not to bring it up to my face to deeply inhale his scent before putting it on. Gathering my pile of clothes that smelled like a campfire, I opened the door and walked back into John's room. He was scrolling through his phone and looked up at me. His shirt swallowed me, but it did show a lot of leg. Still, he didn't need to stare, making me feel even more self-conscious. John put his palm to his forehead and pressed like he had a headache.

"When are your parents getting home?" I quickly re-framed the question, which made it worse. "I mean, I didn't mean it like that. I just realized this looks bad."

John cleared his throat but didn't look away from me. At least he was looking at my eyes now, willing himself to stay focused on me above the shoulders. "It's okay. They're going to be gone until late."

At that moment we heard the front door open and the sound of Alex's voice. John quickly moved to his door and paused before opening it. "I'll go talk to him. Let me take your clothes."

I reluctantly handed over the evidence.

While John was gone I paced the room, realizing I was trapped for an hour or more, and I started to get anxious.

John walked back in, interrupting my rising panic. "He's with his boyfriend, August, so we won't see them. I told them you're here."

"Great."

I sat down awkwardly on the edge of John's bed, realizing too late I should have sat in his desk chair. I covered my lap and legs with the quilt that was half falling off the bed. John came over to join me and sat in the middle of the bed, facing me, legs crossed into a half-lotus position. I stared at his tanned bare feet, wondering for the first time in my life what it would be like to be an ordinary girl.

Since I first saw him, it was as if on some level I knew John would end up knowing everything. What was it about him that made me unable to lie to him? I didn't want to lie to him. In the end the choice I made felt inevitable.

"I didn't say a word about Barton Springs even when I was under arrest, so you know I would never . . ."

"I know."

"Is it that bad if I know?"

"It is. But not if you never say a word for the rest of your life." Before John I'd never had more than a cordial conversation with an outsider, and now I was considering telling him our secrets.

He began by laying out what he knew.

"After jail that night I read an article about your family. There was a comment about a group that was in Peru. You sound exactly the same."

So he had read that far. I looked him straight in the eye but didn't say a word.

He sat back. "So are you actually related to them? It was a tribe most people thought died out."

"It's not a big deal. There are all kinds of tribes."

Holy shit. "Not magical ones."

"We're not magical."

"Then what are you?"

"Are you sure?" I asked. I gave him one last chance to decide whether he wanted to cross over into knowing.

"Yes."

"The tribe I'm descended from lived in complete isolation until they were discovered in the late eighteen hundreds."

"So you're from that tribe in the article. The ones the gold miners killed?" he asked.

"Yes. There was a genocide, but a number of us escaped. I'm directly descended from that group."

"But you can do extra . . ." He searched for the words but couldn't come up with anything.

"Technically, we're a different species." I'd said it. He looked like he hadn't heard me right.

Please tell me he can handle this. All I heard coming from him was white noise.

"Because of geographic isolation and serious inbreeding, at some point in time we shifted as a group. So we're close, but we're not identical to *Homo sapiens*. There's just a shade of difference from a genetic standpoint. We became a separate species evolving in parallel."

John's mind was still a blank.

"No," he said, flat out.

"It's true. Our DNA sequence is different. Just a tiny bit."

"What scientist would—"

"Some of us have become leaders in genetic research."

It was silent for a full ten seconds.

"Who else knows?" he asked, looking at me skeptically but with a touch of awe.

"No one," I answered. "We've managed to adapt quickly and figure out how to hide among the population. We're too smart to get caught. We have every advantage."

"That's hard to believe. Look at that article. And isn't your dad under investigation? You obviously haven't hidden that well." So he'd done his research.

He leaned back, almost like he was scared of me, although he remained in his position on the bed. It was craziness that my biggest fear was that I would repulse him.

"What can you do, exactly?" he asked. I was relieved he'd moved on from the most difficult part, so I was almost happy to answer.

"Better vision, better sense of hearing, sense of smell, all of that. It helps us pick up on a lot and stay ahead. So everyone is just pretty quick—with sports, how they learn, reading nonverbal cues. . . ."

"But there's other stuff. How did your sister survive that day? And how did Magnus, or whatever his name is, destroy that grate?"

"We can amp up adrenaline on command."

"Okay. But how did you know your sister was drowning? Or tonight with the fire? Even if your senses are great, how can you actually sense things before they happen?"

I wasn't entirely sure myself. "I think we're just genetically more complex. Our brains evolved with more biological receptors."

"But how does that work? What does that feel like?"

"It feels like a wave of energy goes through my body and *I know*. Maybe it's picking up a different frequency of electrical waves, the way animals do. You know—how animals can sense an earthquake or storm before it happens? It's all biological. Nothing magical."

"All of you can do that?"

"Some of us."

"But you all have better senses? And you seem to heal quickly."

"Yes. To both."

"What about the tennis balls? That's not possible," he said.

"Why not? Just because you're told it's not possible doesn't mean that's true." I was getting frustrated, beginning to feel backed into a corner. "Look, have you ever had the feeling of being in 'the zone' when you were playing tennis?"

"A few times."

"What did it feel like?"

"It's hard to describe."

"Try."

He looked like he was struggling to find words to describe it. "I don't know. It's quiet. It's like your mind gets out of the way and your body knows exactly what to do. It feels like total focus and tunnel vision."

"And you feel like you and the ball are one and the same, right?"

"Yes," he admitted.

"Exactly. That's what it's like for me."

"But I use a racket. How are you capable of moving matter . . . I don't know . . . energetically?"

"Actually, I have no idea." I made it sound like it was just a fact of life. Which for me it was.

"Okay, if you're making it sound so natural, why are you all so secretive?" He sounded annoyed.

"Why do you think?" I asked sarcastically.

"Seriously, what would happen if people knew? What are you so afraid of?" he pressed.

"I am serious." I turned it back on him. "Tell me what you think would happen."

"I'm not sure," he answered honestly.

"Exactly. No one wants to believe what seems impossible. People don't like to question their reality. It scares them. And they definitely would not like knowing there's someone better out there. We were discovered once and almost annihilated."

"How is any of this possible?" he asked. The difference now was that he sounded like he was marveling at it, not like he didn't believe it.

"I guess it just is."

"So you're . . . Chachapuri?" John tried out the name he somehow remembered from the article.

"That's something that person got wrong. We're the Puris tribe." I'd now actually said our name out loud. That was never done. It felt powerful and horrifying to say it.

No one and nothing had prepared me for this conversation. It was like we assumed outsiders were just too stupid or afraid to ask.

"But how do you feel sticking only to your own people and hiding all this? Don't you feel trapped?"

"No. That's why we keep to ourselves, so we don't have to hide it."

"How's that working out for you?"

"Great," I said flippantly. *Except for the fact that I'm not allowed to live up to my potential. And I can never be with you.*

"Can you just turn all this on and off whenever you want?"

"I'm trying to work out how to be consistent." I pulled my wet, tangled hair into a ponytail and then dropped it back on my neck. I found myself being more honest with him than I'd intended. It must have helped that he had started to seem so open to and relatively accepting of everything I was saying.

"By practicing on me? With tennis?" He looked horrified.

I put up a hand. "No! Well, it's back to Barton Springs. I screwed things up for you, and I wanted to put them back together. And it helped me sort of . . . I don't know. Figure things out."

"You didn't screw things up for me," John said quietly. Then, "Are there more people out there like you?"

"You mean living other places?" I asked.

"Yes."

"Sometimes we play a game and try to guess if someone in the general population has also made the jump—famous athletes, geniuses, celebrities who have that irresistible quality, you know? But no, I don't think so," I said. "Are you almost done?" I asked, letting him know I was.

"Is there more you haven't told me? About what you can do?"

"No." I shook my head, hoping I sounded convincing. There was no way I would ever let him know I was able to read his mind. I just couldn't.

"What about that guy? Was he your boyfriend?" John's voice was suddenly cold. It made me want to laugh that of all the things we'd talked about, that was what got under his skin.

"Who? Angus? No. He's my sister's boyfriend."

I shouldn't have been surprised by his next question.

"Why do you look so different from the rest of them?"

I made a move to get up then.

"Hey! What did I say?" He gentled his voice and tried to put a hand on my arm to stop me. It was the first time he'd touched me since we began the conversation, and I was surprised he still wanted to.

I tried to stifle my reaction. "Nothing. I look different because I have a different mother than my sister. But I didn't know her."

"You didn't know her, or you don't know who she was?" John looked confused.

"Both."

"I'm sorry."

"No, it's fine." I couldn't believe I had said the word *mother* out loud and lightning hadn't struck. But John wouldn't know I'd just broken yet another cardinal rule by mentioning the past. I needed a minute to recover. "Can I get a glass of water?"

"Absolutely. Sorry, I forgot to offer." He had incredible manners. John left and came back with a bottle of water. He closed the door and passed it to me as he sat down again. Our hands touched and I dropped the bottle. We both bent over to catch it—our reflexes equally quick.

I had the feeling he was backing down from his questioning and in the next few minutes I'd know the fallout from his reaction. I realized how much I didn't want to lose him and how ridiculous that was. Of course I would lose him. I had always felt superior, but now, looking at it from his perspective, I saw myself as a freak.

"Look, I'm sorry," I continued. "I'll stay out of your life, although I couldn't help myself tonight when I thought you might be burning up. I know you won't ever say anything to anyone about me. I trust you. But please forget what I told you. I'm not sure why I told you all of this, except you already seemed to know."

"That is the stupidest thing—I'm not going to forget it.

And I don't want you to stay out of my life." My heart suddenly flipped over.

"What are we going to do, John? Be a couple?" The room got really quiet. Maybe I'd read him wrong. "I'll go find my jeans," I said, standing up. Hopefully what I'd said came out as sarcastic and demeaning instead of something, shockingly, that I felt. I was such an idiot.

"No." John was off the bed and grabbing my hand. A current went up my arm and I turned back to face him. We stood there, holding hands for the second time tonight. I couldn't let go. Like he was afraid I'd bolt if he moved too quickly, John came closer until I had to look up. The smallest details came into focus—a small rip in the shoulder of his T-shirt, a thin scar near the corner of his eye. I looked away for a second, away from his liquid eyes that were asking me if I wanted this. I couldn't deny that I was going crazy with joy that he did, in spite of what he knew.

We stared at each other, my heart racing. Then the air shifted from tentative to loaded with overwhelming energy. John's eyes narrowed and he bent his head toward mine.

His fingers slid into the hair at the nape of my neck, and his other hand held my back, gently pulling me to him. I didn't care what I was supposed to do or what I was supposed to want or not want. It was so wrong, which of course made it feel so good.

Both of us leaned in, and his lips touched mine softly. Even though it had only been days since the kiss at school, it felt like this had taken forever.

His arm snaked around my waist backing me up a few steps until I was against his bedroom door. Any kind of softness disappeared fast. John kissed me hard. The very natural and sensual way he moved his hands and lips made it clear he had a lot of experience. It took me a second to adapt to how he was kissing and how his lips were moving, but then I picked it up.

We were breathing hard and didn't stop. My shoulders were flattened against the door. I ran one of my hands through his hair and rested the other on his chest. His hands moved to my hips, and I stood on tiptoe to get closer, which made his shirt that I was wearing rise up.

Eventually it was John who began to back off. I was glad he knew it was time to slow down. His beautiful, soft lips went from ravaging mine to being more business-like. I could tell exactly when his mind became aware of our surroundings. He pulled away and took a ragged breath, which made me smile. He kissed my cheek before taking a big step back.

Then he stared at me, to the point that I asked, "What?"

"Nothing. I . . ." John looked confused at my instant lucidity, like he hadn't quite caught up yet. He cleared his throat. "I . . . was looking at you."

"I know."

"I . . . People must tell you all the time that you're beautiful."

What? I didn't say anything. I watched John, and this same person who had just masterminded the most blatantly sexual kiss ever actually blushed.

"I don't want to be just another person telling you how beautiful you are and you being bored by it."

Oh. "It's not boring coming from you."

John smiled. I loved seeing his smile reach his eyes. The

combination of his politeness with how hot that kiss was pretty much blew my mind.

"You're okay with this?" I didn't know how else to ask.

"I think I've had the chance to adjust to most of it over time. It's definitely weird. But you're still you."

I couldn't believe he'd said that and he knew almost everything.

"But one thing," he said, very seriously.

"What?" I asked, brushing the hair out of my eyes.

"Don't ever use your skills or whatever they are on me again. I don't like it."

"Okay."

"Okay?"

"Yes." *Dammit.*

John had bent his head to kiss me again when a knock vibrated through the door right behind my head.

"Mom and Dad just pulled in!"

"What?" John moved me unceremoniously to the side and opened the door. He walked into the hallway and must have sensed that his brother was right.

"I'm getting your clothes even though they're wet, okay?" I nodded, but John was already sprinting. Great. I was getting busted in an outsider's home. It was almost funny.

John came back and practically threw my clothes at me. "I'll wait out in the kitchen." But he paused, one hand on the doorknob, when I started putting on my wet jeans—impossible—while he was in the room. Then I quickly took off his shirt and, standing there in my bra, threw on my own. He was looking at me like he'd seen a ghost.

"Okay, I'm ready." I put a hand to my hair, which was

damp. This looked bad. Not what he needed after a rocky few months with his parents. "I can slip out the front if I go now." He nodded and opened the door wider. I headed straight to the front door, not looking back. Behind me I heard the door from the garage open and his parents walk into the house.

John followed me out. I walked to my car, and just when I realized I'd left my keys, John unlocked my car for me. I slowly opened the door.

He rapidly came to my side and picked up my hand, placing the keys in my palm.

"I have to kiss you one more time." John lowered his head and kissed my lips before trailing to the hollow below my ear. I practically hung from his neck, my knees going out.

"Oh my God—stop!" I half laughed. John pulled away. I corrected myself: "I just mean I can't take any more if I'm supposed to leave you right now." John broke into a huge grin, as though some part of his ego had been satisfied. He sauntered back to the house, so hot in his T-shirt and jeans and bare feet. I realized I was just standing there watching him. Alex had come to watch us too, hanging in the doorway, fingers hooked on the doorjamb above his head, bowing out his body. John punched him lightly in the stomach, forcing Alex to retreat.

I didn't know if he would pull away after processing everything I had told him. But just then John wheeled around, and I swear it was like he let me read his mind. I had that feeling again that we were connected somehow. His pure happiness was almost exactly like mine.

Chapter Eighteen

Monday morning I pulled into the school parking lot as early as I could reasonably be there. I'd been dying all weekend for a million reasons. But there probably had never been another person alive who'd been more excited and nervous for a Monday morning. I felt like an entirely different person. I felt young for the first time in my life. I'd stopped thinking.

I could hide any kind of secret life. It was possible, I'd decided. No one from the group ever saw me at my new school. They wouldn't dream of coming by to visit me at this place. No one had ever been here except Angus, and he wasn't coming back.

It was insane, but I'd decided I wanted—I *needed*—this experience before I left this time in my life behind. I wanted to be this person for at least a little while. It was just for fun. I deserved it after everything I'd been through.

I sat in my car and listened to music, aware of cars beginning to stream in. I felt when John pulled in. Then he walked toward me with his brother, sidling between rows of cars. I hadn't seen him since Friday night outside his house.

Now I couldn't help it—a smile spread over my face. John's hair was still wet, and he was wearing his sunglasses. Alex looked from me to his brother and beelined off.

"Hey," John said, and leaned against my car next to me.

"Hi," I said, trying not to smile so big. Thank God I had sunglasses on too. Measured, calm, and hard to read was what I usually killed myself to present to the outside world. I knew I had never smiled like this before in my life.

"We'd better get going." John reluctantly straightened and stretched. I watched, openly admiring him.

"What?" he asked.

I shook my head, smiling. "Nothing at all." He smiled back, knowing I was looking at him.

"Let's go." I stepped forward, ready to walk to class. To my total surprise John put his arm around my waist and pulled me to him. He kissed my cheek almost absentmindedly before backing away and taking my hand, leading me out of the parking lot. He knew all these little things about how to act with a girlfriend. They were second nature to him. This was all new to me, but I tried not to show it. I was living in total terror and thrilled at the same time. It was addictive.

It seemed like everyone in the parking lot was watching us. It was official now. I was letting this happen in this world. Luckily it was entirely separate from my real one.

Listening to his thoughts now, I felt it. Something about him had changed. I was sure it had to do with what he'd learned. He would never see things quite the same way. I knew he was worried he was in free fall. But from where he stood today, whatever happened, he thought it was worth it.

Later that day a miracle happened. It rained. It came out of nowhere. I was standing in the locker, about to change into my tennis clothes, when word spread that practice was cancelled.

I was relieved. Word was out about me and John, and I felt the tennis team sizing me up critically, and enviously, all over again. I had begun packing up my bag when I saw my phone light up.

I'm in the parking lot. Are you free?

I suddenly had about three hours completely open. So did John, who usually had zero free time.

He was waiting in his car. John quickly opened the door for me and I slid in. Water streamed down the windows, and we were in our own world. I noticed a blue thread on John's shirt, the thickness of his lashes. Every moment with him slowed down and felt like it was occurring in Technicolor.

John leaned toward me, presumably to either shut my door better than I had or to kiss me hello. A harsh knock on his window jolted him. Alex was standing there, soaking. John turned on the car and rolled down the window.

"You coming to practice?" Alex saw I was in the passenger seat, and I could feel him stiffen.

"No way. Look at this."

"Well, I'm going up there. There's weights and all that."

A moment hung between the brothers. Reading John, I knew he was annoyed, thinking Alex was calling him out on getting distracted and half-assing it. He was also seeing a new side to Alex—his brother's commitment was bigger than his—and John was beginning to feel competitive.

I broke the silence. "Go. I'll see you tomorrow." I made the move to get out.

John looked at his brother when he said, "No, it's all good. I'm not going."

Alex shrugged his shoulders in an *It's your life* gesture and, without saying good-bye, walked off. I heard him mumble, "At least pretend you want it," but I knew John couldn't hear him.

John was quiet for a second and then shook it off. The flash of annoyance he'd felt wasn't gone, but he buried it a few layers deep.

"Are you sure you don't need to go?" I asked.

"It's fine. I can skip for once." It was a giant monkey on his back. Guilt all the time over his parents' hopes for him and the increasing lack of desire on his end.

"Stop looking at me like you know what I'm thinking," he said.

"What? I'm not."

"It makes me nervous, the way you look at me like that sometimes. If you can read my mind on top of everything else . . . I don't know."

I laughed, pretending to think that was funny. "Would that be too much for you?"

"Yes! That would be awful."

"Trust me—I don't know what you're thinking." How was that for a blatant lie?

"Good."

I tried to lighten things up before he could tell my mood

had changed. "But please don't think any pornographic thoughts about me!" I was actually only half-kidding. Over and over again in class, his mind drifted to a very distinct image of us kissing, lying on a bed, sunlight flooding the room.

"Julia, it's a little hard not to. It wouldn't be normal if I didn't," he stated matter-of-factly. There was something very sexy and confident about his not having any room for embarrassment.

I looked at him askance. I was completely out of my element with this banter.

John suddenly laughed. "Are you telling me that you get shocked?"

I didn't like being called a prude. I ended the conversation by leaning over to him and initiating a long, slow kiss.

After a minute he said, "Let's go to my house."

I looked up, suddenly worried on all fronts. I didn't want to get in over my head physically. And I didn't want to see his parents.

"No one will be home until about six. That gives us almost"—John checked his phone—"two hours."

I also didn't want to say no. It was an opportunity that might not happen again.

"Okay. I'll follow you there." Impulsively I ran my fingers through his hair. I couldn't believe I could just reach over and touch him now, whenever I wanted.

John steered us through his house to a screened-in porch.

A long outdoor sofa was pushed up against the wall with some chairs facing it. Of course it had already stopped raining.

Birds were singing and the air was humid and still. Leading me to the sofa, John pulled me down next to him.

"Your parents aren't going to suddenly walk in again?" I asked nervously.

"If they do, we're just kissing. We've been lectured on the rules a million times. My mom's biggest fears are transmitted diseases and someone getting pregnant." There was an awkward silence after that. "What?" he asked.

"Nothing." It was strange to hear pregnancy talked about casually; the topic had become taboo in my family. It was the only area where we were totally helpless. Besides counting on Novak to make every effort to find a solution, it was like we also looked to him to tell us the vision had changed. I came up with a reasonable reply. "I'm just thinking about the long line of girls you've brought home and tried not to get pregnant."

"That doesn't matter. Nobody else matters. And don't worry, no one has ever gotten pregnant." He laughed but I didn't. He reached out and stroked the back of my hair. "What are you worried about?"

Ha. So many things. But instead I said, "I've realized I have a jealous streak."

"I like it. I think it's what brought us together. Remind me to thank Reese again," he teased. Over the weekend I'd asked a few too many questions on the phone about our classmate who was hanging all over him at the party.

"Stop!" I laughed.

We looked at each other without saying a word. John drew in a breath, and I was surprised he was nervous too.

"Are you okay?" I asked.

"Yes." And then, "I can't believe you're here." It was quiet for a second. I couldn't stand the awkwardness, and I made the first move by leaning in. He quickly met me halfway. After a minute, kissing next to each other wasn't comfortable and he eased back on the sofa, pulling me on top of him. It was almost too much being completely up against him. I had worried this was going to move to a place I wasn't comfortable with, but I ended up never having to say a thing.

We stayed right there, kissing for ages, his hands moving all around my back but never anywhere else. The kissing had more of a first-date feeling, not an in-the-moment, this-may-never-happen-again feeling like it had in his bedroom the other night. Physically, it felt like we just fit together. I hoped he'd never had that with anyone before me. I wondered if I could find that in his thoughts somewhere, or if I didn't want to know.

I wasn't sure how much time had passed when I finally, reluctantly, untangled myself. When I pulled back, John said, "You need to leave?"

Standing up, I straightened my skirt. When had I started wearing skirts? Suddenly it felt like everything was changing.

I looked over to see John watching me. "What?" I asked. He shook his head, as if to say, *Never mind.* "No, really? Do I look strange?"

He stood up. "It's nothing. You just look like we've been making out for hours. Your lips are puffy. . . ."

"I'm sure. I've got to get it together in case anyone is there when I get home." I hadn't meant to even mention my family. I was getting flustered.

"Julia," he said. I looked up at him again. "I didn't mean it as a bad thing. You look so hot right now. You're always beautiful, but now you're . . . sexy. Well, you're always sexy, but right now you look like we were just . . ." He cut himself off.

I felt shy for a different reason. I had a hard time accepting the compliment. In the world I lived in, I didn't meet the standards. But now I tried to play it off like I'd heard all this a million times before. It would be so easy to be one of those girls from school who knew exactly who they were—young, cute. Or to be like Liv or even Angus. I realized I walked around feeling different every second of my life. Stuck in no-man's-land.

I felt the vibrations of the garage door only moments before we both heard the door to the house open. *Dammit.* I hadn't been paying enough attention, and now there wasn't time to make a clean exit. I couldn't let down my guard like that again. It was a reminder that I could only be this self-indulgent if I didn't make mistakes.

"What time is it?" John looked at his watch. "I'm sorry. I lost track of time."

I was annoyed I'd put myself in this position. John led the way from the screened-in porch into the kitchen area, where his dad was sifting through the mail.

I'd only seen John's dad from afar at that one terrible tennis match. He was pretty handsome—not quite as tall as John, but still around six feet. He was dressed in jeans and a button-down shirt. He had the same implacable prove-it-to-me look as John.

When John's dad extended his hand to me, I realized I'd been walking around dismissing and underestimating everyone who wasn't part of my family, but in this case, that was a mistake.

"Taro."

I shook his hand. "I'm Julia." He nodded. I could tell he knew who I was and he really wasn't impressed. He looked at John. That was all he had to do and John started talking.

"It was raining, so . . . "

John's dad held up a hand, as if to say, *Don't worry about it*. Then he asked, "Where's your brother?"

"Lifting weights." John looked his dad straight in the eye, and they had some kind of passing communication, until John's dad simply nodded. "Are you staying for dinner, Julia?"

"No!" I shook my head vehemently. "I was actually on my way out." I started searching around the room for where I'd left my bag. I had never, ever in a million years pictured myself interacting with John's parents. It was one thing having people at school see us together—they felt superfluous to me. This was on a whole other level. I couldn't take this back. If they knew me, it became real, not just a fantasy that only concerned the two of us.

"No. Stay for dinner," Taro said directly to me. John looked over at me apologetically but didn't try to get me out of it. It seemed that if his dad said it, it was going to happen.

The front door opened, and in walked a still-sweating Alex, who paused for a moment when he saw me. "Hey, Julia."

"Hi." I was ready to make my move to leave again before I was trapped.

"Stay," John said. The fact that he wanted me there was the strangest thing to me. It was also a little bit sweet. But I didn't know if I could do it.

And then a minute behind Alex, John's mother appeared,

carrying pizza boxes and bags. You couldn't have stopped John and Alex from leaping over themselves to help her.

John's mom, who had been dressed casually the last time I saw her, appeared in a wrap dress that clung snugly to her curves. She was tall and broad shouldered but not overweight. She off-loaded the food onto the boys. They carried it over to the counter and automatically started getting down plates.

She looked over at me, surprised. "I had a school-district meeting, so . . . ," she said, as if apologizing for the takeout.

"Pizza again?" said Taro.

"Next time you make the call," John's mom said, not snappishly but in a matter-of-fact way that made me not want to mess with her. I remember John saying his dad taught high school math, and I knew his mom was a middle school principal, and it made perfect sense. They both seemed tough, but his dad was more stoic, his mother more fiery. I wondered what they were like as a couple. Victoria was extremely strong, but ultimately everything revolved around my dad. Here you got the sense that when John's mom was home, everyone jumped to attention.

"Hi, I'm Kathleen." John's mom extended her hand to me. "I saw you at the tennis tournament but didn't have the opportunity to introduce myself." Was she saying that pointedly to John or me?

"I'm Julia."

"Nice to officially meet you." Kathleen didn't sound at all psyched to meet me. I suddenly felt exhausted, surrounded by a whole new set of people I would have to perform for. The room felt close and overly warm, the small space filled with tall people. There was too much going on, and it might take more concentration than I had to appear normal. It was getting easier after the past months of being on all the time, but I had to be vigilant.

"Excuse me," I said slowly. "I'm just going to use the bathroom."

John led me down the short hall to the guest bathroom. I was irrationally pissed that he'd roped me into this dinner. He knew it too.

When we were alone outside the bathroom door—within earshot of his parents and brother—he said, "I'm sorry. No one really says no to my dad."

"Yeah. I kind of got that."

Realizing how mad I was, John leaned in. "I'm sorry," he breathed in my ear, and kissed the corner of my mouth.

"John!" Out of nowhere his mother was standing where she could see us. "Let her use the bathroom."

John moved away from me, more slowly than I would have thought he would in his mother's presence. He had a rebellious streak, and you could see he knew how to make his mother crazy. I pivoted quickly, closing the bathroom door behind me.

I had to get the hell out of there. I knew I'd feel better if I broke or moved something in their bathroom right now, but I was too scared to try. And it seemed impolite.

I took in the small powder room. In spite of the slightly peeling wallpaper and other fraying details I'd seen, the house was decorated nicely. Sort of the best of IKEA meets ethnic art brought home from travels. I hated the snob in my head. Hated it even as I couldn't help but look at everything through the critical lens of someone who grew up in a house that would be featured in *Architectural Digest* if my family would allow it. Whatever—I wasn't judging, just observing—and I vowed to keep anything resembling judgment off my face while I was here.

John's mom didn't like me. I'm sure she thought I was a snobby rich girl who was pretending to be something other than that with my tattoos and dyed-black hair—which, looking in the mirror just now, I realized actually wasn't so black or severe anymore. And here I was leading her eldest down a bad path right at the precise moment he needed to stay focused.

Funnily enough, beginning last weekend, tennis had started to go well for John. It seemed like right when he quit trying, everything turned around. He had even accused me of messing with his matches after he destroyed some top-ranked players, but I assured him he had no one to blame but himself.

I studied myself in the round mirror. Who was this person? John was right—my lips were puffy, and on top of that, my incessantly growing hair was bigger than usual from the rain. I had less makeup on than I'd worn at the beginning of the school year, and I looked more like myself from two years ago, before the Lost Kids. I looked girlish and even pretty.

I took a rubber band off my wrist and pulled my hair back into a bun, feeling a little more in control and like I was headed into a match. If I was going to do this, I was going to do it well. I could hope I had maybe developed some of Novak's charm overnight.

Outside in the hallway I paused to look at the hanging family photos, mostly snapshots, none of them artistic like the ones on the second floor of my house. In the baby pictures the boys were adorable, looking almost like twins—one was of them in a pumpkin patch, another was of them posing in the snow with a couple I assumed were their grandparents, an older Asian woman and a Caucasian man. There was one of a very young Taro and Kathleen, standing in front of zebras on a savannah. I could picture them having met at Teach For America or the Peace Corps.

"Do you even know what a douchebag is?" John's mother was saying to Alex. "Because I want to make sure you know if you're going to keep saying it. Sorry, Julia," she said when she saw I'd walked back into the kitchen.

I tried not to smile. "Why don't you sit there," Kathleen said, and pointed next to where John was sitting, mortified. As soon as I sat down next to him, John moved his chair closer to mine. *Seriously, John?* I knew he was trying to irritate his mother, and it wasn't funny.

As soon as I was seated, Taro put down his phone and meandered over from the kitchen to the table and stood behind his wife for a second. He put his hands on her shoulders and bent to kiss her cheek. Kathleen absentmindedly looked up at him, but then caught his hand and squeezed it when he walked by. She caught me staring.

It struck me how they seemed to live so easily together. I realized I had never seen a "normal" family interact before, except on TV.

All at once Alex started talking, and began a monologue about his coach that became funny because he was so clueless about how long he'd been talking. His parents just kept nodding and nodding until they started cracking up.

"Take a breath," John said, not unkindly.

"Don't forget to eat, babe," their mom urged Alex, who held a piece of pizza in front of his face for the full two minutes he was talking.

Alex was a little offended and clamped his mouth shut.

"So . . . Julia," John's mom said, "you're a senior?"

"Yes. I am." I hoped I was smiling pleasantly. John's mom had really good posture that made her look excited and alert, like she was ready to spring out of her seat.

"Are you looking at colleges?" she asked.

"UT. That's where my whole family goes," I said, lying.

"That's a great school." Then, looking over at John, she said, "Well, my baby wants to go as far away as possible. Speaking of which, Alex, I got a phone call today from UCLA. The tennis coach wants you to visit."

"Really?" Alex looked at John and seemed hesitant, like he didn't want to step on John's toes. "That would be cool if we both went there."

"I haven't heard a thing from them this fall, so you'll probably be there by yourself," John replied. *Whoa.* Touchy subject. The entire table tensed up.

"Where do you want to go?" Taro asked, looking over at John.

"Stanford."

"Well" was all his mom said.

"Trust me, I know. They haven't reached out since I've been back." John looked his mother in the eye with a *You seriously want to talk about this right now?* look.

"How was practice today?" she asked instead, changing the subject.

John's dad stood, as if trying to draw her attention away from John. "Want another glass of wine?"

"Sounds good. So, John honey, how was practice?" She suddenly knew something was up.

"I didn't go today. It was canceled because of the rain."

"But Alex was there?" No one said anything. Kathleen looked at me and then back to John. After a moment she said, "Got it," which was worse than if she'd been openly annoyed.

John's dad sat back down. "Julia, would you like anything else?" he asked politely.

"No, I'm fine. Thank you, though." I noticed John had stopped eating also. Taro took a sip of his wine and surveyed his family. He was so calm and collected, yet he had a strong presence. It was quiet. He didn't demand power like my dad, who came into every room with an energetic burst and an expectation of being the center of attention.

"Let me help," I said when Alex stood up to start clearing the table. I thought that's what a normal person would do, even though I'd never helped with such a thing in my life.

"No, no. Sit down!" said both parents at once.

"No, really!" I slowly removed plates and handed them to Alex, watching his system for cleaning plates and putting them in the dishwasher. Alex watched me hold a bunch of silverware in my hand and pause while I looked for where the hell to put it.

"It goes in that side basket," he said, giving me a strange look.

I finished what I could and promptly said, "Unfortunately I need to get going."

John's mother said, "Of course. Thanks for joining us." Both of his parents stood and walked John and me to the door.

John practically dragged me out while I said thank you. When the front door closed behind us, he began apologizing immediately.

"Stop. Don't worry. Seriously. Your family is very caring," I said, and I meant it. My existence seemed to drive them crazy, but it was because they cared about John. "And I kind of have a crush on your dad," I teased.

"Ugh, please. You and every student he has."

"Really?"

"No, I don't know. That's what my mom says."

"I really better leave," I said, looking out to the street beyond the house. The sky was starting to darken, the days getting shorter. There was an awkward pause between us, and I looked down at the bright red geraniums, newly planted in pots by the front door. In just about every way, this experience had been the opposite of my home life.

"Call me later?" John said. He matched my sudden distance with his casualness. I didn't need to read his mind to know he was cursing himself that he'd made me stay for dinner. I wanted to tell him it wasn't that. It was that all of it was suddenly too real.

When the gate to my house opened, I was met with the sight of three or four cars parked in the driveway. A yellow Lamborghini suddenly came to life, backed out violently, and then drove swiftly past me, taking me by surprise. The windows were dark, but I saw that the driver was Angus's dad, Lati, my dad's best friend. I may have been wrong, but I thought I caught a glimpse of Angus in the car. I was surprised Lati hadn't acknowledged me or even slowed down. He'd stared straight ahead and driven like he was angry.

They'd been caught.

When I entered the house, Victoria, who was standing with Anne, met me.

I had my answer to "Where have you been?" fairly prepared. But, more kindly than usual since Anne was listening, Victoria said, "Julia, will you please go upstairs?" Just then, Dominik and Carlo, who worked closely with my dad, walked by carrying trash bags, and another man followed with a large external hard drive. By way of explanation, Victoria said, "Your father is home and decided to clean house, so to speak. It's a little crazy down here." Clean meant confiscation. I could tell Victoria had been caught off guard because she was wearing workout clothes. I glanced at Anne, who seemed preoccupied.

"Of course. I'll go up now." I began to walk in the direction of the living room.

"Why don't you go up the other way? They're having a meeting in the living room."

I nodded and changed course to the back stairs. "Good night."

They were severely distracted. Distraction didn't happen very often. It worried me that the boxes were being dumped in this manner. It seemed reactive.

I ran up the stairs wondering what the hell was going on. When I was in front of my bedroom door, my bag weighing down one shoulder, I could hear sounds coming from Liv's room much farther down the hall. I listened for a moment. It was muffled crying.

Old protective instincts took over. If she was crying, I felt like I needed to go to her. No one ever cried. There was no need. Except for me. I was the only one who let my emotions get to me, as Victoria and Novak had witnessed that night in Novak's office. I knew they'd never forget that. Even if Liv could cry, she had never had much, if anything, to cry about. What had my dad said to Liv and Angus? What was their punishment? I wondered how much Novak really cared that Angus had gone beyond his social reach to be with Liv. It seemed like there were bigger things going on.

Just before I knocked on Liv's door, I paused. She certainly hadn't been there for me. I couldn't bring myself to knock.

Hearing Novak's voice below, I walked over to the staircase. I could only see if I stood in full view. I took a step out into the open at the top of the staircase and immediately saw my dad. He was standing in front of an audience of people of his generation arranged in a semicircle around him. They looked up at him as he paced and gesticulated, like he was working to win over a jury. They all sat on the edge of their seats, hanging on his every word. Then everyone laughed. This was Novak at his most compelling and persuasive.

Sensing a presence, my dad suddenly looked up to where I was standing. He looked back at me almost blankly, deep in his train of thought. I immediately stepped back into the shadows.

My phone buzzed. Junk email. Nothing from John.

I swiftly made my way back to my room, afraid to even think John's name in Novak's vicinity.

I had promised myself I could manage the separation between John and this world. Keep them compartmentalized in my mind. Knowing I shouldn't do it, that I was beginning to blur lines, I began a text to John.

Not what I was expecting, but thank you for tonight. You have a very nice family. I miss you already. I immediately deleted it, knowing I could never send it. It looked like my time with him was running out.

Chapter Nineteen

John and I sat across from each other in the library, our feet touching under the table. Our English class had been temporarily moved to the library during construction to repair the leaking roof.

We sat at our own table, no one else bold enough to intrude, but I felt people glancing up to look at us curiously. One girl from class even scooted back in her chair in order to see under our table, then kicked the girl next to her to point out my feet touching John's. I pretended not to notice and definitely didn't move away from him.

"Hey, man." A friend of John's came up behind him and clapped him on the shoulder.

"Hey. What's up?" John said. I remembered his name was Chris. Chris glanced surreptitiously at me. I didn't bother to look up. It was rare that anyone spoke to me. Especially anyone male. But they seemed to like to get close when they could use John as an excuse.

"Not much. You going to the festival? You missed out last year. We're parking at your house and walking from there."

"Yeah. I'm going on Friday."

"Cool. I'm going the first weekend too. So hopefully we can hang out." Chris quickly studied me one more time. John had barely hung out with his friends for a few weeks now.

"Sounds good," John replied. Chris nodded and walked back to where his class was sitting.

I threw down my pencil and arched back, stretching long. When I moved, more eyes looked my way, watching me. I knew I looked like I didn't notice, but I was always aware. I'd never get used to it.

John liked that his family had flustered me. It gave him hope that I wasn't a complete ice queen where other people were concerned. John thought it had been funny to see me nervous. He liked that I wasn't perfect.

And I hated that he thought that. I'd had no idea I appeared nervous that night. Of course, I didn't like that he saw differences between me and my family. They were perfect, and that's what I wanted to be—I had to be—too.

As soon as I left that night, his parents had been all over him. Safe sex, tennis, distraction, getting too attached senior year—those were some of the highlights I got from reading his mind. Right now he was thinking that no one could believe I was his girlfriend, if that's what I was.

Sometimes he looked at me like he would any other girl. He thought I looked like a blend of rich girl and tough girl with my nice clothes and tattoos—that people would always stare even when they didn't know who I was. Many times he would look at me and try to pinpoint other differences. I didn't like that as much.

"What?" I asked. John wanted to ask me something. I

watched him crumple up a piece of paper in a ball and throw it into a trash can at least twenty feet away. He didn't even react when he made the shot. He turned back to me.

"Nothing. Want to go to Austin City Limits with me? The lineup is pretty good." He caught my hand on the table-top and held it for a moment, out in the open.

"This Friday night?" I asked. I slowly moved my hand out from under his.

"Yep."

"I've never been."

"Seriously? You've lived here your whole life and you've never been?"

Of course I hadn't. Too crowded and too much human-ity. "I've never been to a live show," I said quietly.

"That is crazy," he said. "Especially living here. You have to go, then." I knew I had the look of someone who couldn't come up with an excuse fast enough.

"Did you already finish your work?" he asked. John saw that not only had I completed the short essay questions for our class, but I had just finished my AP biology homework. We'd only been sitting there for about twenty minutes. I started moving papers around, uncomfortable with the scrutiny. "How do you do it?" he asked.

"What do you mean?" I looked at him suspiciously.

"Guys! Quiet over there," Mrs. Bartell said from across the room. I wasn't sure if it was directed at John and me. Everyone was talking.

He lowered his voice. "Never mind," he said, annoyed. He went back to pretending to do his work. He was too dis-tracted to concentrate with our feet touching.

After a minute I said, "It's easy. All the information is in my head and I can just visually recall it when I need it. Little kids sometimes have the ability, but then they grow out of it. We don't." I looked down again and acted busy.

In John's mind I kept freezing him out and then giving him a few details, as if I couldn't decide how far I was going to let him in. He was sick of being the one to ask questions, so he decided to ignore what I'd said. After a minute that started to drive me crazy. Without looking up, I slid my foot up his leg under the table. He didn't react. Finally he leaned back in his chair and looked me in the eye. I gave him a *What?* expression. We'd barely had any time alone together for at least a week.

He trapped my foot with his legs to make me stop. The bell rang, and we packed our belongings and trailed out of the library. It was easy to linger and leave last. Most likely I wasn't going to see him for the rest of the day. When we exited the library, we turned to each other like we had the same idea at the exact same time and kissed. It was quick. I didn't think anyone saw. John backed away, leaving me standing there.

"Talk to you later?" he asked.

"Of course," I said, feeling a smile light up my face. I felt his heart clench.

He walked away thinking, *She is going to crush me.*

In honor of Austin City Limits, classes were canceled for the afternoon and I found I had even more freedom than usual. Victoria was taking Liv to Telluride for the weekend. My dad was in Europe again. Or so they said. Maybe they were visiting their favorite places in these last days before we disappeared. I quickly blocked the thought. I didn't want to think about the future right now. Relocation was a ways away.

I was walking toward the parking lot when I saw Mrs. Bartell, happily talking to other staff members. I was surprised to see her with a stroller and a round toddler sitting in it, barefoot and dressed in striped shorts and a burnt-orange University of Texas T-shirt. I had to admit he was cute. I was close enough to give the child a smile, and he gave me a drooling grin back. It was probably because I was studying him that I was able to hear the muffled heartbeat. I stopped right where I was and listened more closely, realizing the odd rhythm belonged to the baby. *Goddammit.*

I didn't know if it was something serious. Maybe they already knew about it. I realized I liked Mrs. Bartell. I looked over at her, debating. I was about to walk away when I looked back at her toddler, who smiled at me again like he was so happy to see me.

"Julia!" John called to me from the entrance to the parking lot. I turned at the sound of his voice and started to walk toward him, my back to the baby.

Halfway to John, I spun around and retraced my steps.

"Mrs. Bartell?" I walked up to her. The other two adults halted their conversation.

"Julia. Hi!" she said, friendly.

"Hi. Can I speak to you privately for a moment?"

"Sure," she said with a question in her voice.

Mrs. Bartell followed me a short distance.

"Your son . . . ," I started, and pointed to the stroller.

"Michael?" she supplied helpfully, surprised.

"I don't mean to interrupt. I just noticed his feet seem swollen. Does he have a heart problem?" I didn't have a plan. I was making it all up on the spot. The toddler appeared to be just fine.

"No. No heart problem." Mrs. Bartell looked at me strangely.

I needed to make her worry. Just enough. "I'm only asking because my cousin's feet swelled up and it turned out there was a serious valve problem."

"He's fine, honey. Thanks for your concern," Mrs. Bartell said, and patted me on the shoulder.

"No," I said sternly. I knew he wasn't fine. Mrs. Bartell looked taken aback. If I didn't say anything, that was it. He was dependent on me right now. I didn't know what to say except to explicitly tell Mrs. Bartell, "He should be seen by a doctor." I looked at her hard before continuing on my way. I tried to shake it off; I would think about my actions later.

John met me halfway and looked up at the sky. "I think it might rain." Then he leaned down and kissed me full on the lips in front of everyone exiting the parking lot. I let him, which should have told me something about how happy I was and how ridiculously not careful I was being.

"Let's go." I impetuously decided to leave my car in the lot, and we walked across the bridge over the river to Zilker Park, where the music festival was kicking off. Some of the best bands from all over the world were playing at the festival. Every time ACL came around, I felt a shift in the air as the city was taken over by the throngs of visitors. If I ever got near the park over the course of the weekend, I always felt a pang that I was missing out on living, somehow. But then I would take one look at the crowds and turn away, relieved I wasn't among them.

John held my hand until he couldn't anymore, and we showed our wristbands at one of the gates and went through. Alex and August were with us, a group of their other friends loosely walking in front of and behind us. There was a playing-hooky feel in the air.

I passed through the barricades and came out onto the enormous green field, downtown Austin in the background, massive stages and smaller stages at different points. It was early enough that the field wasn't covered with people yet, but I'd never been in a crowd like this.

I waited for the usual aversion and fear, but no eyes were on me here. There were so many people, it was the perfect place to blend in. I realized I was free. A stolen afternoon with the hottest boyfriend . . . *Jesus.* I did not feel like myself. I felt one hundred times better.

We stayed with just Alex and August, quickly losing everyone else from school, which made me feel even more comfortable. Hours blended into one another as we moved from stage to stage. With the music reverberating through me, I felt like I was in a dream state. It began to rain, and there was nothing to do but surrender and get wet.

❧⊷❧

Before I was ready, one of the headlining bands began to perform, the last act of the night. By now it was completely body-to-body. It didn't matter. My ability to selectively tune out what I wanted must have kicked into gear, and that's what made the music and my time with John better—more focused and intense. I was fully aware this moment in time would never be repeated.

The field had been trampled and become muddy. People streamed out of the park, ready to come back tomorrow. But this was it for me. John had a tournament, and I would sit home and pretend I didn't have a secret life even while I dreamt about it.

The crowd was moving slowly, so slowly that John leaned down to kiss me. I turned fully and pressed up against him, our wet bodies plastered together. Reluctantly we stopped kissing, and I took a step just a few inches back and faced the exit again, reaching for John's hand. Turning my head casually, I caught someone's eye. It took me a second to register who I was looking at.

Angus.

My brain went up in flames.

Angus was staring at me with an expression on his face I'd never seen before. I dropped John's hand and moved away from him, letting people move between us. The other Lost Kids minus Roger and Ellis came into focus, but none of them had seen me yet. Angus was back with them, post–Liv breakup. And he looked like himself again—no more cleaned-up version.

Oh shit. What were they doing? They weren't supposed to be together in a group like this. It didn't look like Angus could resist breaking the rules. He was back out in the world, craving action.

Angus wouldn't look away from me. I had no choice but to meet his eyes and edge closer to him, pretending I wasn't scared by how he was looking at me—like he now had a different opinion of me. I had something on the Lost Kids, discovering them disobeying Novak like this, but it didn't compare with what I was doing. How in the world could I have been so stupid?

"Julia," Paul said, surprised. The four Lost Kids paused, waiting to see how Angus handled me. They were wondering if they still needed to be angry with me. What was the point? They were back to doing what they wanted to do. None of them besides Angus had seen me all over John.

"Hi," I heard myself shout, doing my best to pretend Angus hadn't seen what he'd seen. The jostle and the murmur of the crowd made it hard to have a conversation. "What are you doing here?"

Why wasn't Angus saying anything? I could feel John watching me, and I prayed he'd stay back in the crowd. Of course the boys would recognize John from Barton Springs. The crowd started to move again. More people filled in the space between the Lost Kids and me.

It wasn't like Angus to be quiet, and it was scaring me even more than if he acted like he was having a field day with my dirty secret. Did he not hear my question? After a long moment he spoke. "Same thing you're doing. Not following the dictator's orders." Angus looked over my shoulder. *Shit.*

John was next to me and then in front of me, aggressively moving face-to-face with Angus.

"I know you," Angus said to him.

"I know you," John said right back. "You're the asshole who lied to the police about me. Thanks. I appreciated that."

"You're more than welcome." *What the hell?* They stood

looking at each other, and while I knew they weren't going to fight, something was going on. The other Lost Kids watched this outsider, taller by a few inches, stand up to Angus. They simultaneously moved in closer.

And then the craziest thing happened. Angus turned away first. "Bye, Julia," he said. He raised his eyebrows at me. "Have fun."

I wasn't sure why he hadn't outed me. I watched them melt away into the crowd, Sebastian looking at me over his shoulder, confused by what had just transpired.

So this was what it felt like to blow your life to bits.

<hr />

It was like my mind wouldn't work with my two realities in the same space, like they couldn't exist together. That had been my mistake. I had lied to myself that they never would. I had acted like I was the puppet master who had total control over keeping them apart.

I followed John out of the park. I had shut down completely. I had no idea what to do.

My word against Angus's. The Lost Kids would believe anything Angus said. But I had plausible deniability in case it ever got to Novak. I was confident Novak would side with me—clearly he already disliked Angus: he wouldn't let Angus near his precious daughter. I tried to imagine Angus telling Novak, but as I slowly began to surface from the swirl of thoughts in my head, in my heart I knew the Lost Boys would never say anything. We had too much history.

I became aware of John again.

John had known I'd been trying to distance myself from

him. He had stayed apart from me, even during his confrontation with Angus. You would think I would drop John immediately after getting caught. That I cared how John felt at this point was insane.

I couldn't believe that John had gotten in Angus's smug face. I wished he hadn't. I wished he had remained anonymous, blended into the crowd behind me. But a little part of me admired him even more. John had reminded me of his dad. He had that same quality of commanding respect.

John wouldn't look at me. Rivulets of mud were running down my legs, and I could feel my surroundings seep back into my consciousness as we walked farther and farther from the park. Now I was all too aware of the crowds, the rain adding to the chaos, the atmosphere wild and party-like.

In my own defense, I'd had to pretend I wasn't with John. It was for his own safety. I couldn't believe that out of thousands of people, I'd ended up face-to-face with Angus. Maybe the boys hadn't seen me kissing John—maybe the crowd had been big enough—but I had seen in Angus's crystal eyes the click of recognition and the mortifying knowledge of what he now had on me forever, delivered to his doorstep by yours truly.

It was close to eleven. I had to concentrate to keep up with John's long strides. I could tell he was keeping tabs on me, looking slightly over his shoulder out of the corner of his eye. Even when he was angry with me, he was protective. I'd just smashed his pride. I knew how he felt since it was an emotion I was all too familiar with—that someone wanted you out of sight.

I couldn't leave him with that feeling. He didn't deserve

it. I didn't want to hurt him. I would try to find a way to explain before I broke things off.

"John!" My voice came out strange and hoarse, forcing him to look at me. He slowed but didn't give me anything else. I had to give him credit—he played mad well. He shut down and moved on. He never looked at Tom or Sarah after he'd discovered the cheating. Not because he was angry. He no longer cared.

When we got to the next block, we were almost alone. Under the glare of the yellowed streetlight, John's house came into view, but my relief that he would now be forced to talk to me dissipated when I saw Alex and a small crowd of friends gathered in the driveway in spite of the rain. *Dammit.*

It turned out John wasn't in any hurry to drive me home. He held court simply by hanging out, his silent presence beckoning others to him. I looked off into the distance and decided to outwait him. Eventually he had to walk over to ask if I needed a ride.

I stood back a bit, leaning against a random car while the group of about seven, including Alex, August, Chris, and their friends, all talked to John. Everyone—except John and me—hadn't come down from the high of the concert yet, and you could feel the music and the afterglow of the immense crowd vibrating through them.

John talked almost exclusively with a girl who seemed to be a friend of August's. I watched him try to make me jealous. His anger obviously wasn't so cold after all.

I tried to see John through this sixteen-year-old girl's eyes. I realized I'd been living a teenage fantasy, knowing exactly what John Ford was thinking. What made him so incredibly attractive was how much of an asshole he could have been, with his looks, his intelligence, his athleticism. So much seemed to come easily to him.

What made me mad was that it was getting to me. Watching him with another girl—and this wasn't the first time—I had this gnawing thought that I counted on John thinking I was everything. It had become something I needed.

I had to go. Now. I would just leave things where they stood before they got worse. I turned to go and felt my movement catch John's attention.

I was so focused on John that at first I didn't react when I saw the yellow Lamborghini Aventador slip to the curb in front of the house. It just seemed so incongruous to see Angus's dad's car in front of John's home.

I hadn't felt him coming, but he'd certainly found me. I should have known this was how Angus would react. He wouldn't leave this alone. It was too tempting to come and fuck with me. And them.

The group stopped talking, the head-turning car doing just that—turning heads. Everyone seemed to lean forward. Angus rolled down the window. I moved as fast as I could down the driveway.

Angus was alone, thank God. I was sure I'd see the five boys together, excited to flex their superiority, ready to tease me. When I leaned down, elbows on the window, I hoped to block everyone behind me from Angus's view.

What I saw in Angus's eyes was the opposite of what I expected. He wasn't here to threaten me or mock me. "What are you doing? This is dangerous for all of us." Angus looked like he wanted to understand. Like he thought I needed help.

For a second I had the same old sensation of wanting to lean on him, that he was the only one who understood me and maybe I could explain this to him. I wanted to say, "I don't know." Instead I said, "It's fine."

His eyes turned cold before they became taunting. "This is not fine. That dude, Julia?" His laugh came out strangled and mean.

I suddenly realized Angus had the look he would get when I flirted innocently with one of the other Lost Kids. He never liked it. He was actually jealous.

I straightened up, taken aback. It seemed like Angus was confused also, like he didn't know exactly why he'd come and he wasn't thinking straight. I wondered if a part of him wanted me and that's what made him get in the car and concentrate his efforts to come find me.

I was so surprised, I didn't know how to handle it. "This is part of something bigger, Angus." There was truth to that, but I was aware I'd just cheapened John.

"Then tell me. Get in the car." Angus softened his voice. He thought he was rescuing me.

I took a step back as the door flew out and open.

I could get in the car with Angus and leave. Angus felt like home. And he seemed to finally be offering himself to me. How ironic that after all this time it was the sight of me with John that did it.

It was everything I had wanted before Barton Springs. I could get in this car now and pretend the last two months had never happened.

Why the hell couldn't I get in? At my hesitation Angus's expression turned guarded. Then his attitude became smug with disbelief.

Behind me, someone was approaching, but I knew it wasn't John. He fully expected me to get in the car with Angus. It was Alex.

"Nice car," he said, a little drunk and slightly belligerent.

Angus held my eyes for a second before making a show of turning his attention to Alex, as if he were doing him a favor by acknowledging his presence. I realized too late I'd made a colossal mistake by not getting in the car, if only to get Angus away. Now I saw the old Angus was back and would cover his hurt by taking this opportunity.

"Want a ride?" Angus asked Alex nonchalantly.

"No," I said, halfway knowing I was making things worse. It just made both of them want to do it more.

Alex was daring. And drunk. Since I'd planted myself in front of the door, Alex had to maneuver around me. I watched helplessly as he bent low into the car and the spaceship door closed behind him. Then they were gone.

John came up behind me on the sidewalk.

"Where are they going?"

"On a drive. They'll be back." I made it sound like it was all fine. John walked away, pretending he wasn't extremely jealous and beyond annoyed that his brother would get in the enemy's car. He wasn't thinking about any danger. I forced myself to move so it didn't look like I was standing vigil. They needed to come back. I couldn't stand one more second of this.

I wasn't sure if Alex was wearing a seat belt. I knew Angus

would scare the shit out of Alex, because Angus was trying to scare the shit out of me. He and the Lost Kids loved to scare me by driving like they wanted to die. And while they had sharp instincts and reflexes, they made mistakes, as evidenced by their fancy cars that had taken a beating. Often they would take a beating too, but nothing they couldn't walk away from or shake off in a couple of days.

Alex didn't have that guarantee. If he wasn't wearing a seat belt and flew through the windshield—which had happened to the Lost Kids before—that was it.

I began to count the seconds in my head. John was laughing with his friends, and I walked slowly over to join him, keeping the wet, black street in my peripheral vision. When I came to stand next to him, I felt him lean his body almost imperceptibly away from mine. At the five-minute mark, I felt his big-brother worry kick up. My worry was getting near hysterical. If something happened to Alex, it would be my fault.

Mercifully, I heard the hum five blocks away, and my heartbeat began to slow. To my surprise the car stopped farther down the block and Angus let Alex out there. Angus didn't want to see me. It was also a threat. He wanted to leave me unsure.

Alex approached and seemed exhilarated rather than stunned.

"Hey!" Alex called to his friends. He ignored me as he passed, taking his brother's cue. I watched Alex try to joke with his brother, to bring him around. John had no idea what could have happened. Thank God it hadn't been John who had walked up to the car.

Angus had succeeded in making his point. These people didn't hold a candle to us, and John ultimately couldn't measure up to Angus. Regular people were vulnerable. Anything could happen to them at any time. And that would be me too, if I got caught and banished from the family. It was a reminder of how quickly all of this could go wrong. It already had. I had just chosen John over Angus.

Chapter Twenty

"Ready?" John stalked ahead of me and unlocked his mother's car. As if he just couldn't go through with being a jerk, at least by his standards, he held open the passenger door for me instead of walking past. The high curb made it tricky to open the door all the way, so I had to squeeze in while he held it. I inadvertently brushed up against him. The last time we'd touched had been seconds before I'd seen Angus at the festival. Now those feelings came rushing back.

I knew this was about to end. If John didn't end it right now, I would have to. But at this point we were still technically together. At least for tonight.

"Did you put your seat belt on?" John asked.

"Oh, sorry." I drew it across me, and when I looked down I realized my shirt was stuck to me.

He quickly looked away and did a U-turn, going the long way to avoid passing near the park. We would only have about ten minutes together.

My confidence that we would talk dissipated completely when John turned on the radio loud. I turned my head and looked at him long enough that he should have looked back. But he didn't. To make things worse, a slow, romantic song came on the radio. John immediately went to change it. "No, don't," I said, and he dropped his hand.

The stoplights seemed endless as the rain started up again and the music filled the car. I leaned my head against the glass and stared out the window, watching the streets of the empty late-night downtown go past.

"John?"

He looked over at me impassively. God, why couldn't I get in his head?

"Do you remember how to get to my house?"

"I do." *Dammit.* This was going too fast. Soon we were entering my neighborhood. He took the corners too quickly, but the neighborhood was dead quiet at this time of night. Large estates and greenery blurred by, his speed unsettling me.

"Don't kill me, okay?" I only half joked.

"Do you even die?" he asked sarcastically.

John didn't bother slowing to look for my house. After zooming past the twenty-foot-high hedges that went on for almost a block, marking the front of the property, John took a clean left at the exact spot and put the car in park in front of the gate. You couldn't see anything of the house from the street from any vantage point.

"Hold on. Let me open the gate." I could tell he was surprised. He'd thought he was going to drop me off here like the last time, like a driver. And that's what I would have done if I hadn't decided to do something completely insane.

No one was home. If he came inside, no one would ever

know. I could easily tamper with the surveillance cameras later. I took my keys out of my pocket and used the remote. After a long pause the gate swung open like wings, revealing the property. All that glass. Seeing it from his point of view, the house was beyond grand. I felt like I was in a conversation with the house and it was asking me what I thought I was doing. It was just a house, I reminded myself. It wasn't alive. But as we drove down the incline of the driveway and the house loomed large, I felt like I couldn't look it in the eye.

"Come in. Please?"

She has got to be kidding.

He was so done with me, I was surprised I could hear him again.

"No one is home," I explained.

"Where are they?" He turned to look at me. I saw him noticing my hair. I'd taken it out of its knot, and now it draped around me, long and tangled. I knew how different I looked from when he'd first met me.

"Telluride, I think." I looked out the window. The lighting scheme in front of the house was soft and perfect.

"Why didn't you go?"

"I wasn't invited." I shrugged.

He didn't ask any more questions.

What am I doing? She has me so ridiculously under her thumb. I've had enough of this bullshit.

"Can you come in?" I tried again, knowing I was now overestimating my draw.

I saw him look up at my house. "No, I'd better be getting back."

"Come in. Please. We'll talk," I said softly. I knew I sounded unsure.

"I can't, Julia."

"Don't be mad at me. I didn't know how to handle it. No one dates someone outside our group. . . ."

He scoffed and looked over at me. "How do you just date each other? Doesn't that get old? There aren't that many of you."

"It works out. There are enough of us. And we just aren't . . . attracted to . . . you know . . . people."

"But you are?" he pressed.

"You."

"And you're ashamed of this?" His severe annoyance was back.

"I'm struggling with it."

I could tell my honesty surprised him. We were quiet for a long moment.

"Why? What do you think it says about you?" he asked.

"That I'm not one of them."

"Is that so terrible?"

"I don't know." I nodded. "Yes."

"Julia, I can't do this when clearly he's who you want. I can't be your boyfriend from the wrong side of the tracks who you're ashamed of. I'm not going to play into that bull-shit."

"John! Jesus. That's not how it is. At all."

"It is, though. I saw how you looked at him at Barton Springs. I'll never have that kind of money or be able to do the things he can do."

"Stop." I shook my head. "Even if I used to like him, I don't now. Look. Since Barton Springs I'm on a kind of probation, and I'm not supposed to be doing this." I gestured between us. "I'm not supposed to be doing anything out of the ordinary."

"Why are you doing it, then?"

I laughed humorlessly. "Believe me, I tried not to. But then you . . ." I trailed off before I said something really bad. "Just, can you come in?" That hung in the air between us. Then I said, "I didn't get in the car with him."

He was still pissed. He knew that by going in he was just getting in deeper. After a long moment he surprised me when he opened his car door.

There weren't really any words to describe what he felt when I unlocked the front door. To John the house was unreal, and kept becoming more unreal as I led him through room after room. What surprised him most was how truly beautiful it was. He thought its size was ostentatious, but other than that it was simple—but so deceptively simple, he knew it was on a whole other level of wealth.

John was quiet when I walked through the living room with the glass wall, facing the lake. He went over to observe the view. We had just been across the water in the park, but here we were a world away. The lights outside showed the rain falling hard. The rectangular pool was lit, and even from afar you could see the surface dancing. The house was never cozy, but this was as close as it got—this feeling of being dry and protected inside.

"I'll show you the upstairs," I said softly.

He followed me up the stone staircase to the long hallway that ran the entire length of the second story. He saw the black-and-white family photos arrayed on the white wall.

"Where are you?"

"Um, here's one." He came over to where I pointed.

"You and your mom and sister?" he asked, looking closely. Most of the lights in the house were off, and it was hard to see.

"Stepmom," I corrected quickly. "Come on. My room is down here."

My entire body relaxed once we were in my bedroom and I closed the door.

"This is your room?" He looked around. I could tell he was surprised it was as spare as the rest of the house. Both of us were trying to ignore the massive bed sitting right there and the fact that we were all alone.

"Yes. Why are you asking like that?"

"It's just—it feels like a hotel suite. It's so perfect. Clean, I mean."

"I know. I'm a little crazy that way. You should see Liv's room. There are clothes everywhere—on the floor, thrown around." I realized I sounded fond of Liv.

How does she even have a hallway in her room? He wandered down the hall, feeling free to look in the bathroom and the small den. He paused in the walk-in closet. My shelves contained almost no colors, just perfectly folded cashmere sweaters and T-shirts in black, white, and gray. On another long shelf were about thirty pairs of jeans. Hung up on wood hangers were dresses and skirts arranged according to category and color. And then the shoes. Now I felt self-conscious.

"Did you freak out when you saw my room?" He was thinking I must have thought his house was the shittiest house I'd ever seen.

"No! I love your room. It feels like you. Seriously—I love

it." He didn't look at me, adjusting to everything he was seeing and how it made him feel. About me. About himself.

"Come here." I led him to a long window seat where you could look out on the lake. "This is my favorite place in the whole house. This is where I'm usually sitting when I'm on the phone with you." He sat down, suddenly conscious of all the whiteness of the house and my room, and the dried mud on him.

That I wanted to show him my home and let him deeper into my life meant something to him. But he hated that he suddenly felt lacking in every way—that he didn't have the money or abilities that matched mine and Angus's. He stood up and shoved his hands into his pockets, ready to go.

"You want to leave?" I tried to cover the hurt I felt.

"I should be getting back," he said.

I've refused to feel unworthy of her this entire time. I've fucking looked Angus in the eye and let him know he wasn't better than me.

But I could feel it all starting to seep into John's head. I'd made it worse by bringing him here. It was impossible for him not to feel like he didn't belong.

"Don't. You do not get to feel that way." I moved over to him, reaching out to touch him. He knew what I was talking about. He moved away before I could reach him.

"I'm going to go."

Dammit. I walked behind him in the hall. I hated what he felt.

"John," I said. "Just wait." He kept going. Now he wasn't even trying to hide that he was pissed. I kept up, right behind him, taking the stairs just as fast.

John somehow made his way to the front door by memory. He started playing with the complicated lock on the stainless-steel door, which slowed him down.

"Listen to me!" I tried to sound authoritative. Then I pulled a low trick. I put my hands on him, under his shirt, on the smooth skin of his back. I knew him; he was too much of a gentleman to jerk away.

"Listen," I said more quietly. John slowly turned and gave me a look that said, *I'll hear you out but you'll get nothing back.* His hands caught mine when they slid to his chest.

"I'm sorry for the Angus crap, and I'm sorry you would think for one second that I'm embarrassed to be seen with you." He removed my hands, not wanting to have the conversation.

I grabbed his arm. I needed John to know it wasn't him. "You are the most beautiful person. And you're the kindest person I've ever met. The problem is, I'm not supposed to feel this way about you." I shocked myself by tearing up. I pushed my fingertips against my eyes, as if that would stop it.

"Julia," he said, pausing, and then he swore under his breath.

Instead of making a move to leave, like I was dreading, he bent his face to mine and kissed me softly. It took only a few seconds for the kiss to change. It deepened, and everything—two weeks of barely seeing each other, this awful night, our intense physical attraction to each other—began to find an outlet.

"Come with me," I panted a few minutes later. John and I were in the entryway. Out in the open. Even though we were all alone, my instinct was to take him to the most private part of the house.

I led him through the kitchen to a back hallway with a pantry and a small wet bar and down some stone stairs.

"A wine cellar?" John looked at the hundreds of bottles of wine—useless to my father in a matter of months. I violently pushed the thought of the June departure from my head. Through the two small windows, you could see the rain sheeting down. The lights from outside combined with the moonlight lit the room just enough.

"Is this okay?"

"It's perfect," John said.

It could have been awkward at that moment, but the inevitability that hung in the air gave us confidence and momentum. There was a table below the two windows, and John must have already made a plan in his head as he led me to it. He picked me up and sat me on the table, my knees moving to either side of him as he stood in front of me.

Minutes went by. We'd stopped kissing, both breathing hard. We got to the point where John carefully held my face and looked me right in the eye. "Are you sure?" I tried not to think of any other girl whom he'd asked the same question.

"Positive. I want to." It was more than physical attraction. I wanted to know John as well as I could, even if he wasn't what I was supposed to want. I didn't want to miss this.

I wanted badly to make fun of him when he reached into his back pocket and pulled a condom out of his wallet. That would come later, when I questioned him about whether he always had it there or he thought tonight would be the night. I could have looked into his mind, tried to see what he was feeling, but I gave him space. Especially right now. I refrained from saying a word, knowing enough to understand this was probably going to be the most romantic moment of my life and I shouldn't even think about pushing it away, as hard as it was to just be present and feel it.

John, with all of his stupid experience, took over, and it was easy to stop thinking. Most of our clothes were off and we were soaked with sweat, and afterward we lay next to each other. Feeling so close to him, I rolled over and pushed my face into the crook of his neck, wondering if he could sense my smile. I'd always remember how I couldn't stop smiling.

I propped my chin on his chest and we looked into each other's eyes. One of John's arms was trapped under my body and I tried to sit up to give it back to him, but he said "Not yet," and continued to hold me close. His breath was still ragged. I rubbed my top leg flirtatiously over his leg that was tangled with mine.

"Stop!" he half joked. "I'm still recovering." I felt such a rush, like I could do anything. I was thinking about that when John suddenly took my face in one hand so that I was looking at him.

"I love you."

Chapter Twenty-One

I deliberately walked in just as the bell rang.

"Hey," he said, smiling at me as I sat down next to him in English on Monday morning.

"Hey," I said softly. Our eyes held for a split second.

We spoke on the weekend, but it was small talk, mostly updates on how he was playing in his tournament. We didn't refer to what happened in the wine cellar.

When he said "I love you," my whole body had tensed, and it hadn't been the same after that. We'd talked and kissed and lingered as we said good-bye in the drying, steaming driveway, but I'd never recovered.

All weekend I'd torn myself apart over what he'd said. It wasn't because I worried he was becoming obsessed with me. My instinct told me that wouldn't happen with John—his thoughts didn't have that irrational quality—and it was only something that ever seemed to occur with Novak's assistants. It was because I'd lied to myself that I had any control over a situation that had always been completely out of control.

As I sat next to him, eavesdropping on his thoughts, I

learned he'd spent the weekend consumed with should-haves. Ultimately, he'd decided he didn't regret saying it, and he wasn't going to apologize for how he felt. At the same time he'd decided he wasn't going to chase after me.

Knowing that he wasn't sorry, that he stood behind how he felt, made it harder, because it made me want him even more.

Mrs. Bartell suddenly kneeled right next to my desk. She looked exhausted. She whispered conspiratorially, "I took my son to the doctor on Saturday, and they sent us straight to the ICU. We found out his heart is inflamed; it's called myocarditis. Thank God we found out, because now we can give him the proper care. He should be okay." She looked at me meaningfully and squeezed my hand. "I can't thank you enough." She stood and headed back to the front of the classroom.

I drew intricate circles on my paper as class started, trying to pretend Mrs. Bartell hadn't rattled me. As class progressed I also tried to pretend I didn't know what John was thinking. He was trying not to replay Friday night in his head, but he couldn't stop himself. The clock said we had an hour before the period ended. He wanted to know how I would act when we had our first five minutes alone together since Friday night.

Mrs. Bartell's classroom phone started to ring. She looked at it, confused, like she'd never heard it ring before. I looked over at John, wanting to say something that might bring us back to normal—somewhere more casual and safe. He leaned in to hear what I was going to say, but suddenly I turned my attention to Mrs. Bartell. I knew that phone call was about me.

"Hello?" Mrs. Bartell said. Even before she hung up, I started to pack my things.

"Julia? You're being called down to the front office." Mrs. Bartell shrugged her shoulders, indicating she had no idea what was going on.

"Thank you." I was ready to go. I doubted anyone else besides John noticed that I'd stood up before Mrs. Bartell said my name.

I didn't look at John on my way out. At that point I still thought we had more time.

I reported to the front office. "Hi. I'm Julia Jaynes."

The young man at the front desk leapt up and said, "Right this way."

Someone was waiting for me. I'd assumed it was only a transcript problem or a schedule technicality.

I was led into a small conference room with shabby chairs and a long table. Three people rose to greet me—two men in suits, along with the school principal, Mrs. Brown. She looked extremely nervous.

Oh no. Had Mrs. Bartell said something?

"Julia, these two gentlemen asked to speak with you. Would you like to speak with them?" I could tell she was trying to clearly express that this was my decision and, for the record, no one here was strong-arming me.

I was confused because I'd seen these men somewhere before. A cloud passed over the sun, briefly dimming the light in the sterile office. In that instant I placed them. One of them was the man who appeared out of nowhere after my car was rear-ended back in September.

"Please sit." The younger man gestured to a seat across

the table. "Would you like a bottle of water?" The other man closed the door behind us but allowed the principal to stay in the room.

I remained standing. I turned to look at Mrs. Brown, who stepped forward.

"I let them know you need to get back to class."

"Yes, we'd like to ask you just a few questions." The older man sat himself down across from where I stood, clearly trying to draw attention away from Mrs. Brown. "Would you like some water?"

Again with the water. Did they want to get my DNA illegally? I shook my head.

"Who are you? I've seen you before," I said accusingly. The two men looked at each other, one annoyed with the other.

"I'm Russell Kelly with the FBI, and this is Agent Rhodes, also with the FBI."

"Is this legal?" I looked to Mrs. Brown.

Before she could open her mouth, she was not so subtly interrupted by Agent Kelly. "We have some questions for you about Kendra Wilson. Do you know Ms. Wilson?"

I needed to not say a word. I knew that.

Agent Kelly paused for effect. "She's missing. She was last seen with your father, at his office. Have you seen Kendra? Her family is frantic."

I had to just stand there, knowing I had a mountain of information that would help Kendra.

"Is there anything you could tell us about her or something you've heard?"

I remained silent, trying not to think about her family.

Knowing they weren't getting anywhere, Agent Kelly

changed tactics. "We also wanted to check in with you. Make sure you have our information in case *you* need help." He passed two business cards across the table. I let them lie there.

"Why would I need help?"

The younger agent jumped in. "We've had a close eye on your father for a while now. We know your family is very insular, and you may need a hand in case you'd like to restart your life away from them."

"Excuse me?" They thought we were some kind of cult I needed to escape from? That made me want to laugh. I was relieved this wasn't going to be a big deal after all.

"Do you know where your mother lives?"

I went cold.

"My mother lives here," I replied.

Agent Kelly said, "Your birth mother is in the San Francisco Bay Area. She used to work for us, and she had an interesting theory about your father—she almost got him to come in to talk with us."

The younger agent interrupted. "But then your mother became pregnant. Shortly after you were born, your father disappeared, and you vanished with him. It took years to connect you with that group in California. Until your father had a problem staying off the radar."

Agent Kelly interjected, "We can put you in touch with her." It went unsaid that they would want information from me in return. I realized they were looking to me for confirmation that Novak was the same person they'd been pursuing in California.

I cut him off. "You can speak to me with my parents and their attorney present."

You could feel the heaviness and annoyance when they

realized it had been a mistake to approach me. They must have seen me as their big opportunity—the clear outsider, the one most likely to talk.

Mrs. Brown looked relieved. She may have been strong-armed into calling me down when they flashed their badges, but it must have occurred to her that she would have to answer to my father.

I turned to leave. Mrs. Brown opened the door for me to exit.

"Her name is Elizabeth Blackcomb. She was born in Bethesda, Maryland," one of them called after me. A good-will gesture in hopes I'd come back for more.

Frustrated, the other agent also called out. "Tell your father it's a hell of a lot harder to hide in the world than it used to be." Like the good girl I'd been taught to be, I kept walking.

❦

I strode in a daze through the deserted halls. I didn't know what period it was or where I was supposed to go. Everything suddenly seemed surreal.

I leaned over the nearest trash can and threw up.

I hovered, holding back my hair. I'd let my bag drop onto a piece of spit-out gum, and I could see the neon green, still with teeth marks, stuck to it.

I'd never dreamed I might learn a thing about her. It hadn't crossed my mind as a remote possibility. I'd been denied any knowledge of her. And now, out of the blue, these men show up and they tell me my mother is one of them. . . .

My heart was beating out of my chest.

I had to remind myself that everything those men said

was bullshit. Still, it was a shock just to hear their words. To hear them talk about Novak having lived in California. For the first time I could picture our lives on a continuum instead of broken into airtight chapters.

Novak had warned me this might happen. I'm sure he knew about the surveillance, and that's why there were all the rules after Barton Springs.

My phone vibrated, and it dawned on me I'd heard the buzzing for minutes now. I knew who it was. I just didn't know what to say. Five missed calls. Novak had never wanted to speak to me so badly.

"Hello?" I answered woodenly.

"You are being picked up in front of the school in three minutes. Your principal called Victoria to let her know what's going on. Don't go back for anything. Your books, nothing. Do you understand?" Novak said.

"Okay." It came out as a strange half whisper.

"Is that a yes?"

"Yes. What about my car?"

"You're worried about your Prius?" He made it sound like it was sweet I cared about such a shitty car. "We'll arrange for someone to pick it up." He hung up.

What was happening? I felt like the Secret Service was coming to airlift me out. And Novak would be waiting at the other end. What was John going to think? An hour ago I was thinking about what to say in response to "I love you," and now I didn't know if I'd ever see him again.

I waited out front, all by myself in the quiet morning, until a Mercedes with blacked-out windows pulled up. I got in and we ripped away from the school.

It was serenely calm when I arrived home, like nothing out of the ordinary had happened. Like a bombshell hadn't been dropped on the story of my life.

It was midmorning and it was nice outside, birds singing. There was a crispness in the air, indicating the shift in seasons.

"Your stepmother is picking up Olivia in case the FBI go to her next, and then they'll join you and your father here. He's waiting for you down by the water. He wanted to speak to you alone as soon as you arrived." Anne smiled at me. She had been the one sent to pick me up, and now she was being oddly kind.

There was no reason I should feel sick. That was the FBI's job—to peel me off from the group and get information from me. They would do that by any means necessary, whether it was pretending my mother was an outsider or telling me my father had considered speaking to them. Both scenarios were absurd. There was no way Novak Jaynes would go down either path.

Everyone had always seemed like they were on a different plane of calm and had a higher level of loyalty to one another than I did. It was like a poison entering me when I started to contemplate the truth. Maybe this was why I looked so much different, why I always felt some of the older members were wary of me, why I cried and blushed, why I would ever be attracted to an outsider. All the weakest parts of me that no one else seemed to have. All the parts I was ashamed of and wished I could fix.

I made my way down the lawn to the water. Why did he want to see me all the way down here? Was he afraid of what I'd learned and what I might say out loud? They may not have been acting like it, but I realized this was what emergency mode looked like.

"Honey." Novak was waiting for me at the edge of the bulkhead. He folded me into a hug.

He murmured, "I'm sorry, I'm sorry." Eventually he held me back from him. "Let's sit over here." He led me to a grouping of sleek outdoor chairs. Already this felt different from how I'd been treated the last time I had been summoned, seated in his office, receiving my punishment.

I sat and blinked, willing myself to hold back tears. I usually rehearsed what I was going to say to my father. Even casual conversations. Now I felt like I couldn't get my head together. Novak pulled a chair close to mine—a little too close—and stroked my hair. In a low voice he said quickly, close to my ear, "Don't worry about them ever bothering you again. They can't find the evidence they want for their case, so they're coming after us personally. They want to prove the other . . . hearsay. Our lawyers are in the process of making sure they never attempt to speak with you again."

Pulling back, he looked at me. "Did they scare you?" Without waiting for an answer, he said, "Your principal did the right thing, calling Victoria. Of course, she should have called as soon as they approached her. It sounds like you walked out almost immediately?" He wanted to know what had gone on in that room. I wondered what Mrs. Brown had told him.

We didn't talk about the past. Ever. This was most likely

the only opportunity I would have for the rest of my life to ask him about my mother.

Instead I said, "I walked out as soon as they introduced themselves."

The pinpoint pupils of his eyes reacted, but just barely. He waited for me to continue, but I stayed quiet. He said, "Those fuckers. Playing with a young girl like that. I'm sorry, Julia." He paused again. This was beginning to feel a bit like a game of cat and mouse. Had he guessed what they had said to me? Would he think I believed them?

Without warning, Novak stood up as though the conversation was over. I was mostly relieved. I had gone this far without knowing a thing about her. It was the right thing to do, even though part of me felt like I'd missed my chance. What the FBI had said wasn't true. There was no possible way. Novak wouldn't be here today, let alone be the head of the entire family, if he had had a relationship with an outsider. Not to mention had a child he'd brought into the fold. No one could overcome that transgression.

I felt much better, the way I usually did after being near Novak. At this point I assumed I'd stay home and return to school tomorrow. So Novak shocked me when he said, "It's not safe at your school. We're bringing you back home, so to speak."

"Back to St. Philip's?" I was confused. It couldn't be this easy.

Novak nodded.

"It won't be for too much longer. Relocation is happening sooner rather than later."

"What? When?" I sounded slightly panicked to my own ears.

Novak's eyes looked surprised at my tone. "Everyone will find out the plan at the same time. And I'll tell them then whether the plan is right for them." So I wasn't out of the woods.

I couldn't get over it. That was it? After everything I'd been through, it was done, just like that?

"Don't look so shocked, Julia. I think you learned your lesson. We've had enough of this business, don't you think?" He gave me his glamorous smile. Then, sincerely, he said, "I'm proud of you. You're extremely strong. Be worthy of your heritage, Julia, and you should have no problems going forward." Putting his arm around me, he kissed the top of my head. He stood holding me like that for a moment while we looked out at the lake, both of us aware that soon enough we wouldn't be seeing it again.

In that moment I felt loved. Eventually I walked with him back to the house. There was no question—I never wanted to disappoint him again.

I should have been ecstatic, like I'd just been let out of jail and unburdened from my mental prison as well. It was the oddest thing; maybe it was leftover shock. It was the only explanation I could come up with for why I was shaking all over.

Novak had almost reached a set of glass doors to the main house when he glanced at me. "Your sister especially will be excited to have you back at school. She's very unhappy with us at the moment. Maybe you can explain to her that sometimes young love is destined to end badly."

NOVEMBER

Chapter Twenty-Two

There was a moment when I wondered if I could just disappear and it wasn't necessary to see John again. I purposely never left anything behind. I never returned texts or left voice mails, and I made sure no one ever took pictures of me. If I stayed away long enough, he could easily begin to feel like he'd made me up. For a week I focused on reintegrating myself, thrilled to be back in my family's good graces. It was a risk to go near him at this point anyway.

I told Angus what happened—about reading John's mind, letting it go unsaid that that was why I'd been with John. Angus was the one who told me I needed to see John in person, that I had to make sure it was handled.

I decided to do it almost two weeks after I'd left Austin High. Following months of heat, it was a freakishly cold fall day, and after the drive deep into Westlake Hills, I arrived at the tennis complex, beautiful with its canyon views and bordered by woods.

It was already dark at five thirty p.m. and the surrounding area immediately off the courts was in the shadows, away from the floodlights. I waited for him there. As much as I tried to separate myself from the task at hand, I felt my stomach drop when I saw him on the court.

I waited patiently. During a break, John walked over to a water fountain in a small wooden hut with an old school chalkboard people used to sign up for courts. He came back out, pausing at the base of the metal spectator stands tucked against the cedar trees where I sat. He was still breathing hard, staring at the court, planning to finish his opponent.

"He's going to serve short to your backhand."

He whipped around at the sound of my voice. I was in the shadows, in the top row of the stands, partially hidden. I stood up, situating myself deeper in the dark.

"Ford! Come on!" They were already calling him back. His heart was racing, but now it was from pure adrenaline.

John stood frozen in place. Being near him, I could tell he was having a hard time sleeping at night. John's perceptions of his surroundings were different now that his world had changed to gray.

I'd been hoping his shock had turned to hate by now, knowing this would be easier if I couldn't read him.

I carefully stepped down the rows and came to a standstill three steps above him. I'd transformed myself in a very short amount of time—hair cut short and dyed jet-black again.

"Ford! Now!" I realized they couldn't see me standing in the dark. Now that he'd stopped moving, he must have been getting cold, his sweat making it worse.

I held my gloved hands together in front of me to stop

them from shaking. "You have to go. I just came to say good-bye. I've gone back to my old school."

He knew me well enough to know that his not saying anything was making me nervous. I had trouble looking him in the eye. He just watched me. I wished I were anywhere else.

She's really doing this when I can't talk? This particular moment. She's such a coward.

I couldn't help it. I audibly sucked in my breath when I heard that. I tucked my hair behind my ear and looked at the ground. I realized he had caught a glimpse of the three Cartier diamond love bracelets on my wrist—jewelry that I knew seemed laughable on a teenager. I lifted my eyes to meet his, as if to say, *See? I'm looking at you, and a crazy energy flowed between us.* My gaze slipped away again. I couldn't look at him and maintain my Jaynes persona at the same time, not when he looked at me like he could see right through me.

"Are you forfeiting?" the other players yelled.

"You need to go." After an uncomfortable second I stepped off the bleachers. Completely out of character, my foot caught and I swayed, accidentally falling against John. He automatically put up his hands to steady me and caught my wrist. I was against his chest for a breath. All of our usual insane chemistry was there. He didn't move, hoping that the contact would bring me back to my senses.

I quickly said, "Excuse me," and he let go of me like I was on fire.

I walked away from the courts, into the dark. Knowing he was watching, I unlocked the car, and it glowed to life. A new BMW, not my old Prius. It was like I'd been let into the club.

"Julia!" I heard him yell hoarsely. I paused imperceptibly but didn't turn around. He called out, "It all fucking happened."

I kept walking. I felt it when John saw him—Angus—in the passenger's seat. I knew it would seal the deal, that John would know this was who I wanted. Someone perfect. That he'd been right all along.

I let myself into the car, and in seconds we were driving away. There was no sign I'd ever been here. There was no real sign we'd ever been together.

As my car tunneled off into the night, I finally let him go. It felt like we'd been physically connected for the past two and a half months and now the connection was severed. We were spinning far, far away from each other.

"Thanks for helping me," I said to Angus.

Angus stared impassively out the windshield. "Sure. He won't be coming back."

"I think I broke him."

"You had to," Angus said.

I mentally cut the cord, and that world no longer existed.

Chapter Twenty-Three

I told myself school was glorious. Compared with Austin High's severe architecture and subsequent cheap fixes, our school was a country club.

In some ways being back was better than I had imagined. I no longer carried the shame of being isolated from the group. It was like being in the right country, where everyone spoke my language—that higher level of frequency that my family communicated on. It felt so good to have that kind of understanding. No more slow, deliberate conversations communicating the obvious, making sure I sounded right, no more feeling so isolated from other people. It was effortless.

And the beauty. It wasn't just everyone's sheer physical beauty. They all seemed to radiate something that gave you a high just from being near them. It was to a lesser extent than with Novak, but each and every member gave off that energy in varying shades. I could feel it much more strongly after having been away.

Things weren't exactly the same as when I left; everyone was more subdued. Life as we knew it was about to end, and everyone wanted to make sure they would be included on the ride. But there was a last-day-of-school excitement in the air too. If I could guess, we would be leaving around Christmas.

Everyone accepted my presence. It said something that Novak had brought me back. I carried an expensive bag and wore the nicer clothes in my closet. My hair was black again, but otherwise I'd toned everything down and resembled my stepmother and Liv more than a Lost Kid.

While I didn't dare hang out with the Lost Kids, I carefully maintained my place, making sure I hung back in class and in sports. I had grown up thinking I had to strive and be the best in everything in order to fit in. That hadn't done me any good. Now I knew how important it was to fade into the background, where I wouldn't draw attention to myself and disturb the ecosystem. That was my best chance for moving on with my family.

Whenever I saw the Lost Kids during the course of the school day, they were only in twos. No groups. They seemed quiet and cleaned up. But after seeing them at the festival, I knew it was an act. Except for Ellis and Roger. They had actively distanced themselves from the other Lost Kids, as ordered. I saw them constantly searching out Angus with their eyes, though. I missed the old days of hanging out with the Lost Kids, when I felt like I had a group and a sort of identity, feeling free in my own way.

I stayed away and they took the hint. If they were being reckless, I couldn't join them. As a result my rashes were terrible. I had zero release, but there was no way I was going to do anything that would make the rashes go away. I kept telling myself nothing was worth jeopardizing what I'd gotten back.

Angus, however, was in my life again. In class he always entered at the last minute, looking like he had just rolled out of bed. His bloodshot eyes would meet mine. We had always had a flirtation and an odd mutual understanding, but now it felt like we were partners of a different kind. He knew more about me than anyone else, and still he was being cooler than he'd ever been, accepting me back without missing a beat. The only thing he didn't know was what the FBI agents had said to me that day.

During the day I convinced myself I was living the dream. Night was a different story. It was harder for me to hold my thoughts back. Those moments just before I fell asleep were the worst. I told myself this feeling that I was missing a part of myself had to do with suppressing my abilities. It wasn't because of John.

I also tried to tune out the constant replay of my conversation with the FBI agents. Once morning came, however, thoughts that had run through my head seemed irrational.

Every time I left my driveway, I'd see work vans parked along Scenic and wonder if they were watching us. I couldn't let them mess with my head. I was so close. I was doing so well here. As long as I could operate perfectly within their framework, and Novak never discovered what I'd done while I was away, I'd make the cut. This was all I'd ever wanted, I told myself. This was enough.

My greatest comfort was knowing Liv had a say, whether she knew it or not. Happy Liv meant happy Victoria. If I was left behind, I didn't think Liv would forgive them. Even though she was behaving like a complete bitch.

In my first week back, Angus grabbed my arm, pulling me as I walked down the hall to the next class. I yanked my arm back.

"What are you doing?" he asked.

I kept walking. I knew what he was talking about, but I didn't need to answer to him.

"Hey! Why are you acting like that?"

"*Acting* like what?" I was annoyed, but we were speaking softly and quickly. Our friends in the hall were speaking in the same manner, so fast and low that outsiders couldn't hear. To the other students, it must have looked like mass mumbling.

"Like you're not the smartest one in the room. Of all of us."

"I'm not."

"Yes, you are. You're still pretending."

"Novak never gave me permission to do everything I can do. I just need to stay off the radar."

"Aren't you sick of pretending, Julia?" Since I'd been back, Angus had been more sour than usual. I didn't blame him, since Novak had knocked him back down the social ladder after his attempt to date Liv. Angus was the one in isolation now—forced to stay at home anytime he wasn't at school. Like a wolf that needed to roam, though, he snuck out whenever he could.

"Since when haven't we had to pretend, Angus? We're always pretending. All of us. Hopefully we'll do less of it in the next place."

"For a few years, maybe. Everyone's whispering that Relocation's going to be different this time, but really? Some things will never change," he said bitterly.

"It is the way it is. And let me tell you, it's a lot less pretending here than it is out there." I waved a hand in the direction of Austin High.

"You seemed happy," he said.

I let that go and started walking.

"Julia." I could tell from his tone that he was sorry. He stopped and I turned around. Liv was standing in the doorway of a classroom, watching us. She turned her back after shooting Angus a semblance of a dirty look. I was aware that we looked like we were having a lover's quarrel.

Angus saw Liv's reaction but didn't seem to care. In fact he seemed to have moved on from Liv completely.

"How's that going?" He nodded in Liv's direction.

"Not great."

"What's up?"

"She's been cold since I've been back. I'm not sure why *she's* the one being cold to *me*," I said, annoyed. Angus was the only person who knew I had any issues with Liv. Since I'd been back, Liv was either ignoring me or challenging me. It made me want to smack her. "I'm sure it has to do with you and me being friends. Even though you were my friend first."

"And that you wanted me first," Angus teased.

"Shut up," I said, but I laughed. He was so incredibly cocky, it was funny. We smiled at each other, which might've made things worse if Liv happened to still be watching.

"Have you heard from him? John . . . ," Angus said, testing the name and testing me.

The question caught me off guard. It took me a second to recover. He had to stop. I took a step toward Angus, my face close to his, almost like I was going to kiss him. He didn't move a muscle.

"Angus," I said as softly and meaningfully as I could, "it never happened."

We held eyes and I willed him to get it.

He moved first, but it was to kiss my cheek. "Heard that."

I wouldn't think about him, I wouldn't think about him.

Two weeks later, our lives changed abruptly. We were told we were done with school and that we needed to stay home. If we went out, we needed to tell someone where we were going, and we needed to stay close.

At first it felt exciting, like we were preparing to leave for a trip. After days went by, though, the mood changed. It began to feel like we were languishing in a compound, waiting for the FBI to bust through the door. I began to see my same rash appear on Liv, and even on some of the adults who came by the house, as if something was building up in their system from being restricted. You could feel the frustration with Novak increase by the day: What were we waiting for? Why were we still here?

Novak had clearly relocated headquarters from his office to the house. Only the members of his inner circle came to see him. When I was in the vicinity of Novak's office, I'd hear fragments of the same general argument every time—Novak defending his position on why we hadn't left yet. From what

I overheard, Novak wanted more time to get a last piece in place.

I wasn't worried until I heard about Kendra. I'm not sure I ever would have found out if I hadn't been at dinner with Novak at the time. We were gathered at the dining room table—Novak, Victoria, Victoria's parents, Liv, and myself. I was feeling proud that I'd been asked to join them.

"Novak." All of us looked up at Lati, Angus's father, standing in the doorway with George's father, Darien. Novak immediately stood and followed them out of the room.

When Novak came back moments later, Victoria looked at him questioningly. He shook his head at her.

"What is it?" demanded Victor, who was Victoria's father. He was still vigorous and youthful looking. The older generations were our most dangerous giveaway—their longevity, their resistance to disease. Puris exceeded the life expectancy of normal humans by twenty years easily.

Like it was a simple matter, Novak stated only a tad regretfully, "Kendra's dead."

"What? How?" Liv asked.

"Girls, time to go," Victoria said.

In a very un-Novak moment, he flatly said in front of us, "She tried to jump our fence and was electrocuted. It was a problem in the hookup. There must have been a live wire. Darien was reviewing our security and alerted Lati. Don't worry. It's being handled."

"What about the police?" I asked, stunned.

"They won't find out. We're taking care of it."

Like, disposing-of-her-body taking care of it? "But won't her family come looking for her?" I asked.

"We'll be long gone by then."

"Will they ever know what happened to her?" Liv asked.

"Enough," Victoria said. Liv and I looked at each other. There was something so wrong about Kendra's family not knowing she was dead. I would never have guessed that Novak would do something like this and the rest of the family would go along. There had to be a way to get word to Kendra's parents. Otherwise, they would spend the rest of their lives searching.

Victor spoke up. "I'm done—with the lawsuits, the broken families, the suicides. Just let it go, Novak." Victoria's father was the only person I'd ever seen disrespect or corner Novak.

Novak looked at Victor coldly. "For two decades I've been executing this plan. I haven't come all this way for our people to end up in a beautiful casket. We need to continue our line. And we need them to do it."

It was the babies again. And the fact that there weren't any.

"We'll be together. Maybe that's enough," Victoria said—astonishingly, siding with her father.

"What's all this been for if we're just going to let ourselves end? I'm telling you, I know this from my visions. These lost souls are drawn to us—to me—for a reason. Some outsiders have our genes already, but the traits are dormant. If we apply just the right amount of stress, if we surround them, these traits will reveal themselves."

"Novak, do you want to be arrested on federal charges? You have nobody else cultivated—male or female—and we need to leave. No one thinks it's a good idea, even if they seem to have similarities to us. You made a compelling case for taking Kendra with us on Relocation, but then look: the same thing happens every time. There aren't others like us." Victor waved his hand in the direction of the backyard.

"There are. I *feel* it," Novak said.

"You aren't hearing what I'm saying. These people you identify are only outsiders and none of us want them. We don't want to dilute our blood." There was a dark pause, and maybe it was paranoia, but I felt like Victor purposely wouldn't look in my direction.

I looked down at the napkin in my lap, staring at the pattern and texture, realizing the position of Novak's assistant had been slotted for someone he identified as a lost soul with the potential to evolve into one of us. They needed breeders essentially. I felt resentment to my core. Novak had really been willing to take Kendra, but he'd threatened me, his own daughter, about needing to earn the privilege?

Novak leaned forward, changing tactics and recapturing his patience. In his charming, coaxing manner, he said, "No one will be sorry. I promise you. I'm almost there."

Ultimately I didn't even know how anyone could wrestle a plan away from Novak. All of us were at the mercy of his decisions. Everyone at the table seemed to comprehend this at the same moment, and for the rest of dinner there was only silence.

In the days following I stayed at the house, not wanting to ask Victoria permission to go out only to be denied. If I wasn't in my room, I was down at our dock, staring at the lake, trying to counter the ominous feeling in the house that this exit wouldn't go according to plan.

To make things worse, a couple of days after that dinner,

I was positive someone had been in my bedroom when I wasn't there. After walking around the property, I returned to my room, and as soon as I entered something in the air felt different, like someone had just left. Nothing was out of place, but I instinctively knew my things had been touched. I picked up my phone and knew someone had held it minutes before.

I scrolled through quickly to see if there was anything incriminating Victoria might have found. I'd erased texts and phone messages the moment I'd arrived home that day after the FBI questioned me at my school. I had only one photo of him, but I knew it was obscured and no one would be able to tell who it was. I never planned to look at it again, but I also didn't delete it. If I went to delete it, I'd have to see it.

Relieved, I knew there was nothing there. I almost put the phone aside when something bothered me. I stared at the phone. A moment later it dawned on me.

Petrified, I scrolled down, down until I saw it: Deleted Messages. They were all there. I'd never completely discarded them. It had been thoughtless, just like everything else I'd done while I was away.

I walked over to my door and locked it softly, then slowly sat down on the very edge of my bed. I turned the volume to the lowest setting and held the phone to my ear, forcing myself to listen to the only three messages he'd ever left me.

Hearing his voice, he was real to me again, suddenly pushed back into the foreground. The first message was from the very beginning, when he first began to call me. It was formal and he spoke fast. The second one was when we were in the thick of dating for those short weeks and he actually said "Hey, babe" on the phone, teasing me because I hated it. His last message was the day after the wine cellar. I remember watching the phone ring, but without a plan for what I was going to say, I let it go to voice mail. I remember noting he had waited until noon to call, most likely so he wouldn't appear worried about telling me he loved me.

His tone was straightforward, hiding any vulnerability even though he had to be unsure of how I felt about him. *"Hey, it's me. Thanks for having me over last night. Call me."* He didn't deny the night before, but he didn't bring it up explicitly either.

Victoria had finally won. The messages made it so obvious. If getting close to an outsider wasn't enough, I'd brought him here, to our house. If Novak found out—if he didn't already know—come Relocation, my time with the group was over. I knew firsthand, you couldn't defy Novak and get away with it. The worst of it was, I had done this to myself.

Chapter Twenty-Four

Victoria gave Liv permission to take a drive as long as it was short and she stayed relatively close. I was surprised when Liv knocked on my door and asked me along. I'd barely ventured from my room, almost scared to move, waiting for Novak to come find me. When Liv asked if I wanted to come, I leapt at the opportunity, thinking no one would confront me as long as I was with her.

With the music thumping, we blazed down the road in a car borrowed from Novak. The life outside the car window felt bright and new after days being holed up. The two of us hadn't been alone in months. It felt manufactured, but at least we were trying.

"Whoa, slow down, Livvy." Cars honked as Liv went through a red light. She laughed her lilting laugh. Liv seemed happy for the moment, like she used to be before Novak separated her from Angus.

Liv didn't listen to me and continued driving like a maniac. We tore down West Fifth, aimless on a Friday afternoon. Traffic was piling up and Liv was swerving around cars. I'd been a passenger in cars driven recklessly countless times, but I trusted the Lost Kids' skills a hell of a lot more than I trusted Liv's, since she was a new driver.

Seeing my look, Liv said, "What? I've got it. This is how you like to drive."

"Yeah, but I—" I stopped myself. She didn't drive looking ahead and in all three mirrors at once like I did.

"What?" Liv looked over at me too long, her eyes off the road. "You're better at it than me?"

"No. Of course not." Immediately I felt a pit in my stomach.

She slowed and draped one hand on top of the steering wheel, stuck in traffic now.

"Can I ask you something?" She looked over at me, her tangled hair hanging loose halfway down her back. Liv looked more Lost Kid than I did at the moment.

"Of course."

"Why are you holding back?"

"What are you talking about?" I looked out the window.

"It's like you're deferring to me all the time." We were moving again, and Liv took her eyes off me. "What happened at Barton Springs—both you and Angus—no one ever talked about it."

"Ha. I'm sure Angus did." I didn't mean to say that. I avoided mentioning his name in her presence.

"You're advanced like Dad, aren't you?" The impact of her words got lost in my realization that Liv had driven way too close to Austin High for my own comfort. We were nearby at just the time school would be letting out. I didn't like it.

"No! Not at all."

"Are you okay with that?"

"What? Not being like Dad? Of course. I mean, it's a pipe dream we probably all have, you know? To be that special person among special people. And you all know so much more than me and the boys. I'm just happy I can be back and live this life, be with all of you. . . ."

"I don't know, Julia. I want to make sure you're not holding back on my account. It's okay if you're better than I am. I don't care. Honestly. Even if they want it for me, it's become clear I'm never going to have abilities like Dad's."

What did she want me to say? Admit to being better at everything just so she could run off crying? What did she care? I couldn't act on it anyway. I'd always be a second-class citizen. I pushed the bitterness down quickly, surprised at how fast it had come up. "You have it all, Liv," I said lightly, hoping that would placate her.

"I really don't."

I let it drop. I wasn't going to discuss her heartsickness. Angus and I would each have given our right arms to train with Novak. It was funny how, after everything she'd been given, all our future leader seemed to want was Angus.

"Liv, what are you doing? Why are you driving so close to—" I broke off.

"I want you to point him out." She sounded like she was trying to work something out in her head.

And then I realized she was the one, not Victoria, who'd been looking in my phone. "Turn around." My voice expressed the dire need for us to turn the hell around.

Liv swung to a stop right across the street from the west parking lot and turned off the engine. I felt like if I moved, someone would notice us. Kids were trailing out into the festive Friday-afternoon atmosphere of the parking lot. John would be getting in his car right now, leaving for tennis. Already a few boys had noticed the Porsche and were pointing.

Liv had stopped talking and was watching me. I looked out the window, knowing exactly where he'd be. Liv followed my gaze. I saw Alex by John's car, laughing about something. He and August were talking to someone—Reese, the girl who had been with John at the party the night of the fire. John would be joining them any moment.

"Do you see him?"

I started to panic, something in me never wanting her to see him. "Just drive!" I didn't dare look again.

Liv didn't move.

"Drive, goddammit!"

"Oh my God. Okay, okay, I'll drive. Calm down."

Liv restarted the car, the loud Porsche engine drawing attention. She pulled out, and I didn't breathe until we had blended into traffic.

Why was she doing this? Did she hate me that much? Was she so jealous I was hanging out with Angus that she was actively trying to get me expelled from the group? That wasn't the Liv I thought I knew.

I tried to compose myself. If it was Liv, not Victoria, who knew about John, maybe there was a way out of this. Neither of us said anything for a few minutes as Liv drove toward home. Eventually she was unable to help herself.

"Why won't you say anything? You're just going to sit there? Tell me about him," she said encouragingly, as though she wanted to hear about a harmless crush.

"Have you told anyone yet?" I asked icily, rounding on

her. Maybe there was still a chance and she was just being mean, trying to rub my face in my disgrace.

Liv froze at my tone. I had never spoken to her like that.

Her demeanor suddenly changed. "Why don't you just say everything you want to say, Julia? You've clearly wanted to say something to me since the day Dad announced the groups."

"What is wrong with you? Are you pissed I'm back? Do you feel guilty about something?" My tone implied she should. I couldn't forget how she hadn't tried to stop Novak from sending me away.

Stop talking, Julia.

Liv was so quiet, I glanced over. Her thick hair mostly hid the side of her face, but I could tell she was trying to control a temper she didn't know she had. She lost the battle.

"I can't believe you would fucking say that to me. You really think I'm a terrible person, don't you?"

Whoa. "I'm sorry. I don't, Liv. Not at all. You just have so much, and if anyone finds out about this, that's it for me. I won't be going with you." I hoped I sounded placating.

"Don't condescend to me, Julia."

"Excuse me?"

"It was chance you were put in the other group. It wasn't me who asked you to step aside. But since then you've acted differently toward me."

Liv pulled through our gate and roared into the elevator. It began its descent. It was claustrophobic in the car within the elevator and I just wanted to get the hell out.

"You hate me," Liv said.

"Liv, shut up. I love you more than I love anyone else." It was true.

"Then you must resent the crap out of me. Why won't you admit it? They had me replace you in everything you were better at."

I had thought I had my feelings under control. It scared me how suddenly I saw red. And then the rush of it overtook me. "What do you want from me? I've given you everything. I'm sorry I can't also give you Novak's skills or Angus. You have never, for one single day, had to worry about anything. Let me tell you, I have worried every day of my life. If I was better at everything, it doesn't even matter. You at least know who you are. Just let me go with the group, Liv. That's all I want."

The elevator landed gently in the undergound garage. Liv, in shock, remained motionless in the driver's seat. I got out, slamming the car door and walking directly to my own car. I had to keep going. If I stopped, it would sink in that I'd completely alienated the person who held my future in her hands.

❧◦❧

I had thought I was okay. I really had. I'd sworn to myself I would never do this, even though, lying in the dark, I'd planned it a hundred times.

I found myself in front of the double doors of the public library, feeling like I must have floated there. It was almost empty inside, and I made my way to the bank of computers, taking the seat farthest from the one other person there. I typed in "Elizabeth Blackcomb." I wasn't about to do this on my phone.

The old computer took its time, and I had a second to

come to my senses. I wanted out. Then, before I could stand up to leave, a row of images appeared at the top of the search results. I could see the correct Elizabeth Blackcomb was among them. She was my doppelganger. The eyes of the woman in the photo were the same shape as mine. Novak used to tease that they were Elvis's eyes.

I scanned the results below and one stood out. "Elizabeth Blackcomb, government-sponsored remote-viewing program, research and experimentation in the use of psychic phenomena for intelligence gathering." That was enough. I didn't want to know any more. I got up and walked out of the library as fast as I could. I'd never be able to forget what I'd just seen.

Maybe the FBI had planted this, knowing I would eventually go looking. It was still possible she was one of us, that the group had rejected her for doing something wrong and it just so happened both of us looked different from everyone else.

But unfortunately, in my heart I knew those FBI agents had been telling the truth.

I sat down on a stone wall, staring at the ground like a zombie, while Angus paced in front of me, talking and skipping stones impressively across the glassy water. The sun was almost gone from the sky, and you could barely see the stones when they were five skips out.

I wasn't going to tell Angus, but I was scared to be alone. Angus was cagey but excited to leave his house. He'd had to sneak out to meet me at the boat dock.

"So, what happened?"

I looked up at Angus and could see he was annoyed I wasn't fully present and listening to him.

For a second I wondered what it would feel like to say her name out loud, to see if Angus thought I was a lost cause. "Nothing."

"Oh, now I have to hear it." Angus came and sat down beside me, stretching his legs out in front of him. He instinctively knew it was easier to talk if we weren't looking at each other.

"Liv," I said, then shook my head. That would feel good to talk about at least.

The way I said her name made Angus start laughing. He stopped when he saw I was in a shitty mood. "What happened?"

I couldn't look at him. He was going to think I was so stupid for getting caught. "Liv is trying to make me look bad. She found out about . . . John." I hated saying his name out loud.

"How?"

"She went into my room and went through my phone."

"Julia . . . "

"I know, I know. And then I lost my temper. I'm worried she's going to tell them, and that's all Victoria will need to get rid of me."

"Liv's not going to do that."

"I don't know. We're not close anymore. God, Angus, I just want us to leave and to know I'm included." I sounded desperate.

"Ha! Tell me about it. I'm losing my mind, trapped in that house. Look: I'm like you now." Angus unzipped his jacket and lifted his shirt, showing a rash all over his chest.

He lowered his shirt and offered me his arm. "Hit me. Seriously. Hit me hard." When I looked at him like he was crazy, he gave up and looked into the distance. "I can't fucking feel anything anymore."

I didn't say a word, and Angus picked up that I was really scared. "I wouldn't worry about it. Liv told me they're too busy trying to find people to bring with us."

"It's ridiculous," I said.

"Well, creatures will do pretty amazing things when their species is in jeopardy. Novak has fucked us. By keeping us so tight, this branch is dead," Angus said.

"I get it in theory. No kids in seventeen years is a problem. Who knows? Maybe there's something to his lost-souls theory and there are more of us out there."

Angus shook his head in amazement. "Because of a theory Novak has? There aren't people like us out there, whether you call them reincarnated souls or people with similar DNA. They don't exist. He's just going to abduct people who kind of look like us and seem better than average and try to mix our gene pool with theirs. Not that anyone will last a second with us. They'll end up like Kendra."

"He's not going to abduct anyone! Jesus."

"What do you think he's going to do? He thinks they need full immersion to make this 'transformation' happen. Not to mention, we need to get out of here. At the very least they'll be better off with us than with the rest of humanity," he said.

I knew Angus was a snob, but that angered me—the thought that we would take away someone's rights and think they were better off. I couldn't help myself. "These people we hate so much? Has anyone ever thought they could be living special lives here?"

"Maybe one percent of them do. But one hundred percent of us live exceptional lives. At least those of us who are told we can," Angus said bitterly.

"Angus, it will be different in a new place. We just have to get there." I put my face in my hands, my nerves completely frayed.

Angus put his arm around me. "Stop worrying. She won't say anything. She's just being pulled between her powerful parents and her loyalty to you."

I raised my head. "I don't know. It was bad. I lost it," I admitted.

Angus laughed. "We're human, Julia. Maybe different or special or whatever. But still human."

I'd never thought of it like that. To me it had always been just them and us, no gray area between.

I put my head on his shoulder. "You all seem perfect."

"Well, we all know there's more than meets the eye. Seriously, I wouldn't worry about Liv. You know that saying—she needs to kill the king in order to grow up and take her rightful place. You acted like her mother forever, and now she's rebelling, trying to prove herself. You're older and a badass."

"I don't think so."

"What? The badass part? Jesus, Julia. You always have been. You don't see yourself. You're the OG. That's never going to change."

I lifted my head and looked at him like he was crazy. "This is very different from what you were saying to me a few months ago."

"Things change." *Novak's mind changed* was what he really meant. I wondered at the timing of it. Would Novak have brought me back if the FBI had never spoken to me? Was I back because he was afraid of what I might know?

Angus leaned forward, elbows on knees, and stared up at me.

I wasn't good with compliments, but, weirdly, what he said about Liv made sense. I looked up at the sky. "Well, she's playing around with something dangerous."

"It'll be fine. Liv is smart."

We made eye contact and I smiled, feeling just a tiny bit of relief in spite of the day's events. Angus suddenly stopped smiling but held my gaze.

He sat up and very slowly extended his arm toward me, his fingers sifting through my hair. Angus had always been a flirt, but this felt different. Like I was precious, he carefully pulled my head toward his, his lips brushing my temple. Then he tilted his head to the side and leaned in to kiss me.

His lips were soft, but they felt totally foreign. Last summer I had been so ready for this, wanting to melt into him. Angus was a skilled kisser, but now I felt removed. After a moment I pulled back, not wanting it.

Angus straightened up, immediately defensive. "What?"

"You surprised me."

"How could that have been a surprise?"

"Angus, you have led me on for two years." I felt angry. Why now? He'd shown up too late.

"I was an idiot."

"No, you just didn't know if you liked me that way."

"Like I said, I was an idiot. I have always liked you that way. I just needed to realize it." I knew he meant it.

"No, Angus." I put my hand on his knee. "This is because I've apparently had a status change."

He grabbed my hand, holding it—a complete contrast to his harsh words. "Fuck you, Julia. It's not. I have always loved you."

"Angus, you were with my sister." I pulled my hand away and stood up, as if that made it a done deal.

He leaned back, as if in disbelief that Liv could really be a deal breaker. "Julia, she liked me, and I felt like I should like her back because of who she is. You're right: I got caught up in the status bullshit. But I don't feel for her the way I feel—

I held up a hand. "Don't say it. Liv cares about you. A lot."

He narrowed his eyes at me. "So nothing can happen between us simply because I dated Liv for two seconds."

"It was for more than two seconds. And I wouldn't do that to her, anyway. Not right now."

"I never had sex with Liv."

"Ugh! Why are you telling me this? I don't want to know."

"Just letting you know it was never serious."

"It was to her."

"She'll get over it." Angus stopped abruptly, like something had just occurred to him. Slowly he stepped toward me, trying to get me to look at him full in the face. There was surprise in those light eyes when he asked, "Did you have sex with him?"

"Angus, shut up!" I made a move to grab my bag and jacket.

"Wow. You did." His voice was more amazed than disgusted.

I expected him to say something demeaning. Instead he said quietly, "I just thought—I always thought I'd be your first."

He left me sitting on the stone wall. I watched him walk away, feeling like I had nothing left.

DECEMBER

Chapter Twenty-Five

When Liv said she was taking me out for my birthday and it was okay with Novak, she could have taken me anywhere. I didn't care, I was so desperate to leave the house after weeks of staying close to home, quarantined and feeling so messed up, the same scared thoughts spinning. I was surprised when she pulled up in front of a large music venue on the east side of town. We had never been to a music venue or to the east side. This seemed extreme, even for my birthday.

Things still felt uneasy between me and my sister. In the line to get into the show, we were mostly silent, Liv fidgeting in the cold of the late night, impatient and out of her element, and me glancing at her sidelong, in awe that the two of us could be related in any way. Whenever I closed my eyes, I saw the photo of Elizabeth Blackcomb all over again.

I felt humiliated that I had walked around thinking I was one of them all these years, that if I just tried a little bit harder I could fit in, though I never did. Turns out I was the child of someone who had probably suffered like Novak's assistants had.

But I was starting to feel wronged too. I was the one tainted by Novak's sins. I was the one who would forever have to pay for Novak's transgressions while he was revered.

Relocation would happen in a matter of days now. You could feel it. I knew it was the perfect time for them to be rid of me. But if Liv was here, tonight wasn't the night.

Liv kept looking around, as if she was trying to find someone in the crowd.

"Are you waiting for someone?" I asked, but she just shrugged.

I stared off into space, the crowd making me edgy. For a second I thought I was mistaken when I recognized Angus's battered BMW as it slithered into an illegal parking spot directly in front of the building. The driver's door flew open, and Angus took a giant step into the street without a glance. A car veered and honked, narrowly missing him. Angus kept walking, calmly raising both arms, giving the double middle finger to the car as it passed. I looked over at Liv, who also couldn't help but smile.

"What's he doing here?" I asked.

"It's your birthday. I thought you'd want him here." Liv looked over at me, and while she seemed distracted her eyes were kind. I smiled back. It was hard to believe Novak was fine with us being out like this, but Liv seemed confident.

I hadn't seen Angus since our conversation by the water. He sauntered up in the dark, definitely looking more beat-up—dark blue rings under his eyes and the rash partially on his face now. You could see Liv's beginning to creep up her neck. My rashes were gone altogether. Maybe it was psycho-somatic. Now that my identity had fallen by the wayside, so had my abilities and any urge to use them.

"What? No special line?" Angus said by way of greeting.

"No special line." I could tell Liv was nervous, but her entire being changed around him. She was excited to see him.

"Happy birthday," Angus said to me, his eyes intense. He seemed to want to make peace.

"Thanks." I smiled, but it didn't match my eyes.

"It's fine," Angus said directly to me.

"What's fine?" Liv asked.

"Everything," Angus said. The line began moving. Then he said, "Julia's worried about being here."

Liv got indignant, feeling second-guessed. "I told you we're fine! I thought you'd love to see Sweet Spirit. We've never been to something like this, and I thought we could try it before we . . ."

"No, I'm very excited. I love them. Thank you," I said. I couldn't help but wonder why Liv would put herself in a situation like this. She didn't want to be here. Angus and I could handle it—we'd been out and about a lot—but all this humanity was a lot for Liv, with the standing throngs and lack of personal space. Wind whipped through the line again, and, freezing cold, I braced myself. The image of John standing in line with me at ACL, holding my hand, popped into my head. I kept losing control of my thoughts.

It was an all-ages show, so we passed through the door, each getting an X on our hands, which I assumed marked us as minors. We entered the crowded outdoor space of the restaurant and music venue with its stage at the far end. I felt a pull and looked up to the third-story balcony.

"What are they doing here?" I asked, seeing the Lost Kids gathered in a large group for the first time in months. Even Ellis and Roger were present. Angus seemed surprised to see the group also, and I felt both of us go on edge at the exact same time. This was starting to feel weird.

"I thought everyone deserved a night out." Liv had to speak louder now that we were inside and the band was beginning their show. "So enjoy, because this will be the last time."

"We know," Angus said.

"Not just in Austin," Liv said cryptically.

I suddenly realized she had a secret she wanted to tell us. Both Angus and I didn't say anything, just waited.

Our patience was rewarded. "We're going into seclusion."

"What do you mean, 'seclusion'?" Angus asked after a beat.

Liv leaned in. "Once we go in, we won't be coming out. Ever. Novak's built a place to sustain us for the rest of our lives. He wants us away from all this"—Liv gestured around us—"people, cities, their stuff. We won't be coming out for generations. Assuming there will be generations after us."

"We can't get out?" I could feel Angus's panic.

"We won't want to. It's going to be like paradise. And safe. No more looking over our shoulders."

Angus up and walked away from us, stunned.

"It'll be better," Liv said to me, sounding like she was convincing herself. "We can live how we're meant to." She sounded like she didn't wholly buy the idea and wanted to see my reaction.

"That's crazy. Maybe our ancestors lived in isolation, but none of us have. How long have you known this?" I asked.

"A week, maybe."

It didn't feel right. I always thought this Relocation would be a kind of remote pastoral haven—an attempt to get back to a homeland from our past—but this felt different. It sounded unnatural and scary, like being trapped behind a pane of glass. I knew I shouldn't be having this reaction in front of Liv. Without looking back, I blindly walked into the crowd alone, like I wanted to hide among the people we'd always wanted to get away from. Not knowing where I was headed, I worked my way front and center, to the foot of the stage.

The lead singer rasped into the microphone, stalking the stage, and I stared. She stilled, and I could swear she looked directly at me. She was raw and powerful, and I'd never seen anyone own both. I didn't understand why I was so transfixed by her. Maybe it was that she seemed so free. I realized I admired her.

I was uncertain if I was going with my family to this strange new reality, but either way everything was about to change. This life was over. For the first time I felt a whispering of second thoughts about Relocation.

I could have stood there forever, watching the singer and losing myself, letting her be my surrogate for expressing feelings I didn't understand. Involuntarily I looked away when Angus nudged me with his shoulder, interrupting. He looked destroyed, his eyes red. I knew he was desperate to talk about what Liv had told us.

With his head he gestured to my right and aggressively shouted into the noise, "Your boyfriend's here."

"What?"

"That guy John is here."

I shouldn't have looked. I should have walked to the car, protecting myself. I'd put so much effort into building walls to keep him out, I wouldn't have thought they would come down at the sight of him. Just like he burst into my consciousness at Barton Springs, he broke through now, and I had no time to prepare myself.

Alex was the one who caught my eye. He looked away first and stared straight ahead at the stage. August was also there, and of course Reese, who clearly had never stopped circling John. Then Alex nudged John, the way Angus had me, and tilted his head in my direction. John scanned the crowd in response. I knew I should look away, giving him the option of pretending he didn't see me.

I saw the split second he registered it was me. He was amazing—he hid his reaction at once. There was nothing behind his eyes when he looked at me. Then John moved away from his group, slowly parting the crowd as he headed toward the back.

"Don't do it, Julia," Angus said without even looking at me.

It was useless to tell me not to. As soon as I saw him, I knew I would talk to John.

Without a word I drifted away from Angus. It took forever to navigate my way, but finally I opened the door to the dark interior of the wood-paneled bar with its smell of beer-soaked floorboards.

There he was. Waiting for me, wanting to get this run-in over with.

I drank John in—he looked so good to me. He seemed

taller, his dark-brown hair shorter. He was even better looking than I recalled. He wore a navy blue hooded sweatshirt and jeans, his hands shoved deep in his back pockets. He felt so untouchable now, like he was someone else's.

Wordlessly he turned and walked into a smaller side room with a pool table. It was almost empty, and the sounds from outside were muffled.

I followed a few steps behind. John walked only partway into the room, as if he wouldn't commit to staying long.

John's expression was absolutely neutral, making me feel as self-conscious as I felt around my family. He spoke first. "I saw your boyfriend."

I couldn't help the smile. "Funny, he just said the same thing about you," I said, regretting it the second it came out of my mouth.

"Happy birthday," he said, and I melted. The damage this was doing to me by the second was incredible.

"How did you remember?" I asked.

"It's so close to Christmas, it's hard to forget."

A realization dawned on me. "You got into Stanford."

"How did you know?"

"There's no way your parents would let you out this late on a weeknight unless . . ."

"I did. I got in."

"Congratulations." It was my first real smile since I'd broken up with John. I didn't even try to temper my reaction. I was so happy for him.

"It wouldn't have happened if you hadn't fixed that match," he said flatly.

"No, don't, John." I felt him react when I said his name.

"You earned Stanford on your own. It was just that one match." I felt both our minds go to what was also only one time. I blushed and he knew why.

John's words so far were polite, but he wouldn't give me a thing—no indication of how he felt. Without a map I felt insecure, like I'd never talked to him before. I wanted to know if he hated me, if he thought about me.

I blurted out, "I'm sorry I—"

He stopped me. "It's done. Don't worry about it."

"Hey, man." We both looked up. Alex stood there, wanting to get his brother away from me, the bad influence, the bitch.

"Hey." John nodded to Alex and straightened. I realized he was going to join his brother, leaving me so soon. Why wouldn't he? There really wasn't anything to say. I'd made that clear at the tennis court.

John had been the only time I'd ever let go. Now a terrible, self-destructive part of me wanted to grab that feeling again, one last time.

We looked at each other, and maybe because he was saying good-bye he allowed our eyes to meet. I took a step closer into his space, and watching his eyes, I saw it. He felt it. It was still there.

His brother saw it too. "John."

The moment was over. John said a simple "bye," and then he was gone.

I stayed where I was for long minutes, until a crowd found the empty room. Numb, I eventually walked up the dank indoor staircase to the third-floor balcony, which put me outdoors again, the band on display below. It was darker now, the winter air filled with cigarette smoke. I saw Liv and Angus and reluctantly made my way over.

"How far away is the nearest town?" Angus was at Liv's elbow, and she was leaning up against the railing, watching the band and attempting to ignore him.

"I told you, I don't know where it is! It's not detectable by satellite. That's all I know."

"But we can never leave?"

"Look, maybe you're claustrophobic and that's what's bothering you, but it's not like you're going to be shut in a box, Angus."

"Maybe there's enough food and water to wait out a war or Armageddon or something, but it's still a metaphorical fucking box, Liv."

"Don't come, then. You want to be left here?" Liv turned to face Angus. "We'll be free there." She reached out to him. He ducked a bit when she touched his hair.

"What if it's no different from here? Novak's in charge. You think your dad's going to suddenly let me be with you?" he scoffed.

"If you want." She was embarrassed. "We were only in groups here because we had to be careful."

"What's really going to change? He doesn't like me. And it will be worse, because I'll have nowhere to go."

"You won't want to go. Jesus. Oh, thank God you're here," Liv said when she saw me. "He's driving me crazy," she said in front of Angus. "He's psyched himself out, thinking he's going to go live in some cage."

Angus did look like he was panicking. "Julia." He held up his palms as if he thought I would bring some sanity to the situation. My mind was still downstairs, though.

Liv was back at the railing of the balcony, scanning for something. "Ah!" she said suddenly. "He's here," she breathed.

"Who?" I asked.

"John Ford."

What had she just said? I felt Angus freeze. I paused, thinking I'd heard wrong.

Liv turned to me. "Have you seen him yet? He's why I brought you here."

It felt like ice water had been poured through my veins. "What are you talking about?" I finally said.

"John Ford. From Barton Springs. The person you dated this fall."

"You knew he'd be here?" Angus asked.

"Yeah, I've been watching him." Liv sounded proud.

I found my voice. I moved closer to her, looking her directly in the eye. "Liv." I felt like I was choking. "Let it go." I couldn't fathom why she would do this to me.

"Julia, you did it." Liv looked at me like she was about to reveal a birthday surprise.

"What are you talking about?"

"He's fine. After dating you, he's fine. You found him."

I felt every hair on the back of my neck stand up. "You were searching through my phone, weren't you? That's how you knew."

"You aren't getting what I'm saying. I'd been thinking about him, ever since Barton Springs. I thought I was dying, and then he touched me. It was like he healed me, Julia. When I stood up, he was right there and he had his hand on my arm. And then Angus pushed him just like he pushed that policeman, but nothing happened to him. I've been thinking about it since then, but I knew everyone would think I was crazy.

"I looked in your phone one day, not even thinking I'd find anything that would help Novak, and then I realized that same person from Barton Springs was in your life. All of a sudden, it occurred to me that Novak's visions are correct. John is one of these lost souls! I *know* it. Think about it— what happened to me at Barton Springs, and then you dated him. He had extended periods of direct interaction with you and he never broke with reality like Kendra and the others."

I stared at Liv, a beat behind.

Angus jumped in first, fully aware. "What are you going to do, Liv? Abduct him?"

"No. I want Julia to be the one to introduce him to Novak. She's the one who did this. She should get the recognition."

I found my voice. "Do you hear yourself? So we're going to take him like we own him, no trace left behind, and just hope he can make the leap and become like us? You know that has never, ever happened, Liv. It's a pipe dream of Novak's."

Angus backed me up. "You want babies who are half, Liv? By some poor guy who ends up a basket case like all the other ones?"

"Shut up, Angus. It's not like that. I'm telling you, he's important. I'm sure about him."

What she was saying was so outlandish that it took me a second to realize my little sister might actually have the power to make this happen. Liv had done this to me before with Angus. And now she was doing it again. She was interfering in my life, but now someone could legitimately get hurt. Not just someone. I turned the full force of my rage on my stupid little sister.

"Look at me." I got right up to her face and spoke slowly. "You're wrong." Liv began to shake her head to argue with me. "No." I shut her up. "Do you know how I know that? The reason he didn't change is that I'm not the same as you. I had no effect on him because I'm like him. Novak might be my father, but my mother was just a normal person off the street. All I did was spend time with another average person. But if you bring that out in the open, it gives Novak one more reason to say I'm too different, and he'll leave me behind."

I'd never seen Liv turn bright red. I couldn't tell if it was because she was angry or because she was ashamed. But she was definitely looking at her own sister with new eyes.

"Do you understand? You point him out to anyone, I'm not going with you. I don't know—maybe you don't want me there now that you know. But no matter what, if you take John, you'll be disappointed. And you'll end up stealing his life for no reason."

I didn't want to look at Angus now that he knew the truth as well. I kept my eyes on Liv, waiting to see what she'd do. Liv kept looking at me like she was seeing me for the first time. Then she said, "Of course I want you to go."

My entire body flooded with relief that Liv was backing down. "You'll drop it?"

"Yes." But her voice was tentative.

"What?"

"Nothing." Liv shook her head, "Novak doesn't know, but I told a few people—George, Emma—and they're coming tonight."

"They know who he is?" I began to look around wildly.

"No. But Julia, they'll recognize him from Barton Springs. I repeated what you and I heard at dinner that night. I told them enough that they're going to want to take him to Novak if you don't. They all want to be the one to find someone."

"They're here," Angus said.

I looked below. The Lost Kids were gathered in a group near the stage, and some of the crowd had their phones out, taking photos and video now that a sighting of our group was unmistakable. I saw George, Marko, Emma, and the rest of the kids on the periphery, looking up at us in the balcony.

You could feel Angus go into protector mode, wanting to get down to his friends. But I needed him.

"Liv, take them somewhere. Okay? Just get them to leave. Tell them you were wrong." I spotted John not too far from the Lost Kids down front.

Liv seemed to feel my urgency and turned for the stairs. I knew I should send Angus with her, but I needed him too much.

Alone, we turned to each other. In spite of everything else, we had been partners in crime long enough that he knew what I was thinking.

"We need to leave now," I said.

"Good luck getting them out of here."

"No, I mean we need to leave Austin now. I'm not letting this happen because of something my sister got into her head."

Angus chose that moment to remind me of our conversation at the dock. "If Liv is right, he would be guaranteed an exceptional life."

"She's dead wrong. You know that. Even if he didn't end up like Kendra, he would lose his mind remembering what he had here."

"And we won't?" I knew it was the question Angus had wanted to ask me all night.

"We only cope with this world—we never get used to it. And now we're going to a more suitable place. At least *you're* going, if that's what you want. So help me, Angus. Please. If anyone has a chance for a good life here, he does." I knew my voice had an edge of hysteria, but I would beg to the ends of the earth until he helped me.

He stared below, the music pumping louder and building, the crowd moving up and down to the escalating song while I waited for his answer. Then he said, "Fine. But it has to be now, and it can't be something that points back just to you. Make sure it's long enough to be caught on video. Like Novak has always said, 'We're just one video away from leaving Austin.' What?"

"That's why I need you. I'm not sure I can do it anymore."

Angus, of all people, hadn't seemed to blink when I told Liv about myself—I hadn't given him the chance—but I realized now that he didn't seem surprised.

"Come here." He gestured me over to him.

"What?" I asked, annoyed, but I closed the gap between us.

Angus looked me straight in the eye. "Don't let this mess with your head. If anyone can do it, it's you."

My panic was rising. Seconds before, I would have

jumped in front of a train to stop anyone from touching John, and now I realized I had no idea what to do.

Angus's eyes were soft now, and he said coaxingly, "Move something. You've shown me that a million times."

I studied the space frantically. I had no ideas for what I could try to move. I assumed anything that could get attention was far too big for me. I fixated on a lone monarch butterfly floating in the sky just above me, thinking it seemed such a strange place for one to be.

Angus didn't say a word. He just waited patiently, putting it all on me. I watched curiously as two more monarchs joined the first.

"Angus . . ." I closed my eyes and buried my face in his shoulder. I didn't know what I possibly had left inside me.

"It's fine. You have it," Angus whispered in my ear. Maybe because there wasn't any other choice, I went directly to the stillness, in the middle of the noise, in the middle of the crowd, waiting for something out there—any energy I could connect with, anything that would give me an answer.

I didn't move. Then I felt Angus begin to laugh, and I heard the band jaggedly cut off their music, one instrument at a time. A silence spread over the crowd. People weren't looking at the stage; I felt them looking up. "Oh my God, Julia. Come on. You have to look." Angus's voice was full of wonder. He nudged me, and, terrified, I lifted my head.

Instinctively, I looked to the sky. Butterflies, thousands of monarchs, hovered in a cloud above us. Lone butterflies on the fringes descended into the crowd, landing on raised fingers. In the hush around me, I felt the shared privilege of seeing something miraculous. I looked below, and I clearly saw John. He looked straight at me, as if he knew this was my doing.

My concentration was broken. With no warning, the butterflies chose a direction and flew under the eaves, out of sight. I'd never done anything like that; I'd never been able to influence animate objects.

Angus looked at me and shook his head. "That's beautiful, but it's not going to do the trick. I can do better."

And then he leapt up onto the railing in front of us.

"What the hell are you doing?" I began to grab at him. Hundreds of eyes were now trained on Angus. I saw the Lost Kids turn their bodies fully toward him, as if awaiting orders. Angus looked from them to me, like he was telling them I was now in charge.

Angus ignored my hands. He suddenly jumped and, turning partway in midair, caught the metal railing at the edge of the balcony with his fingers. He dangled there for an instant, giving anyone with a phone enough time to catch his show. People were shouting, and the crowd parted below, anticipating Angus's fall.

Angus launched himself from the third-floor railing, soared through the air, and dropped down, stomping the ground on impact. A boom emanated from the ground, and the crowd flew back at the force. The lone oak tree cracked, its roots pulling slightly up. The only people left standing were the teens from our two groups, there in the open for everyone to see.

Everything around me moved in slow motion, dust from the dirt floor below making the air hazy. People around me in the balcony began to fight for the exit, instinctively worried about the foundation of the building. And then I was stuck—stuck in the now-panicking mob, stuck in the tight stairwell when I needed to get to John and Angus to make sure both of them got the hell out.

It was madness when I made it to the ground level, searching for John through the bodies and commotion. The lights came on, and in the glare I caught sight of him brushing off Reese's back. John's eyes were scanning the crowd, looking for me, I realized. When he saw me, in a telling gesture, he began trying to make his way toward me.

I automatically took a step forward before stopping to take a cautious look around. I saw George to my left, near me, looking like an eerily still Adonis, his eyes fixed on John.

I wanted to meet John halfway, but I needed to save him. Angus had put me in charge of the Lost Kids, and right away I knew what to do. The butterflies had been the precursor to this. For the first time ever, I silently called for my friends, attempting to summon them.

I knew when they heard me. I felt connected to all of them in a way I never had before, like I had been let in on something I hadn't fully known existed. With the strange exception of Roger and Ellis, the Lost Kids parted the crowd and effectively formed a barrier in front of John, protecting him. Roger and Ellis elbowed their way through, joining the formation a few seconds late.

John thought he was purposely being blocked from me, and in disgust he turned away. He was done with me, in spite of his breathtaking impulse to make sure I was okay.

John was near an exit. He flowed into the crowd streaming out. I looked to George. He hadn't moved. His eyes were focused on the oak tree, which was now tilting precariously, splintered and creaking.

It wouldn't take much more than a mental nudge and the old oak would come down in John's vicinity. It would be as easy as moving a pencil. I wondered if George would dare to try and if he really had it in him to hurt all those people.

George did it. With a snapping noise, the tree began to shift.

For me it felt the same as righting a glass of water the second it tipped.

Imperceptibly to anyone else, I caught the tree in my gaze and held it until I finally won the battle with gravity, redirecting it to crash, with a huge thunderclap, on top of a fence near the exit, demolishing it. A branch fell just in front of John, catching his side. I knew he was hurt, but he kept walking, so it had to be superficial. Nothing slowed him down as he tried to get out of the venue and as far away from me as possible.

George looked both annoyed and confused that his effort hadn't worked. He turned to find Liv, giving up now that John had set foot outside the building. We needed to get out of here immediately ourselves.

John was safe from us. No one would have time to look for him now. This was it, after what Angus had done. Austin was over.

Silently I willed the boys to go too, to leave Angus in my care, to get home now. I knew they wanted to help Angus, but they seemed to understand my urgency, turning to the exit, disbanding. Again Ellis and Roger were a step behind, like they were on a different wavelength from the other Lost Kids.

For a second I stood there, not quite believing all that I'd done. And on my eighteenth birthday. I felt proud and a little awed. As always my next thought was, *What will Angus think?* I turned to see him standing in the middle of the venue at ground level, surveying his damage, Liv by his side.

When I reached them, I gently took his arm. "Angus, why? Why did you do that?" Then I saw the blood trickling out of his mouth and ear, and one foot rotated almost ninety degrees.

"I wasn't about to let him go to paradise with you," he said, laughing.

"Come on, Angus. Why?"

"I can't let Novak own me," he said, as if it were the most obvious thing in the world. His words were confident, but his eyes were scared.

"Come on. Let's take you home." I hugged him to me.

"Julia, he needs to go to the hospital," Liv said softly.

"No," I said. "No. Goddammit." I racked my brain for other possibilities, but I knew it was inevitable. His injury was beyond something one of us could fix or that he could heal on his own. Once the hospital had him under their authority, they could get his DNA, and Angus would be a liability to us. In one rash, rebellious gesture, it was all over for Angus. And he'd known it when he jumped.

Angus, unsteady on his feet, plopped down on the ground. "I just need a minute."

"We're going to get you taken care of," Liv said. He actually nodded.

"I hope George saw it. That fucker. At least he finally knows I'm better than he is." Angus laughed again.

Just then George came to Liv's side. "Come on. We have to get you out." He tried to take Liv's hand to lead her away.

She pulled back her hand. "No, I'm staying."

"He blew it for all of us." George wouldn't look at Angus, as if he knew Angus would be dead to everyone now.

"Liv," I said, "let me handle it."

"I'm staying with Angus. Go." She raised her voice to George. "I don't want this hurting anyone else."

After George left, the three of us sat together, waiting for the crush of firefighters and police. You could hear the sirens faintly, then closer and closer, and then they descended. When Angus had been worked over and strapped down, Liv and I followed the stretcher out the front of the building to the ambulance waiting at the curb. On the street I paused midstep when I saw the black Mercedes with darkened windows. It slowed, drifting by, taking in the scene before gathering speed. Novak already knew.

Chapter Twenty-Six

Several cops milled around in the dingy reception area, knowing it would be a long wait until the doctor allowed them to question Angus. They occupied their time by playing and replaying the video of Angus that was apparently all over social media. You could tell whenever Angus landed in the video because each time the cops would exclaim as a group, "Oh shit!" and then one of them would say, "There's no way. . . ."

The downtown emergency room was quiet this late at night. The occasional patient was led or wheeled past Liv and me into a numbered room lining the linoleum corridor. The staff allowed us to stand outside the room where they'd taken Angus. Angus's father, Lati, was now in the room with him. Liv and I stood unmoving, our eyes fixed on the mauve wall in front of us, waiting. Then Liv nudged me with her elbow. They'd arrived.

I saw my stepmother first, standing in the bleak fluorescent light, consulting with a young doctor. It was just like at the police station months ago, but now it was a doctor that

Victoria was handling, not the police. She was making it known they were major donors and she was a physician. Special treatment, no police, more control over the situation, extra time. I was surprised she was attempting to work a situation that was a lost cause. This was far different from any close call that had come before: you couldn't explain away what Angus had done or tell people they hadn't really seen what they swore they had. It was time to leave town.

Though Liv and I knew he was coming, we almost missed seeing Novak enter Angus's room. He strode so quickly down the hall, he appeared as a blur. After a lifetime of caution, he didn't care anymore. He wasn't hiding now that he'd be leaving.

A primal, guttural noise like I'd never heard came from the room. It immediately went under your skin, like nails on a chalkboard. The doctor who'd been speaking with Victoria abruptly began running down the hallway with a few nurses following her. It was coming from Novak. In my entire life I'd never even heard him raise his voice.

Liv and I both saw our chance to get into the room to see Angus. We slipped in, standing behind the group gathered inside.

Angus's clothes had been cut in the ambulance, and from what I could see his legs were black and blue. He looked right at me. I felt him warning us to get out. He didn't want us to see what was coming. Backing out, I grabbed Liv's arm and we walked down the hall, instinctively flattening ourselves against the wall to escape notice. Victoria lingered in the middle of the suddenly empty hallway. She looked at us but didn't move a muscle.

"Mr. Jaynes, we need to ask you to leave. Now!" the doctor was saying.

"How fucking dare you!" my dad snarled.

"Sir . . ."

"Get him out of here," I heard someone say. Then my dad appeared at the doorway of Angus's room, his face almost reptilian with the skin pulled tight, his cheekbones two jutting knots. And then, as if on command, his facial expression relaxed and he walked calmly into the hall. That was how quickly Novak regained control. It was the most frighteningly unnatural thing I'd ever seen. Victoria quickly crossed to Liv and dragged her toward an exit, leaving just me.

I watched Lati follow Novak into the hallway and lead my dad a few feet away from the room, where he thought they could have a private conversation. Their lips moved quickly. It was almost soundless. I focused everything I had on following their conversation. Angus would be straining to listen from inside the room.

"I'm done with him."

"Come on, Novak. We're leaving anyway. It was a boyish stunt."

"I warned him to shut it down."

"We don't know what happened yet. Maybe he fell."

"I heard about what he did five seconds after he did it. He didn't fall. He performed for hundreds of people. Years of planning and searching in this godforsaken place, and now we need to leave before I said we were ready. And we have no one."

"He's talented, Novak. We can use it." Lati's voice was calm, but the first note of alarm was moving into it.

"*I* can't use it. He can't be trusted."

"Look, the pressure built, and he broke. They've been held too tightly here. Remember how much easier it was to blend in when we were growing up? We had so much more freedom than these kids; there was none of this technology hanging over us, ready to document our every move. And this forced division of our kids? When we get to the next place, we won't have these concerns, and he'll be fine."

That sat terribly in the air for a moment. The pause held Angus's life in the balance. Finally, Novak looked Lati dead in the eye and said, "You're not coming with us."

Lati's tone remained calm. "What are you talking about?"

"You heard me. I suggest you and your family leave town as soon as possible. If it hasn't happened already, they'll make sure they get a sample from him—hair, blood."

Lati acted like his friend was joking. "This is me, Novak."

"Shut up right now, and you can take your money with you. You'll need it. You know more about where we're going than anyone—make a scene or talk to anyone and you're cut off financially. And you know I will have people watching you for the rest of your life." Novak turned to leave.

Forty years of friendship erased.

Lati followed him, drawing closer to where I stood. "No one threw *you* out when you jeopardized everything."

Novak jerked around. "You'll survive. You'll be on the run your entire life, but you'll survive."

You could see the moment Lati realized it was final, and he changed tack completely, years of stored-up hate pouring out. "As a leader you're full of shit. You have all the skill but none of the compassion of our great ones." Lati gestured to Angus's room. "I let you convince us to alter the development of our most talented children who were 'interfering with your visions.' What bullshit. Who would we be if we hadn't been trained? I know what you're trying to do: eliminate your and Liv's competition so you can stay in power. We've always elected our leaders, and you're trying to create a fucking royal family. And at the expense of our children, Novak. My son and your daughter. I'm glad Angus somehow found a way around you. You and your fucking predictions you're making come true. Really, you're just like *them*, another greedy billionaire trying to stay in power."

Lati took one more step even closer to Novak. "The funny thing is, now everyone is starting to doubt your visions. We've stayed here too long, sitting on our hands while we've waited for you to hear voices. There isn't a chosen one out there for you or Liv. It's just a story, Novak. No one can come wholly over to our side in our exact image. You have a daughter who's proof it doesn't work like that. If you want a next generation, they'll be like her. A version of us, but not the same. We're lost whatever you do." Lati began backing away.

"If what I'm planning is so fucked up, why do you want to be part of it?" Novak smiled at Lati. "It's because you know nothing in the 'real world' comes close to it. You know you will never feel complete again. Good luck taking care of your family when this world goes to shit. It's coming sooner than you think." Novak pivoted to walk down the hall and saw me standing there. He knew I'd heard everything.

He paused imperceptibly before passing me without acknowledgment.

Shell-shocked, I stood motionless in the hallway, the entire world tilting on its side.

I lost all touch with my surroundings and any sense of time. But then Liv's voice penetrated my stupor. She'd reappeared at my side. Through a fog she was saying, "They said we need to leave." She pulled on my sleeve, trying to get me to follow her out the ER entrance.

"No," I said, coming alive.

I didn't want to see him. Novak had messed with our very nature. He had made me believe I was nothing special, and then he'd deliberately separated me out in hopes of stunting my abilities permanently. You didn't do that to your own child. Or anyone else's. The authority he thought he had, even over our bodies, made me want to be sick.

"Come on. Julia, what's wrong with you? We're all waiting for you." I realized she'd missed the entire thing. Liv still had her hero. She grabbed my hand. Why would they be waiting for me? We weren't a family. I was a failed experiment from Novak's youth.

They were waiting in the shadows, to the side of the building entrance. Novak and Victoria were the portrait of themselves, not at all disheveled despite that it was almost dawn.

For the first time in my life, I would only look at Victoria, though I felt Novak waiting to catch my eye, his presence thrumming through the air. It was going to be different now that it was out in the open between us. He didn't have to pretend. I knew who I was, and I knew he'd tried to stunt me and the other Lost Kids. It looked like he had managed to succeed with Roger and Ellis.

I knew it was time to receive my punishment again, like I had after Barton Springs when I'd had the gall to act like one of them—worse, to be as powerful as one of them. But apparently that was a punishable offense for others as well. Even without proof of any wrongdoing this time, how would he not group me with Angus? It was what I deserved, regardless. Angus and his entire family would suffer because he'd stood up for me. I dragged my gaze upward to meet Novak's eyes.

Novak shocked me by tilting his head to the side, his eyes gentle. "There's no point discussing tonight. Any of it. In a few hours it will feel like it happened a lifetime ago." I could feel him trying to manipulate my emotions by using that remarkable power he had. I was amazed he was looking at me like this, with love instead of disgust.

He reached out his hand. I stared at it for a second and then realized I had no choice but to take it. Grasping it, it felt so strong and reassuring. I could feel my heart rate slowing.

"We love you girls more than anything. You know that, right?" Novak asked. Why was he including me? And did he so overestimate my love for him that he didn't realize he'd just broken my heart?

Victoria moved closer to Novak, interrupting the moment. "Look, the survival of this group is what's most important, and we are all in danger right now. We need to leave," she urged. It sounded like Victoria expected me to go with them. At that moment I didn't know if I could make myself get in the car with them, regardless of any nirvana awaiting me on the other side.

Novak didn't seem in any particular hurry as his gaze moved speculatively over me. Once Novak made the call, Relocation would spring into action, and he would have to admit defeat—that his hand had been forced by a kid he thought he had under control.

"When are they getting out?" Liv asked, referring to Angus and Lati. She still had no idea.

"Novak," Victoria interrupted sharply. "Everyone's been told they have two hours. We need to get inside our house. Now." Victoria began to walk, expecting us to follow her.

"We shouldn't leave a car here," I said suddenly. "I'll take Liv's car home."

"I want you to ride with us," Victoria said to Liv. She wasn't going to let Liv out of her sight.

"I need your keys," I said to Liv.

"Julia," Novak said. I froze. Then he said, "We'll see you at home." Novak turned, and the three of them walked into the dark, Liv looking back at me. She didn't know she was being robbed of the chance to say good-bye.

I kept my head down and walked directly to his room. It was insane, but I couldn't leave without seeing him.

Carefully, I opened the door without knocking, wanting to get out of the hall before someone stopped me. Immediately Lati snapped his head around and stared at me hard, quickly ending his phone call. The lights were dim. Lati sat on Angus's bed, and Angus looked like he was asleep. I closed the door softly behind me.

"You can't be in here, Julia," Lati said.

"What happens next?" I asked quickly.

Unfazed, Lati accommodated. "Our ride will be here in ten minutes. My son will not be spending the rest of his life as an FBI lab rat."

I wondered who was helping them. It was nice to know

not everyone was abandoning them because Novak said so. "Where will you go?"

"Your father's not the only one who can make plans," he said.

"Can he be moved?" I asked, looking over at Angus.

"His foot has been reset. No internal injuries. So, yes. Amazing. Too amazing." Lati shook his head, looking down at his son.

Lati brushed his knuckles against Angus's arm, his relief palpable. He didn't seem angry, in spite of what he was facing, all because of a spur-of-the-moment choice made by Angus—a kamikaze fuck-you to my father.

"Did you know my mother?" I asked, point-blank. Lati looked at me, realizing I had overheard the conversation. He hesitated.

"She was an outsider," he said eventually. "I always thought it was unfair he wouldn't tell you."

"How?" I asked, incredulous. I knew this might be my only chance to get any information.

"I don't know very much, in spite of the fact that we were close friends. Best friends." Lati's pause reflected how quickly things had changed. Angus stirred, and for a second I feared Lati wouldn't say anything more. Then he looked up at me. He could probably see the desperation in my eyes, and he relented.

"The year before the Relocation to Austin, Novak started disappearing for long periods of time. Then one day he came to the group, telling us he'd found someone like us. Novak said she'd been searching for similar people, that she'd been drawn to us, and by being near him she'd developed some of our traits.

"Novak brought her to us only one time, and everyone was skeptical and suspicious of her. But Novak was hell-bent on convincing everyone she should be part of the group. It was clear he wanted to marry her. Then months later, with no warning, we needed to relocate. Novak showed up with an infant—you—and we were given strict orders never to question it."

If Lati knew anything about her working with the FBI, he didn't say a word. "How did he get away with it?"

"Novak was too valuable to let go."

"Valuable how?" There was so much that had been kept from me.

"He was an outlier. At a young age he was capable of things it took most of us a lifetime to master. He surpassed all of us with what he was able to do with his mind—telekinesis, and his complete control over physical response."

Of course. What had he called the same in me? Nothing important, nothing worth mentioning. He had made me feel so small.

"He began correctly predicting near events. And then Novak said he could see farther and farther into the future. After that people were listening to him more than to Victor. Novak came back to the fold and married the leader's daughter, but you were part of the deal. Eighteen years later he's still trying to save face and prove there are more of us out there. Some people are more receptive now since we've been unable to reproduce."

"Julia." Angus had opened his eyes. His voice was rough and low. He gestured for me to come to the bed and reached out to try to touch my cheek. I leaned in closer.

"Angus, I'm so sorry. That was my problem, not yours. I never should have—"

"Shhhh. If it weren't for my family, I'd do it again. I don't know—the thought of him trapping me somewhere . . . I just couldn't go. I fucking hate him, Julia." Angus's anger could have seared the wall. He tried to collect himself. "Besides, I couldn't let you hurt yourself after you told me you don't have pure blood like me," he joked.

I wanted to laugh but I couldn't. "Did you always know I wasn't like you?" I asked.

"No. Maybe I guessed. It doesn't matter," he said. I laughed at that. He pulled me down closer and said, "You're still you. And you're still one of us. *Them*," he corrected himself.

I nodded, but I knew it wasn't convincing. I said, "You were right about Novak. We were the best. Thank God you taught the boys."

"Thank God you taught me."

Lati stood up, wanting to usher me out. "You need to get out of here and get back to Novak."

"How am I going to do that, knowing what I know? And why would he take me?"

"He's raised you as his daughter, in our group, in front of everyone, and you deserve to be part of Relocation. Somehow, by luck and chance, you're here. If you could wish anything for this one chance on earth, wouldn't it be for a long, peaceful life? To experience bliss? Isn't that what all of existence strives for? What we've created can ensure a beautiful future, secure from the outside world. You have to go. You can't let him take away the extraordinary things about us. Don't let what you just heard change anything."

"What does that mean exactly, 'secure from the outside world?'"

"You know I can't talk about it. Even now."

"Where is it?" I pushed.

In a firmer voice he said, "You need to go. Say good-bye."

I looked at Angus, realizing I might never see him again. "I won't forget you."

"Promise me you'll take care of the boys," he said seriously. I nodded. Angus's eyes glowed bright blue as he did everything he could not to cry. "I love you, Julia."

I could tell he was scared.

"I love you too. You're my best friend."

"Julia," Lati said, impatient now.

"Maybe you'll get the best of both worlds," I said to Angus coaxingly.

"I don't think it works like that."

I couldn't stand seeing him broken, and it scared me, not being able to help him. I lay my head on Angus's chest. Everyone in the room knew it was futile, that we couldn't go back in time, but Lati and Angus were quiet for a moment.

Angus caught my hand as I stood to go. "Julia, don't accept their story that you're less. You're more of everything. All the best parts."

I'd never thought about it that way, that I was more than the image they had of me. I smoothed the hair from Angus's forehead carefully. I leaned my face down to his and whispered in his ear.

"Angus," I said, with wonder in my voice, "don't worry. You are going to feel so alive."

The path to the car was blurry, the tears falling freely as soon as I was out of Angus's sight. Still, I was sure I recognized one of the FBI agents who had questioned me. He walked right past me, striding into the building with purpose.

Chapter Twenty-Seven

I parked across the street, one house down, but with a clear view of their driveway. I sat watching in the black winter night.

I knew that in all probability he was safe inside, sleeping. No one would have pursued Liv's theory about John once Angus jumped. There wasn't any time. We had to run now. I knew the smart thing for me to do was to run too. I was crazy for making this stop.

I started the car, the dashboard lighting up. I felt like I was outside myself, watching to see if I could make the final break and pull away from the curb to drive home through the streets of Austin for the last time.

But I had to check.

I turned off the engine. Walking briskly down the sidewalk, I was in front of John's house in a second, but not without a neighbor's dog starting to bark. I walked back to their rotting wood gate and tried to open it with a push of my hand. It didn't budge. I slammed my shoulder into it, and it made a loud scratching sound on the concrete. Breaking into a cold sweat, I glanced at the neighbor's windows, but no one came to peer out to see what was driving their dog crazy. Letting myself into the backyard, I nudged past the recycling and garbage cans.

It felt surreal—an out-of-body experience—being at John's house early in the morning, his backyard cold and quiet. My eyes locked on the weathered French doors leading into John's bedroom, and I slowed.

I tapped so lightly on the glass, he may not have heard. If he didn't open the door in ten more seconds, I'd turn around.

Nothing. I drew a shuddering breath and turned to leave.

"Julia!" I heard his voice, low and husky so as not to wake the house. I whipped around to see John standing in the doorway, shirtless, in boxers. *Oh, thank God.*

"I'm sorry I woke you up." I could go now, knowing I was leaving him right where he was supposed to be. I still didn't move.

"I couldn't sleep. What are you doing here?" he whispered, his eyes tired and sexy behind his glasses.

"I wanted to make sure you were okay. That's it," I said, as though it were perfectly normal that I was knocking on his door at dawn, so many weeks after we'd broken up.

"It's freezing." John opened the door wider, silently asking me in. He seemed half-asleep, and his defenses were down. I'd lost my jacket at some point in the night, and cold was coming off me.

I knew I shouldn't do it. No one would wait for me.

I brushed past him. Stepping into his room, I was enveloped in warmth. His bed was rumpled and the sheets had the impression of his body. Just being this close to him made me aware of every pore in my skin.

312

John seemed to be waking up and realizing I was actually here. I could feel when the wall went up. He swiftly put on a pair of jeans over his boxers and grabbed a T-shirt.

Earlier in the evening felt like playacting compared with this. Maybe his family was asleep in the house, but this time we were really alone, no one watching over our interaction.

"Are you okay?" I asked. "I didn't get a chance to talk to you after . . ."

"I'm fine. That was crazy. It's all over the place now. Videos of it." He backed as far away from me as he could get in the small room, hands shoved in back pockets in his usual stance. He had a long gash on his arm from the tree. "What happened? Why did he do that?" John asked.

"It was—I don't know—things got out of control. It had to do with a fight we were having among ourselves." My eyes rested on the framed photo of John and Alex. If I never did another good thing in my life, at least I'd saved John's. It blew me away how much potential he had here. His family, Stanford, tennis. Meeting John had made it impossible for me to continue ignoring the value of other people's lives. I thought about how his life, how every outsider's life, would keep moving forward, in contrast to mine. In five years John would be finished with college, and who knows what he would have seen and done in that time. And who he'll have been with.

"Was that you? The butterflies?" he asked. I nodded, and he gave a small *Of course* smile. I realized we were both holding our breath.

"What else don't I know?" he asked.

"I think now you've seen it all." Though I actually didn't

know what I was capable of anymore. I'd unnerved him. I backed away a few steps.

"So what happens now? How do you explain what happened tonight?" John asked.

I stopped smiling. "We can't. It's done. We're leaving."

"When?"

"Right now."

"What? Where are you going?"

"I don't even know." I tried to sound matter-of-fact instead of scared.

John's eyes widened, and then he quickly looked down, studying the floor. When he looked up, he'd concealed his emotions again. We both stood in the awkward silence.

"This was a bad idea." I turned to leave. Suddenly he grabbed my arm and I turned back around, hearing my own intake of breath.

And then we both slid.

He lowered his head to mine at the exact moment my arms reached up for him, winding around his neck. Just one last time. I didn't care if he was with someone else—I didn't care about anything. He and I were together in that moment. After the emptiness of being cut off from his thoughts, I felt a deep thrill in finally knowing what he was feeling. We both let go of everything pent up between us and the pain of the last weeks. My hands snaked into his hair. I'd forgotten exactly how he felt and how well he kissed. That coupled with the fact that I would never see him again made the kiss surpass anything I'd ever experienced. And probably ever would.

When we broke apart, he rested his forehead against mine.

"When I saw you tonight, I thought you'd moved on," I said, thinking of Reese.

"I've been trying to," he said, his expression unreadable again, but his hand shook as he smoothed my hair behind my ear. "I thought you'd moved on."

"I've been trying to." I met his dark eyes. For a second I fell into them and pretended he was still mine. "I'm just going to go. It will be easier that way." I reached behind me for the door.

"You're eighteen today. You could stay if you wanted to," he said in a neutral voice that matched his expression. He sounded like he didn't care one way or the other. The only sign that he gave a shit about what he was saying was that he'd started speaking at normal volume.

"Shhh. You'll wake your family," I whispered.

"At least acknowledge it before you go, Julia—what's fucking both of us up. We never talked about the moment we first saw each other at Barton Springs. Something happened. And ever since then, I've known we're supposed to be together. You felt that too. It's why you're here, right?" He didn't wait for my response, his tone annoyed now.

"I'll go to college, get a job, meet someone someday, but they'll always be second best. You'll be with one of your boys like Angus, and you may be happy that you're so superior, but a huge part of you will be locked away. So you choose, Julia. I know which life I want. It's the harder one, but the second I met you I accepted it."

John was looking at me. He'd spoken so clearly and honestly, and after everything he still wanted me.

I'd have been lying if I told myself I hadn't thought about

it. I hadn't stopped thinking about it all night, ever since we arrived at the hospital. But I kept coming back to the same set of facts.

"I'm too different. I would just ruin you, John." I shook my head.

"You already have."

"I'm eighteen—I have nothing to my name. What am I supposed to do? I *need* to be with them to be safe."

"Who told you that? Are you so sure about these rules? Who's telling you that you should only function in a tight group? That could be a complete lie."

"I can't not see my sister again."

"This is your one life. Not your family's. You act like there's this wall between you and the rest of us, that you live some sort of mythical parallel existence. But you can't just ignore the reality all around you. You don't want to."

"I've always been taught that the group comes first. It's so ingrained, I can't imagine anything else. I don't know anything else. And I can't be myself out here." I gestured around.

"You can't be yourself with them, either. You were happy when you let us happen instead of keeping everything controlled. I hate watching you when you shut yourself off and act uninterested in the rest of the world just like the rest of them. I was drawn to you at Barton Springs because you're *not* exactly like them."

He had hit the nerve of my lifetime.

"I am them. You have no idea how selfish I can be."

John looked at me closely. "What?"

"No. Nothing." I wasn't sure if I should do it. I hadn't planned on ever telling him.

From the way I'd said it and then backtracked, he guessed it had something to do with him. "Tell me."

I almost walked away. But then I decided he should know.

"Tell me," he demanded.

"Sometimes I could hear your thoughts."

I saw it on his face. It was like he'd been aware that a piece was missing, and right then it clicked into place. All the times I'd messed up—things I'd known that he'd never told me, his random thoughts I'd finished out loud, how I'd always seemed so in sync with him.

"You had no problem doing that to me? Like I was your toy? After I asked you to leave me alone?"

He was suddenly angrier than I'd ever seen him. "Why did you even come here, Julia? Just to mess with my head one last time?"

"I'm sorry."

"Everything you've done has been selfish. You came slumming to public school and wrapped me around your finger, telling me things that blew my mind . . . and then you dumped me like you couldn't have cared less. I thought that was the extent of it. But this?"

"I didn't plan for it to happen, and I tried to stop it, but I couldn't or didn't. I don't know."

"So I'm completely exposed to you? I never gave you that permission."

I grabbed his face with both hands, forcing him to look at me. He jerked out of my grasp. "Listen, it hasn't happened since we broke up. And before that it only happened when you were open to it. When you were angry, I was cut off. But for better or worse, I know you. I know what's inside you. And I can say you are the most perfect person, John."

He shook his head in disgust. "You had no right."

"I didn't have a choice. It happened."

"So I was your experiment. Is that why you talked to me when you ignored every single other person at the school?" Again, he knew.

"Maybe it started that way. . . ."

"You need to go."

I stood for a moment, but he wouldn't look at me now. On some level I'd known telling him would make it easier to walk away. I'd made it so I could go, free and clear. He'd be happy if he never saw me again.

"You are the only one who accepted everything about me."

I let myself out and walked away from him, knowing this last memory of him would feel like a never-ending wave, crushing me over and over again.

Chapter Twenty-Eight

I should have been present on the drive home, memorizing every detail of Austin, the last city I'd ever see if what Liv said was true. Instead my mind raced, occupied by John, and I arrived back on Scenic Drive before I was ready. The grand black gate swung open, and I hesitated at the entrance. I felt my knees go weak when I drove over the threshold, knowing I'd just begun the metamorphosis.

At first I was terrified that they'd left without me. The house was eerily quiet.

I was relieved when I heard Victoria moving around the rooms downstairs. Realizing my late arrival might go unnoticed, I quickly made my way up the back staircase to my bedroom, not knowing what to expect.

I opened the door and drew up short, seeing Liv sitting on my made bed. My bedroom looked exactly the same as I'd left it. Nothing had been moved.

"Oh."

"I didn't mean to scare you. " She stood and walked to the center of the room. She'd showered since the hospital and changed into a long black dress, a tall contrast in the all-white room. Her feet were bare, and she was looking relaxed, like nothing had happened tonight.

"Where were you?"

"With Angus."

"They told me in the car. They said not to tell anyone else until we've left," Liv said. She went over to the window seat and kneeled on the white cushion, staring out at the lake. "What did he say?" She tried to keep all emotion out of her voice, but she didn't want me to see her expression. I noticed her light-pink nail polish had been half picked off.

I knew what she wanted. "He said to say good-bye to you," I lied.

"I'm going to fix it." There was bitterness in her voice.

"Liv," I warned.

She cut me off. "He and I are supposed to be together. I know how that sounds. . . ."

"I believe you," I said. I did believe she felt that. "I just don't want you hurting yourself. It sounds like we'll be confined. It could drive you crazy, wanting something so badly that's on the other side."

Liv faced me, and there was a steeliness in her eyes I'd never seen before. She played with the necklace she was wearing. The small gold nugget hanging from the chain caught my eye. It looked old and was very beautiful.

"Why did Angus do it?" she asked.

"He's a free spirit; I think he was scared of losing control. He was afraid he was about to be sealed in a crypt."

"But now we'll have control! We'll be in our own world instead of hiding in theirs. He was supposed to come.

He will come." I was worried at both the grief and the determination I heard in her voice. I realized out of everything of mine she'd had, the only thing she'd actually wanted was Angus.

Angus would have been here if she hadn't spoken out of turn about Relocation at the club. But I couldn't help feel that if it felt so wrong to him, maybe it was better he knew ahead of time. Maybe Angus and his family would struggle forever to conceal their abilities, but at least now it was solely up to them to decide how and when to use them. I couldn't stop looking out the window, wanting to go outside again, off the property. It was amazing what you craved once it was no longer an option.

I realized Liv had been talking and I hadn't been listening. My mind wasn't in this room or on Relocation. I kept thinking of things I should have said to John.

"Julia!" Then she gentled her voice. "Stop worrying. You're here, aren't you?"

"Sorry." I shook my head. "I'm all messed up from tonight."

"I am too. And I don't want to be," Liv said. I didn't know if she was referring to me or Angus or both. I wouldn't tell her the rest of what I'd heard tonight—about what Novak had tried to do to us in order to prop her up. Maybe it was misguided, but I wanted to protect her.

"You must see me differently now," I said, surprising myself. It was a break with my tradition of never discussing anything uncomfortable with Liv. She had blinked for just a second when I'd told her about my mother, but then, surprisingly, she'd stood by my side the rest of the night. And she was here now.

"No. Maybe for a second, but what's really changed? You're my sister."

I took a second to make sure I had control of my voice. "Thanks, Liv." She nodded, a little bit shy at my choking up. In some ways there was still something so pure about my sister. She hadn't grown out of her big heart yet.

"Look, I'm sorry about tonight and how I put you on the spot like that. I had no idea. . . . I was really convinced about you and him. And I thought I was doing this big thing, showing everyone that you were the one who found the answer for Novak."

"Thanks for thinking I had that much power, Liv."

"It was also a way to tell you that I've always seen us as equals. I still do."

Hearing someone I loved say those words out loud fixed something that had been broken inside me for a long time. I walked over and stood next to her. I surprised her by doing something I don't think I'd ever done. I put my arm around her and rested my head on her shoulder. She stiffened for a moment, and then laid her cheek on my hair.

"We were put in an impossible situation once we were in different groups. I think we managed pretty well until recently," Liv said, pulling back first.

"We really did."

"I'm sorry. It was a huge mistake not standing up for you when you were sent to that school."

"Do not worry about it, okay? It's over." I made it sound like an unspeakable time to be put behind us. I imagined for a moment that I'd never gone away and never had a concept of the things I'd experienced. I would be a different person if this whole fall hadn't happened. To me that person from last summer felt half-dead. The thought suddenly scared me. Badly.

My eyes were tired after a night of no sleep. I didn't like the way I was feeling—this rising panic. I didn't know what was real and what was an irrational reaction like Angus had had.

Liv sat back down and pulled her knees to her chest. "Do you mind if I wait in here with you?"

The energy and momentum was picking up downstairs. We could both feel it.

"Please."

"I'm scared," she admitted.

"Me too." She had no idea.

"I knew it was coming, but I have no idea what happens now or how it all goes down," she said, glancing over her shoulder at me. "I asked my mom if I should pack anything, and she just said, 'No. It's all been taken care of.'"

I quickly scanned the room for any mementos I wanted to hold or look at one last time. There weren't any. My life here hadn't been full of many memories worth holding on to. It was people I was leaving behind. One who understood me and one who felt like he was an actual part of me. The entire drive home, I'd been haunted by John's vision of our future together. He was right about the first moment we saw each other at Barton Springs. I'd felt the exact same thing.

I realized I was pacing. I felt like I couldn't sit down with Liv, that it would be dangerous to stop moving.

I reminded myself I wasn't at a crossroads. This wasn't a choice. It was my fate and it was an exceptional, privileged one. Like Lati said, I deserved to be here and I'd fought hard for it.

"What do you know about where we're going?" I asked.

"I think it's been built underground. I know there's a large aquifer."

"Like a bunker?" I sounded very freaked out to my own ears. I suddenly took notice of the sunlight pouring through my windows.

"A terrarium, I think. I don't know the details, just that it's a beautiful habitat. Novak said they've been building this for two decades. I think we'll be completely cut off. Novak said no more outside influences. Can you imagine—no internet? Oh, Jesus. I'll miss that. What are you going to miss? Tell me while you still can."

John. Angus. The world. "I don't know. I never even imagined it would be this extreme. Music, I guess. This view. The lake. This house is the only home I've ever known."

"I love this house. We used to play hide-and-seek for hours."

We both smiled, remembering. Any good memories I had of my childhood were because of her.

Liv suddenly got a sparkle in her eye. She may have been scared, but this was right for her. She was so sure of her place in this family, in their world. What was that like? I couldn't imagine.

"This was a great life. The next one will be so much better," she said with confidence.

For you it will be, I thought to myself.

"No matter what, you and I have each other. We'll always have each other. Right?"

"We will," I promised.

"That's the important thing. It's more important than anything or anyone else," Liv said.

We were interrupted by a knock on the door. Since I didn't move, Liv stood up and walked over to open it.

"Liv!" I said. She turned back around. "I love you."

"I love you too," she said, like it was a given.

It was well organized. By the time all the teenagers were led to a corner section of the living room, it was almost dawn. Liv was across from me in the circle. I stood next to Paul and Cyrus, who looked just as tough as always, Lost Kids to the end.

There was no time to talk. Each Lost Kid kept an eye trained on the entry as it grew later and later and Angus hadn't shown. We met one another's gaze, and silently they asked about Angus. I shook my head. I saw the disbelief. When would we stop looking around for him, thinking he was about to join us? It already felt like a spark was missing. I didn't care what they said: how would it not feel that way forever?

We were asked for our cell phones. It was actually kind of heartbreaking—everyone scrolling through their photos one more time as fast as they could and with one last, long look, arms extended, reluctantly dropping them into an oversize Ziploc.

I resisted the urge to look. I'd spent the whole morning trying to imprint the past on my brain, and I couldn't do it anymore. It was my turn next to drop my phone in the bag, but I felt a tap on my shoulder.

"Your father wants to see you," Victoria said softly, and she began walking toward Novak's office.

So here it was. I had started to assume I was safe once they gathered me with the rest of the kids. I should have known this was coming. Despite what Lati said, how could it not have been? Maybe Novak had found out about my relationship with John, or that I had been responsible for making Angus jump. There were so many strikes against me, the biggest one being pure biology. I had no choice but to follow Victoria's tall stick figure, feeling icy all over. This summons felt all too familiar. On some level it was a relief to face it.

I walked far behind Victoria, until she turned and motioned for me to walk faster. Outside my father's door Victoria turned to face me. Her china-doll face was arctic as always, but she seemed softer toward me than usual. She felt guilty, I realized.

"You shouldn't have let him do that to us. To me," I said, openly standing up to her. "You knew I never had a problem stepping back for Liv."

The look in her eyes told me she knew it had been wrong. She never got the chance to reply, however, because the door opened abruptly and Novak impatiently loomed inside, making a sweeping gesture for me to enter. I paused, taken aback that his face looked so much older—like he had the weight of the world on his shoulders. By the time I realized what I'd seen, his features had already rearranged themselves into his normal appearance. Victoria turned to go.

"Victoria!" Novak said. She turned back. "Tell them I'll meet them in the garage." He murmured something else to her in a Spanish-sounding language I'd never heard before.

"Please sit." Novak closed the door behind us with just a glance. The door to Novak's office vault was open, and for the first time ever I saw inside. The small room was empty except for a long white feather that lay on the ground.

Novak looked the part of the relaxed billionaire in his dark jeans, Lanvin sneakers, and cashmere hoodie. He seemed distracted, but when he took a seat across from me and looked up, it was like he had cleared a slate to focus on me completely. I felt like he'd be able to see in my eyes every incredible thing I'd done tonight.

It made me want to crawl out of my skin. I didn't want his attention. I felt like I didn't know this person anymore. If I ever had. I'd learned he was the ultimate chameleon. I was aware of every second that ticked by until Novak spoke.

"I wanted to touch base with you before we left." Novak began swiveling in his chair, back and forth, back and forth, like he hadn't a care in the world. I realized I was getting the Novak who played the role of charismatic leader and kind father, his eyes now light and sparkling. The only sign that he was agitated was the deep scratches he was etching into the marble tabletop with his thumbnail.

"No need to panic, baby." Novak laughed. "You're here because I wanted to give you this." He took something gold off the desk and walked over to me. Looking more closely at what was dangling from his hand, I realized it was a necklace identical to the one Liv was wearing.

"May I?" Without waiting for an answer, Novak bent low, draped it around my neck, and deftly clasped it. Hairs raised on the back of my neck as his fingers brushed my skin.

"What is it?" I asked, wishing I didn't have to talk.

"It's our original gold from Peru. We've been without a home for over a century now. This is a reminder of who we are and where we came from. It's traveled with us all these years."

I touched the gold chain and the pendant, the nugget of gold. "Why are you giving it to me?"

He sat back down across from me on the other side of his desk. "I know what you overheard earlier. I brought you here to reassure you that you have a place in this family. At eighteen it's become clear you have more of our traits than theirs. After months at that school and staying in line, you've proved yourself to everyone."

I'd been on display. I'd always felt different, but I hadn't known I was being watched all these years while they waited to see how I would turn out.

"I know how frustrating it must have been to have these spurts that add up to nothing without training. And I know it was hard to watch your abilities dissipate. My plan has always been to teach you, once we reach the new place, exactly what to do with the gifts you have."

"My remaining gifts?" I asked in a neutral voice.

Novak didn't like the question. "It's a large responsibility to carry on our legacy. Not everyone will always agree with how the leader chooses what's best for our survival." Novak wouldn't even make apologies for what he'd done to me and the Lost Kids. He seemed so confident I wasn't a threat, that the school had been just the place where he could diminish my skills at the precise moment when I'd shown the most potential. He believed I worshipped him and this family so much that I hadn't dared overreach, that I'd sat at that school and let my potential ebb away. He had no idea I'd managed to attain control over my abilities without one shred of his guidance.

"Who was she?" I asked, surprising myself. I'd wanted to hear this from him my whole life.

The only sign of a reaction was a slowing in his near-violent swiveling motion. He'd had time to think about his response. "I mistook her for someone she wasn't. I also learned very quickly that life outside is nothing compared with this. This family and what it means is bigger than any individual desire I may have had. I don't belong just to myself."

So that was all he would tell me about her: nothing. Lati had given me more.

Silence hung between us. "When I was a baby, why did you take me?" I asked, not liking how small and confused my voice sounded.

"I didn't have a choice," Novak said bluntly, and I saw the veil slip.

Novak stood up and looked out the window, no longer wanting to face me. Finally he said, "She fell in with the wrong people. It was dangerous for you to stay."

"So you never wanted me here," I said flatly. I'd been forced not only on the entire group but on Novak as well.

He continued to stare out the window. "It's been a challenge. Each Relocation, the past almost vanishes. It's like a part of us is supposed to die so we can enter the new life completely. But here you've been, a constant reminder for me of a youthful mistake. You look almost exactly like her."

"Why are you bringing me, then?" I didn't know why I was pushing him.

"Thankfully I was able to pass enough of our genes on to you. We're the last Puris, Julia. It is a beautiful, sacred legacy. When we complete Relocation, things will be different for you. That's all I will ever say about that again. Do you understand?" Novak said, indicating the conversation about my mother was closed forever.

My whole life I'd been running alongside them, hoping they'd take me, and now I'd been officially accepted by Novak himself, not merely tolerated. My future, my life, was guaranteed. I would learn the secrets. I would have to conceal some of my abilities, but that wasn't anything new. I should have been relieved that I'd earned my place after all these years.

I didn't move. "Where are we going?" I'd heard rumors for months, and bits of information from Liv, but I wanted confirmation from him.

"For your own safety only a few people know the geographic location. You'll go downstairs and take a sedative, and when you wake up you'll think you've arrived in Eden." I could tell from the arrogance in his voice, Novak was very, very proud of himself and what he would reveal to everyone.

"Where we're going—can we leave?"

"No," he said, simply, then immediately sensed my fear. "Don't worry. Once you're there, you won't want anything else again. It will be back to how it was before our people were discovered—no conflict, no suffering. We can focus on our gifts. That shared enlightenment is so beautiful, Julia. The energy radiating from the group—it can light an entire room. Even if it's not exactly the same for you, you'll be living in a better place."

There was a knock. "Novak!" someone barked from outside the door, clearly anxious at Novak's leisurely pace. It was like he was continuing to resist the timetable Angus had put him on.

"Excuse me one moment," Novak said, formally. He walked out swiftly, leaving me alone. I sagged back into the chair.

Out of the corner of my eye, I caught sight of myself in a large mirror hanging behind Novak's desk. I turned my head to see myself. I did look exactly like the woman in the picture, only my features fit this family's now. Aquiline, symmetrical. My eyes were unreadable. Like Novak said, I had enough of them in me.

I remembered the moment in the bathroom at John's house when I'd stared at myself in the mirror. I'd looked so different then, like a girl I didn't know. My features had been softer, my cheeks flushed. Mostly I remembered how my eyes had looked. Alive.

I still had my phone. An oversight.

Any second someone would walk in. It would be my last rebellion. Quickly I stood and turned my back to the door, scrolling through the phone, hoping I could find the one picture I wanted to see.

I'd taken it through the picture window of the library, capturing John outside in the gold light of a fall afternoon. He was sitting on a bench, head barely turned, just the hint of his profile showing. I'd caught him in this fleeting moment— young and beautiful, waiting for me. One minute later I'd gone out, we'd had a brief conversation, and then we'd said good-bye. This was how he would always be in my mind, frozen in time.

I panicked, and my eyes flitted back to the mirror. This time they landed on the necklace. I touched it gently, wanting to feel the connection to my family and confirm my role in this line, hoping it would tell me that all the possibilities that lay outside the walls of this house paled in comparison with what this move represented.

And then I had the sensation of bright, enveloping energy Novak had just described, that same feeling I had the first day I read John's mind.

It flowed through my entire body, and I just knew. It was more than the bliss I was capable of feeling when I was with the group. In that moment it was like I knew the answer to every question I'd ever asked. It was a glimpse of enlightenment.

I understood the pain of defecting, the reality of never seeing the group, my people, again. I also knew I couldn't look in the mirror again and be half myself. I couldn't pretend that there wasn't a whole other world besides ours and that I was only as powerful as Novak allowed me to be.

It had built to this over time. It had happened little by little. In the end it took just one second, and I was no longer the same person who had entered this room.

I love you, I texted. I needed him to know right then. Just in case.

Before I could turn off the phone, it vibrated in my hand.

I stared at the words on the screen.

I'm here. Outside the gate.

I heard a stirring in the hall and whisked my phone into my back pocket. Novak walked back into the room.

"Apparently everyone downstairs is growing impatient."

He perched on the edge of his desk and leaned back, crossing his arms over his chest, painfully unhurried.

I opened my mouth but didn't say anything, praying he would ask me to leave his office. But Novak was acting like he had more business with me. My mind was outside, on the person who was far too close. I noted uneasily that all four orchids in the room were dead, the formerly white petals now brown.

"Sit back down for one more moment, Julia." Novak gestured for me to sit. Dying from fear and anxiety, I carefully sat down on the very edge of the hard chair.

Novak continued, "Needless to say, my timeline has been rudely altered. Now it's extra important that you be an example. After we arrive, I want everyone to see what a close approximation you are to us." He paused. "You have a distinct role to play, but you need to be sure you can do this. You need to let Angus go."

Novak looked deep in my eyes, "If you think you're capable of doing this for me, everyone will be less resistant to my vision for our future. Everything will go smoother the next time the opportunity presents itself. I'll be going in and out for a time, since I'm the one who seems to draw them."

"Excuse me?"

"You're eighteen now and you're my daughter, so I'm going to trust you. You know I've had visions of outsiders joining us, but one in particular has come into focus. He was the whole reason we've been waiting. And then that little shit Angus . . . I was so close. I could feel it the same way I predict everything else. It was supposed to take place soon. We were going to hear him here." Novak touched his forehead.

"Liv or I—one of us was going to hear this person's thoughts and know he had the potential to become one of us completely. Everyone would finally understand how we might survive. But now we have to leave." Novak stood up from the desk in disgust.

It took me a beat to fully realize what he was saying. What that said about me. And what that said about John. We had been waiting for *him*. The key player Novak needed for the final Relocation was the person waiting for me just outside the property. I was the one who had brought him to us. I was the one who had carried out Novak's prediction— the least likely person in Novak's mind. Liv had been right. She was the only one who'd seen it.

Novak suddenly looked at me. "Did you hear anyone's thoughts? Before you went to that school?"

Truly my father's daughter after all, I felt a mask descend over my entire body, shielding my emotions completely. "No." I shook my head. I felt very scared and kept still, watching to see if I could untangle our fates.

Novak shook his head like it had been a crazy idea that I could do something so incredible. "It was Angus. By breaking the rules he interfered with my vision and he altered the course. We need other people to continue our species, but this person was special. He was key to the growth of my direct line. He was meant for Liv."

By chance or fate, I was the daughter who had found John. It was in my hands. I wouldn't hand over his life to Novak. He'd been wrong about my mother, and people would think he'd been wrong again. Novak would never know. He underestimated me too completely.

Novak seemed to grow calm. "It will happen." Then he gave me a quick kiss on the top of my head. "Apparently I've got to go. And so do you. I'll see you there?" He didn't wait for my answer. I watched Novak's lanky body stride to the door and exit into the hallway, leaving me alone in his office.

I waited for a moment. I knew exactly what to do. Very slowly and methodically, I unclasped the necklace and placed it on the tabletop. Walking behind Novak's desk, I automatically unlocked the tall window to the left and exited onto the fire escape that lay in wait, as if this moment had already been written.

Once I was outside I started moving quickly, knowing every second mattered. I flew down the metal staircase, trying to keep a light step. I got to ground level, now almost entirely illuminated in the pinkish light of morning. Head down, my heart beating out of my chest, I needed to make it to John on the other side of the gate. I rapidly walked through damp grass to the side gate. When I crossed back into the safety of the shadows, I looked up at the house in spite of myself.

Through the glass wall the living room faintly glowed and I saw the entire family together, on display. Some adults were milling around, some draped across furniture. I saw my friends gathered in a corner, heads together—the kids I'd been with my whole life. I was breaking my promise to Angus. The Lost Kids were now on their own.

I felt someone watching me and looked up, my breath catching. Liv stood at the office window.

Our eyes met. Liv turned her head—as if about to call out

to someone—but then she stopped herself. Frozen, I couldn't break her gaze, not knowing what she was going to do.

Then, very slowly, Liv lifted her hand and gave me the smallest wave good-bye. She would let me go. I stood there memorizing her, the other love of my life, for just one more moment, knowing I was breaking a promise to her most of all.

It was hard to believe this was the last time I would ever see her. I gave a small wave back, willing Liv to know how much I loved her. I broke eye contact first and walked away.

I had to let her go. If I didn't put this vanishing world behind me, I wouldn't be able to save myself and another person I loved.

Chapter Twenty-Nine

I grew more nervous the closer we got. I knew John could feel my fear when I gave him the code to the gate. I wasn't sure if it would work, or if I should even have been coming back to this house.

John's parents, thinking my family had fled the country before the SEC formally charged Novak, had gone into protective-teacher mode, wanting to help me as if I were one of their at-risk students. They tried to tell me I should go to Chicago with them for Christmas, or at least stay at their house. I told them first I had to see if I still had a home. Rationally I knew that my family was long gone, but of course a tiny part of me wondered if anything was waiting for me here.

The glass house was absolutely silent. For a moment I wanted not to go in, just to turn around and drive away. I used another passcode to open the front door and didn't turn to look at John when that code worked as well. I couldn't look at him. I was too scared.

I felt John watch me for a moment. Then he walked

through the doorway first, reaching his hand out for mine. I took it and entered, quickly turning off the alarm.

Absolutely everything was gone. No furniture. No pictures. No carpets. Completely empty and professionally cleaned. They'd had it swept of any trace of them. John and I stood in the entrance and stared.

"It's true," I said. "They made it like it never, ever happened."

"How did they do this so quickly?" John asked.

I didn't answer; I just started walking upstairs. All the family photos were gone from the hallway.

When we got to the door of my bedroom, I paused before opening it. All I had now were the clothes I was wearing. I expected nothing to be there. No trace left of my childhood. The last time I'd been in there, I'd been with Liv. That already felt like it belonged to a different lifetime.

I opened the door, and we were both taken aback to see furniture in this room. The only room in the house. They had wanted their DNA removed from the house, but I was on my own. The room was untouched since the last time I'd been in here, the white throw pillows from the window seat on the floor where Liv had tossed them.

John walked over to the bed and stood staring at it.

He was looking at the gold necklace, deliberately laid out on my pillow. Someone—Liv, Novak—had put it there for me. I had needed to leave it. It didn't feel like my birthright. Why didn't they take it?

"What are they trying to tell you?"

"I'm not sure." I didn't like it and I didn't want it, but I assumed it was a parting gift. I was banking on Novak being relieved I'd left, that I'd shown my true colors and, heart-broken, had gone after Angus. I was also counting on him fulfilling his goals far from John and me. I didn't want my family to die away, but John wasn't the answer. Liv hadn't read his mind; I had. And if he was meant for me instead of Liv—well, we could see how that played out in John's world, not in Novak's.

I didn't want to touch the necklace, but I quickly picked it up and put it in my pocket, then turned to face John. I took a huge breath and exhaled.

"You okay?" he asked, concerned but not overbearing. He always seemed to respond to me just the right way, like he could read me.

"I'm really good." I still couldn't believe he'd come for me. I smiled thinking about the moment we finally gave in to this connection between us.

In the back of my mind, I thought about Angus and Liv, and I knew I would never stop. I was worried about Angus, and I wondered if and when I'd ever find him. I told John I wouldn't stop searching, much to his annoyance. I couldn't read John's mind and wasn't sure if I ever would be able to again, but I could sense his resentment and fear when he thought of me finding Angus, my last connection to what I'd given up.

I was also anxious about Liv. Whether it was rational or not, I knew a part of me would forever feel selfish for choosing myself over her. The two people she loved most were on the outside now.

We had stayed up all night. It felt so good to tell John about the edge I'd been living on these past months, explaining more about myself and why I'd acted the way I had. I told him about Angus's family and about my mother. I also told him it was wise to have a healthy dose of paranoia, because the police and the FBI were probably watching me. I was sure that at any time now I would be questioned about everything I knew. And by association John would be as well. Just like the day we met and he found himself at the police station. Over and over again he assured me I was worth it.

I had held back a few things. I would never speak a word of any details I knew about Relocation. It wasn't worth the risk for him or them. I had heard the threats Novak had made to Lati, but mainly I would stay silent for the rest of my life to protect my sister and my friends.

I'd also decided not to tell John how he appeared in Novak's vision. There was no need to burden him like that. It was done. I wanted to put behind me that John had ever been in danger and that he had any connection to us.

I saw the manila envelope on my desk at the same time John did. My name was scrawled in Victoria's handwriting.

"Will you open it?" I asked. My nerves were getting the best of me now that it looked like I was safe.

"Are you sure?"

"Yes, go ahead. They would never leave me a personal note."

John opened the envelope and took out a set of documents. After a minute of scanning them, he started laughing.

"What?" I crossed over to him and gently laid my hand on his arm, peering at the thick stack he held in his hand.

"You won't need to worry about getting a scholarship. You can officially pay for college." It was an irrevocable trust. The house was in my name, as well as multiple other properties and assets, making them safe from being seized and frozen. There was another envelope as well. It was full of cash. John handed that to me before he put the papers back in the envelope, threw the envelope on the desk, and turned to face me.

"Are you okay?" he asked.

"Yes, it's just weird, that's all. That envelope is the last I'll hear from them. It's the last thing I have that they touched. I'm free."

I put my arms around his neck and leaned back, gazing up at him. I couldn't believe he was mine. I couldn't stop looking at him or touching him.

"You really think you can get into Stanford?" he teased.

"I don't know. I may need to try Berkeley. Maybe we need a bridge between us," I joked. He had been so worried I'd regret my decision, especially once I came back to this house. I could see he was relieved that I was so purely happy.

"So, California." John said, and began to kiss my ear. I obliged him by turning my head to the side, giving him better access, so in love.

"California." I said it like it was a foregone conclusion. "But it's not because of her. I've gone this long without knowing her."

John stopped kissing me and I opened my eyes, not liking the interruption, not wanting to talk about her. He had an expression I'd never seen on his face before. It was an expression I'd only seen on Novak's. As if he were trying to tune into a faraway frequency.

"Julia?"

"What?" He was scaring me.

"That was crazy." He shook his head like he was coming out of it.

"Tell me." I took a step back.

"Nothing. I'm fine now. I just had this crazy, vivid daydream."

"What did you see?"

"No, it's . . . I just saw this incredible underground world. I felt like I was there. God, where did that come from?" He rubbed his face with his hands. "Sorry. I'm so tired, I think I fell asleep standing up."

He shook his head and looked at me, beginning to laugh at himself. I watched his smile fade. "Why are you looking at me like that?"

Carefully, I reset my features. "It's nothing." The lie came easily—I wanted to believe it so badly. I reached out to John, pulling him towards me. "It's nothing at all."

Acknowledgments

Thank you, Amanda Eyre Ward. Without you, this book would not exist. Thank you for helping me tell this story.

I am so grateful to my agent, the lovely Kerry Sparks, for ushering *Select* out into the world and holding my hand every step of the way. I also feel an enormous amount of gratitude to Shelby Boyer for her time spent shepherding this project.

My deepest appreciation to Charlesbridge and to my editor, Monica Perez. Thank you, Monica, for your enthusiasm, insights, and thoughtful guidance.

Many thanks to early readers Sophy Hagey, Debbie Dunn, Vivian Raksakulthai, Debby Wolfinsohn, Nancy McDonald, and Megan Frederick. Also, thank you to Elizabeth Kramer, Leigh Sebastian, Eddie Kaye, Dini Snow, Susan Hewlitt, Maureen Carlson, Andrea Dunlop, May Cobb, Jenny Holt, and Sookie Rothenberg.

Thank you to my sister, Kjersti McCormick, and my mother and father, Kathleen and David Weisenberg, for listening and being so supportive over the years.

Astrid and Margot, I owe you so many thank yous for the patience you had while living with this book and for somehow staying excited and sweet.

And most of all, thank you to my husband, Jeff Gothard. You are the most capable person I know. Thank you for your kindness and willingness to be right there for me with support, ideas, and constant feedback. This book has your stamp on it in so many ways. I am so grateful for you.